MERCURY
INK

SIMON
PULSE

MICHAEL VEY

FALL OF HADES

BOOK SIX OF SEVEN

ALSO BY RICHARD PAUL EVANS

MICHAEL VEY
THE PRISONER OF CELL 25

MICHAEL VEY
RISE OF THE ELGEN

MICHAEL VEY
BATTLE OF THE *AMPERE*

MICHAEL VEY
HUNT FOR JADE DRAGON

MICHAEL VEY
STORM OF LIGHTNING

MICHAEL VEY
FALL OF HADES

BOOK SIX OF SEVEN

RICHARD PAUL EVANS

MERCURY INK

SIMON PULSE

NEW YORK LONDON TORONTO SYDNEY NEW DELHI

SIMON PULSE / MERCURY INK

An imprint of Simon & Schuster Children's Publishing Division

1230 Avenue of the Americas, New York, NY 10020

This Simon Pulse/Mercury Ink paperback edition May 2017

Text copyright © 2016 by Richard Paul Evans

Cover illustration copyright © 2016 by Owen Richardson

All rights reserved, including the right of reproduction in whole or in part in any form.

Simon Pulse and colophon are registered trademarks of Simon & Schuster, Inc.

Mercury Ink is a trademark of Mercury Radio Arts, Inc.

For information about special discounts for bulk purchases, please contact Simon & Schuster Special Sales at 1-866-506-1949 or business@simonandschuster.com.

The Simon & Schuster Speakers Bureau can bring authors to your live event. For more information or to book an event contact the Simon & Schuster Speakers Bureau at 1-866-248-3049 or visit our website at www.simonspeakers.com.

Cover designed by Jessica Handelman

Interior designed by Mike Rosamilia

The text of this book was set in Berling LT Std.

Manufactured in the United States of America

2 4 6 8 10 9 7 5 3 1

Library of Congress Control Number 2016943336

ISBN 978-1-4814-6982-1 (hc)

ISBN 978-1-4814-6983-8 (pbk)

ISBN 978-1-4814-6984-5 (eBook)

To the Kyngs

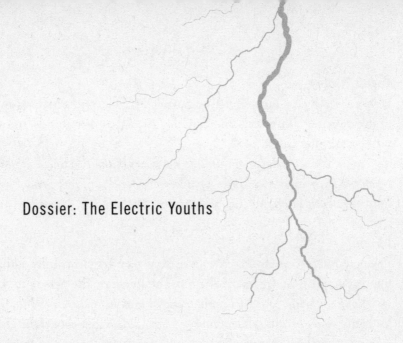

Dossier: The Electric Youths

Michael Vey

Power: Ability to shock people through direct contact or conduction. Can also absorb other electric children's powers.

Michael is the most powerful of all the electric children and leader of the Electroclan. He is steadily increasing in power. He also has Tourette's syndrome, a neurological disorder that causes tics or other involuntary movements. Elgen scientists believe his Tourette's is somehow connected to his electricity.

Ostin Liss

Power: A Nonel—not electric.

Ostin is very intelligent, with an IQ of 155, which puts him at the same level as the average Nobel Prize winner. He is one of the original three members of the Electroclan and Michael's best friend.

Taylor Ridley

Power: Ability to temporarily scramble the electric synapses in the brain, causing confusion. She can also read people's minds, but only when touching them.

Taylor is one of the original three members of the Electroclan. She and Michael discovered each other's powers at Meridian High School, which they were both attending. She is Michael's girlfriend.

Abigail

Power: Ability to temporarily ease or stop pain by electrically stimulating certain parts of the brain. She must be touching the person to do so.

Along with Ian and McKenna, Abigail was held captive by the Elgen for many years because she refused to follow Hatch. She joined the Electroclan after escaping from the Elgen Academy's prison, known as Purgatory.

Bryan

Power: The ability to create highly focused electricity that allows him to cut through objects, especially metal.

Bryan is one of Hatch's Glows. He spends most of his time playing video games and annoying Kylee.

Cassy

Power: Ability to electrically contract or "freeze" muscles from remarkable distances.

One of the most powerful of the electric children, Cassy is also the only one to be found by the resistance before the Elgen. She has lived with the voice since she was four years old. Her job, in addition to special missions and acting as the voice's bodyguard, is to keep track of the electric children. She is well versed on each of their powers and on the backgrounds of both the Glows and the Electroclan. She is a big fan of Michael Vey.

Grace

Power: Grace acts as a "human flash drive" and is able to transfer and store large amounts of electronic data.

Grace was living with the Elgen but joined the Electroclan when they defeated Hatch at the Elgen Academy. She has been working and living with the resistance but has not been on any missions with the Electroclan.

Ian

Power: Ability to see using electrolocation, which is the same way sharks and eels see through muddy or murky water.

Along with McKenna and Abigail, Ian was held captive by the Elgen for many years because he refused to follow Hatch. He joined the Electroclan after escaping from the Elgen Academy's prison, known as Purgatory.

Jack

Power: A Nonel—not electric.

Jack spends a lot of time in the gym and is very strong. He is also excellent with cars. Originally one of Michael's bullies, he joined the Electroclan after Michael bribed him to help Michael rescue his mother from Dr. Hatch.

Kylee

Power: Born with the ability to create electromagnetic power, she is basically a human magnet.

One of Hatch's Glows, she spends most of her time shopping, along with her best (and only) friend, Tara.

McKenna

Power: Ability to create light and heat. She can heat herself to more than three thousand kelvins.

Along with Ian and Abigail, McKenna was held captive by the Elgen for many years because she refused to follow Hatch. She joined the Electroclan after escaping from the Elgen Academy's prison, known as Purgatory.

Nichelle

Power: Nichelle acts as an electrical ground and can both detect and drain the powers of the other electric children. She can also, on a weaker level than Tessa, enhance the other children's powers.

Nichelle was Hatch's enforcer over the rest of the electric children until he abandoned her during the battle at the Elgen Academy. Although everyone was nervous about it, the Electroclan recruited her to join them on their mission to save Jade Dragon. She has become a loyal Electroclan member.

Quentin

Power: Ability to create isolated electromagnetic pulses, which lets him take out all electrical devices within twenty yards.

Quentin is smart and the leader of Hatch's Glows. He is regarded by the Elgen as second-in-command, just below Hatch.

Tanner

Power: Ability to interfere with the electrical navigation systems of aircraft and cause them to malfunction and crash. His powers are so advanced that he can do this from the ground.

After years of mistreatment by the Elgen, Tanner was rescued by the Electroclan from the Peruvian Starxource plant and has been staying with the resistance so he has a chance to recover. He carries deep emotional pain from the crimes Dr. Hatch forced him to commit.

Tara

Power: Tara's abilities are similar to her twin sister, Taylor's, in that she can disrupt normal electronic brain functions. Through years of training and refining her powers, Tara has learned to focus on specific parts of the brain in order to create emotions such as fear or joy.

Working with the Elgen scientists, she has learned how to create mental illusions, which, among other things, allows her to make people appear as someone or something else.

Tara is one of Hatch's Glows. She and Taylor were adopted by different families after they were born, and Tara has lived with Hatch and the Elgen since she was six years old.

Tessa

Power: Tessa's abilities are the opposite of Nichelle's—she is able to enhance the powers of the other electric children.

Tessa escaped from the Elgen at the Starxource plant in Peru and lived in the Amazon jungle for six months with an indigenous tribe called the Amacarra. She joined the Electroclan after the tribe rescued Michael from the Elgen and brought them together.

Torstyn

Power: One of the more ruthless and lethal of the electric children, Torstyn can create microwaves.

Torstyn is one of Hatch's Glows and was instrumental to the Elgen in building the original Starxource plants. Although they were initially enemies, Torstyn is now loyal to Quentin and acts as his bodyguard.

Wade

Power: A Nonel—not electric.

Wade was Jack's best friend and joined the Electroclan at the same time he did. Wade died in Peru when the Electroclan was surprised by an Elgen guard.

Zeus

Power: Ability to "throw" electricity from his body.

Zeus was kidnapped by the Elgen as a young child and lived for many years as one of Hatch's Glows. He joined the Electroclan when they escaped from the Elgen Academy. His real name is Leonard Frank Smith.

PART ONE

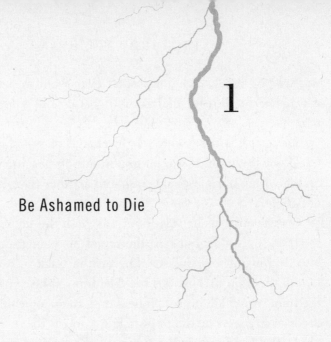

1

Be Ashamed to Die

When I was just eight years old, a few months after my father died, I was going through a box of his things when I found a wooden plaque engraved with these words:

> Be ashamed to die until you have
> won some victory for humanity.
> —Horace Mann

At the time the plaque didn't mean much to me—other than that it had belonged to my father—but it must have meant *something* because I never forgot its message. Lately I've found myself thinking about it a lot. Maybe because it's now my reality. You could say that I'm fighting a battle for humanity. Of course I could die and not win any victory, but I think that's got to be worth something too.

I once heard a story that really bothered me. I don't know if it was true or not. I hope not. I don't even want to share it with you, it's that awful. But for the sake of my story I'm going to. It goes like this:

There was a man who was in charge of switching the railroad tracks for the train. It was an important job because if the train was on the wrong track, it could crash into another train, killing hundreds of people.

One evening, as he was about to switch the tracks for an oncoming train, he suddenly heard the cry of his young son, who had followed him out and was standing on the track he was supposed to switch the train to. This was the dilemma—if he switched the tracks, the train would kill his son. If he didn't, the people on the train, hundreds of strangers he didn't even know, might die.

At the last moment he switched the tracks. The people on the train went on by, not even knowing the disaster they had missed or the little boy who had been killed beneath them. The father went home carrying his son's broken body.

I hate that story, but it makes me think. I've wondered if, given the same situation, I would change the tracks or not. It's easy to act noble and say you would when you're not there, but what if it's someone you can't live without? What if it were Taylor standing on the tracks? Or Ostin? Or my mom?

That takes me back to my father's plaque about winning a victory for humanity. The war we're fighting against Dr. Hatch and the Elgen is one the world doesn't even know about. And just like the guy with the train, if we pull this off, no one on earth, not even you, will ever know how close they came to complete disaster or who was "killed beneath the train." Like Wade. Or maybe, in the end, all of the Electroclan. If we don't win, no one will even know that we tried. How's that for a stupid dilemma? At least we'll have no reason to die ashamed.

My name is Michael Vey. If you're still following the insanity of my life, then you've been all around the world with me. From my home in Meridian, Idaho (which I doubt I'll ever see again), we went to

California, where we broke into the Elgen Academy and I was captured and put into Cell 25. (Yeah, I still have nightmares about that.) Then we broke out, attacked Dr. Hatch, and freed all his GPs, aka human guinea pigs.

You went with me to Peru, where we brought down the Elgen Starxource plant after Dr. Hatch tried to feed me to, like, a million rats. It's also where we lost Wade.

We traveled west to the Port of Lima, where we sunk two of the Elgen's boats—their main command ship, the *Ampere*, and their battleship, the *Watt*. Unfortunately, Dr. Hatch got off the *Ampere* just before it blew up.

Then we went to Taiwan, where we rescued a genius little girl named Jade Dragon before the Elgen could get what she knew out of her head—mainly how to get their MEI machine to make more of us—electric people. It was after our escape from the Taiwan Starxource plant that we found out that the Elgen had attacked Timepiece Ranch, our home base and the resistance's headquarters in Mexico.

We flew back to the ranch—or at least what was left of it after the Elgen helicopters bombed it to ashes. We thought that everyone was dead, until we were found by Gervaso, who took us to the resistance's new headquarters at Christmas Ranch near Zion National Park in southern Utah. Then Taylor, Gervaso, Ian, and I went back to Boise, where we rescued Taylor's parents.

Still, in spite of all we've done, the Elgen just keep growing stronger. Now we have a plan to stop them once and for all. We're going to the Elgen base in the South Pacific island nation of Tuvalu, to steal the *Joule*—the Elgen's floating piggy bank. As if that's not crazy enough, that's just one of our missions. Hatch has locked up three of his own electric kids for treason—his most powerful: Quentin, Tara, and Torstyn—and we're going to try to free them. I can't believe I'm even considering this. Along with Bryan, those are the same three who made fun of me just before Hatch tried to feed me to his rats in Peru.

This is the first time that all of us electrics (except Grace) will be going on a mission together. Even Tanner and Nichelle. Nichelle will be extremely valuable if Hatch's electric kids decide not to cooperate. Still, this will be really dangerous for her. She betrayed Hatch the last time they met, and he's not exactly the forgiving type. I'm guessing he'll do anything to make her pay for what she did. Then again, I suppose that's true for all of us.

I know, the whole plan seems crazy. If I had to lay odds on it, I'd say we've got a 10 percent chance of winning this one. I wouldn't tell everyone else that. If I did, I'd have to drop that number to 1 percent, because if you think you're going to fail, you most likely will—at least that's what our gym teacher at Meridian High always said. But whether you think you're going to lose or not, sometimes you do what you have to do because it's the right thing, and let the chips fall where they may.

I think we're about to drop a whole lot of chips.

PART TWO

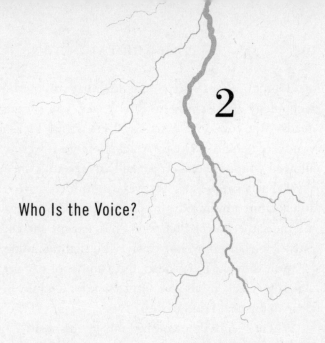

2

Who Is the Voice?

Two Weeks Earlier

Schema hadn't spoken for nearly a minute when the voice leaned back in his chair. "What's wrong, my friend? Cassy got your tongue?"

"It's not me, sir," Cassy said, brushing her short blond hair back over one ear. "I'm not doing anything."

"I know, Cass," the voice said. "The chairman's in shock. I suppose he wasn't expecting to see me."

"Coonradt," Schema said.

"*Doctor* Coonradt," the voice corrected. "At least that was once my name. Many years ago. Now I'm simply 'the voice.' That is all you will call me."

Schema looked even more confused. "But I don't understand. . . . You were dead."

"Because you killed me?"

Schema said nothing.

"Don't bother to deny it. I know that you tried. You used my own technology against me. And, in a way, you succeeded. Coonradt *is* dead. After you killed Carl Vey, I knew that I was next. I knew that you were behind his heart attack, because it was my technology that allowed you to do it—a mistake I've regretted since I invented it.

"What a simple, perfect way to murder, to give someone a heart attack from a hundred yards away. It's the perfect weapon. In a way, it's the same power that Cassy has, except she comes by hers honestly." He glanced over at Cassy, who slightly nodded.

"You thought I was dead, but rumors of my death were exaggerated. I was sick, mind you. Quite sick for a while. But then it became clear to me that I had to die."

Schema shifted uncomfortably in his seat. "If you knew what I'd done, why did you rescue me from the Elgen? Why not just let Hatch kill me?" He looked into the voice's eyes. "Why haven't you already killed me?"

"Because I want your help to stop Hatch. You have information that will help us dismantle what Hatch is building."

"My enemy's enemy is my friend," Schema said softly.

"No," the voice said in a low tone. "You are not my friend. You are an *opportunity*. I'm offering you an arrangement, not a friendship. You can help us or not, it's your choice. But now that you know my identity, if you choose not to cooperate, you will be silenced."

Schema blinked. "Silenced?"

"I believe that's the word you once used to order my murder," the voice said. "Hatch would have fed you to his rats. I, on the other hand, am much more merciful. But if you reveal my identity, thousands, maybe millions, will die. Your life is not worth that. So make no mistake, you will be . . . *silenced*." The voice turned to Cassy. "Go ahead and attach the arrestor."

"Yes, sir," Cassy said. She walked out of the room.

"What's an arrestor?" Schema asked.

"Your new companion."

Cassy walked back into the room carrying a small box. She stood in front of Schema. "Take off your shirt, please."

Schema looked at her, then back at the voice. "What are you doing?"

"Let me be clear," the voice said. "Your very existence hangs by a thread. Don't get into the habit of questioning orders. I am not your employee or your subordinate. I do not have time to trifle with you. You will obey me without question or die quickly." His eyes narrowed and he spoke slowly, carefully enunciating each word. "Do you understand?"

"Yes."

"Then take it off."

Schema quickly pulled off his shirt, exposing his tan, flabby body.

"Now put your arms through here," Cassy said.

The device she was putting on him looked a lot like the Elgen RESAT. Schema put his arms through the straps, and Cassy slid the device forward. A thin, rubber-coated box about the size of a cell phone rested over his heart. Cassy locked the straps, then took the other two straps from the box and brought them around Schema's ribs and snapped them shut in back.

"You are familiar with the RESAT machines, of course," the voice said. "This is patterned after them, but based on the same technology that you used to kill Carl Vey. Except I've made a few improvements." The voice lifted a small remote. "If you are a half mile or more from the central monitor, which is secured somewhere in this building, the arrestor will automatically activate, immediately stopping your heart. If I push this button, right here, the arrestor will activate, stopping your heart. If you try to remove the device, the arrestor will activate, stopping your heart.

"Of course Cassy can do any of this without technology, but I wanted insurance in case you think you can escape while we're not around. You will wear the arrestor until I take it off you."

Cassy fastened the final lock, then stepped back. The machine hummed quietly as two diodes began blinking.

"It's on," Cassy said.

The voice lifted the remote in front of him, his index finger hovering a quarter inch above a red button. "One push, and your heart ceases to beat."

"I get the idea," Schema said, sounding more annoyed than scared.

"Of course you do," the voice said. "You've held others' lives in your hands for some time. How does it feel to be on the opposite end of the leash?"

"Humbling," Schema said. "But Hatch already put me on that end of the leash."

"Yes, he has. And it's time to talk about him. Time is of the essence. We have a plan we are about to put into motion." The voice leaned forward. "We are going to the heart of the Elgen. We are going to steal the *Joule*."

Schema looked unimpressed. "That's a foolish idea. The *Joule* is tighter than Fort Knox. Trust me, the ship is impenetrable."

"*Nothing* is impenetrable."

"The *Joule* is. Its security systems can't be breached. And it keeps its periphery. If anything comes within three hundred meters, it submerges. Its protocols are unbending."

"Which is why we need you to help us steal it. We need to know the ship's security features and its crew's protocols." The voice leaned back in his seat. "If you help us steal the *Joule*, you get your life back. We'll give you a hundred million dollars from the boat and allow you to regain control of the Elgen company."

"I want Hatch's head on a stake."

"You can get his head yourself. Take your money and buy an army. But first we need to steal the boat. We need protocols and security features."

"I'll do what I can," Schema said. "But Hatch has probably already changed the protocols."

"We'll take what you can give us."

"I can get you the boat's schematics. . . . There are plans—blueprints."

"Where are they?"

"They were on the *Ampere*."

"We sunk the *Ampere*."

"I know. I was there. But the plans are still on it. And the *Ampere* is resting in only seventy feet of water. The Peruvian government hasn't started to move it yet. The plans are protected in a waterproof safe in the captain's suite. If you can get to the *Ampere*, I can tell you how to get into the safe."

The voice nodded slowly. "All right, that's a beginning." He turned. "Cassy, please tell Maggie to come in."

"Yes, sir."

"Then come back yourself. I want you here for this. I want you to know everything about our plans."

Cassy's eyebrows rose. "I'm going to be involved in this mission?"

"Maybe. This might be too big even for the Electroclan."

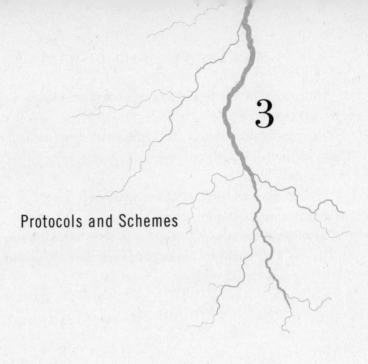

3

Protocols and Schemes

Cassy followed Maggie into the room, and the two women took seats next to Schema.

"Tell us everything you know," the voice said. "Use the board."

Schema walked up to the whiteboard mounted on the wall on the west side of the room.

"Use the stylus. Just write. It will automatically record everything on my computer."

Schema lifted a silver, pen-like instrument. It beeped slightly when it touched the board's surface. "This is what I know. First, the *Joule* always stays at least six hundred meters from any shore."

"It was docked in Peru when we sank the *Ampere*."

"I'm telling you the protocols I know," Schema said. "Like I said, Hatch could have changed them. In Peru, it was likely that with the number of guards and ships in the area, Hatch felt invulnerable and got lazy and impatient, so he moved it in to load before crossing to Tuvalu."

"All right, so he's human—almost. Are there any other exceptions to that protocol?"

"During maintenance. But the *Joule* is only maintained in the Elgen shipyard."

"Where's that?"

"Off the western coast of Italy, near Fiumicino."

"That's a long way from Tuvalu."

"If there was an emergency, they'd have to improvise."

The voice thought for a moment, then said, "We could create an emergency. That might be usable. Continue."

"Most of the time, the *Joule* stays partially submerged and only rises for supplies or when the crew changes, which is every three months."

"When is it due a crew change?"

Schema bowed his head to think. After a moment he looked up. "If they've maintained their schedule, then they changed crews just two weeks ago."

"That won't help us. What about their supply schedule?"

"The galley crew leaves the *Joule* on surface boats and handles the food and necessities. No non-crew personnel are allowed within three hundred meters of the boat. Ever. If the guards or land crew see any unknown person or if the crew reports anything suspicious, the land crew is abandoned and the *Joule* submerges. Everything is done by a strict schedule that is only known by crew and top Elgen brass. The only exception allowed is if the admiral-general visits. Or an EGG."

"How often do they do that?"

"They don't, that I know of. But they could." Schema lifted the stylus and wrote. "Number two, the crew constantly monitors the waters around them. If anything comes near, the boat submerges. I mean *anything*. It once submerged for a school of barracuda. Also, if there is an emergency onshore, it submerges.

"Number three, the *Joule* always travels with a battleship escort."

"This isn't going to be easy," Cassy said.

"Easy?" Schema said, smirking. "It's *impossible*. I told you, she's impenetrable." Schema looked at them. "Trust me, the security is perfect."

"Nothing is impossible. Nothing is perfect. There must be some way."

Schema thought for a moment, then said, "The only chance would be with help from the inside. It would have to be someone high up."

"How high?"

Schema shook his head. "Hatch or an EGG. Nothing less. But you'll never get an EGG. They're the elite—sworn loyal to death. They'll never turn."

"One already has."

Schema looked at him disbelieving. "Hatch has lost one of his EGGs?"

"His chief EGG," the voice said.

"David Welch?"

"Yes."

Schema's brow fell. "That's unbelievable. And Hatch hasn't already killed him?"

"Welch is on the run. For now."

"Where is he?"

"If we knew that, we might not be having this conversation."

"Welch knows everything. If something had happened to Hatch, Welch would have taken over the Elgen. Welch could get you onto the *Joule*."

The voice thought a moment, then said, "All right, our priority has changed to find Welch." He turned to Maggie. "Get me Simon at Christmas Ranch."

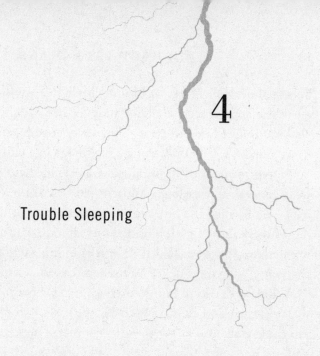

4

Trouble Sleeping

Hatch inspected his personal guard, then returned alone to his room to read. A half hour later his door opened and Hatch's servant, a beautiful, long-haired Filipino woman, walked in. She left a glass of Scotch on the table, then bowed to him. "As you requested, Excellency."

"Thank you," Hatch said.

"My pleasure, sir. May I do anything else for you?"

"Go to the dispensary and get me Ambien and Seroquel."

"Ambien and Seroquel?"

"They're sleeping pills."

"Yes, sir. How many?"

"Just bring me the bottles."

"Immediately, sir."

Hatch went back to his book as his servant hurried from the room. For the last week he hadn't been sleeping well. Most people living the

17

horror and violence of his life wouldn't sleep well, if they could at all—their consciences wouldn't allow it. But Hatch wasn't wired that way. He didn't lose any more sleep over sending someone to the rat bowl than he would destroying a digital foe in a video game.

Hatch thought of himself as a warrior in that way, or, even more so, a general. It was logic. You couldn't become overly sentimental over one soldier if you wanted to defeat an army. Sentimentality didn't work in war. Hatch prided himself on being above such "small-mindedness," as he called it. If you couldn't sacrifice a few men for the many, you could never be trusted to lead.

What was costing him sleep was just *one* man. Welch. As his former top man and EGG, Welch knew things. No, Welch knew *everything.* He not only knew the Elgen's plans; he knew their strategies and methods of achieving them. He knew their technology. He even knew their finances. Most of all, he knew Hatch. Welch was a threat greater than the resistance because he was the ultimate insider—a cancerous tumor inside the Elgen brain. Welch in the wrong hands, or speaking into the wrong ear, could spell disaster for the Elgen, and for Hatch personally. As long as Welch lived, Hatch's plans were in peril. Welch needed to be exterminated no matter the cost.

Hatch regretted not just shooting Welch the night he was arrested. He wouldn't make that mistake again. But first Welch needed to be found, and that was no simple matter. Welch had overseen nearly all of the Elgen hunts for more than a decade and was personally responsible for finding six of the Glows. He knew the Elgen search techniques better than Hatch did. Finding Welch in Taiwan would be like finding a grain of rice in a rice paddy—a grain of rice that knew you were looking for it and knew how to be invisible. No matter—he would be found. And next time Hatch wouldn't wait for a show execution. The million-dollar reward he had offered was for a dead Welch, not a live one.

PART THREE

5

Destiny

Former EGG David Welch was barely twenty-one years old the night his destiny collided with the Elgen. In fact, his birthday had been the day before, and he was still tired from staying up too late with his college roommates.

The moon was unusually bright that night, and even that played a part in his fate. Welch was delivering pizzas for a local company, Sasquatch Pizza, when he was sent out on a delivery to the Elgen building.

He had parked his car, a '72 Camaro in need of a paint job, in the restricted delivery zone in front of the new Elgen building. He thought that the building and grounds were impressive, with a seven-story-high tower and laboratory with a bronze-colored, mirrored glass exterior.

The entire twenty-four-block area had been developed as a research park, and he was always glad when he got called there on a delivery, as many of the people who worked at the buildings were rich and tipped well. Once, someone tipped him a fifty-dollar bill—a near fortune for him.

That night he was about to get out of his car when he noticed a shadowy figure creeping through the cactus garden near the building's front windows.

Recently some of Welch's coworkers had been robbed making deliveries, so he kept alert. Welch lifted the vinyl pizza carrier bags from his backseat and got out of his car, locking it behind him— something he rarely did.

The figure in the shadows seemed too active, too intent, to be a homeless person looking for somewhere to sleep. Welch wondered if they were trying to break into the building. That too would be odd, since there were obviously people inside, who, Welch reminded himself, were waiting for their pizzas.

With his arms full of pizza boxes he started up the front walkway toward the entry. That's when the darkened figure cocked back its arm and threw something at the front window, breaking a large, jagged hole in the glass. The sound of shattering glass was followed by the wail of an alarm.

Welch's first thought was that he would be blamed for breaking the window, as he appeared to be alone and was within throwing distance of the window. A man in a gray-and-black security uniform appeared near the front window, looking directly at him.

Then the vandal sprang from the garden, sprinting diagonally across the building's front walkway in Welch's direction. Instinctively, Welch dropped his pizzas and took off to intercept the man. Welch was built for pursuit. Even though he was large and muscular, he was also quick. He had played both linebacker and lineman on his high school's football team.

Welch leveled the guy, who was barely half his size and at least ten years older than him, with a waist-high tackle. Then he picked him up by the waist and carried him over to the front entryway, where there were now three security guards rushing out of the building.

"I caught this guy," Welch said. "He threw a rock through your window."

"It was a brick," the head security guard replied. He was a stern-looking man with a broad, flat nose from being broken multiple times. He was a few inches shorter than Welch but even broader of shoulder. He looked at the man in Welch's arms, then shook his head. "You can put him down. But don't let go of him."

Welch did as the guard said.

"His name is Dominic. He used to work here in the accounting office. They canned him yesterday. I think he just lost his severance." He turned to the guard next to him. "How far out are the police?"

"About five minutes."

"Let them know we have the perpetrator."

The disgruntled employee, Dominic, suddenly tried to free himself from Welch's grasp. Welch clamped down on him until he cried out, "This is brutality! I'm going to report you! I'll sue!"

The head guard laughed. "What a wuss." He looked into the man's face. "Unfortunately for you, Dominic, this man doesn't work for us. He can do whatever he wants."

"I'm going to sue you for everything you've got!" he shouted at Welch.

Welch laughed. "What I've got? I've got a lot of school debt, a broken-down car, and some textbooks. I don't think a lawyer would work for that."

Dominic continued to rant. "I'll report you to the police. You have no right to hold me against my will."

"That's where you're wrong," the head guard said. "We have every right to hold you. And prosecute you."

"You'll pay for this. I'll make you—"

At that moment Welch belted him across the face, knocking him out. The man dropped to the ground. Welch looked anxiously up at the guards. "Sorry. I hate whiners."

A broad smile crossed the head guard's face. "Nice punch."

The other guards nodded in agreement. "Well done."

"You think I'll get in trouble?" Welch asked.

"Nope," the head guard said. "We saw exactly what happened. Dominic threw a brick through the window. When you tried to stop him, he assaulted you. It was self-defense."

"That's what we saw," one of the other guards said.

The head guard nodded. "We'll erase that part of the security tape, just in case."

"Thanks," Welch said.

A police car pulled up to the curb and two officers got out. They walked up, looking at the unconscious man on the ground. Finally one of the officers asked, "Is that the guy?"

"That's the loser we caught vandalizing the building," the head guard said. "He threw a brick through the window."

The officers looked over at the building. "That hole?"

"Yes, sir."

"Why is he unconscious?"

"The pizza guy tried to stop him and the man attacked him. It was self-defense."

The officer looked at Welch, then at the man on the ground, then back at Welch. "He attacked this guy? He's half his size."

"He was out of control," the head guard said. "He was trying to get away."

"If you're willing to testify, we'll book him for assault as well," the cop said.

"Of course we will."

One of the officers squatted down and shook the man. Dominic groaned.

"Sir, please roll onto your stomach. We're going to handcuff you."

Dominic was still too dazed to offer any resistance. The police officers handcuffed him. "Can you stand?"

"I—I don't know," he stuttered.

The officers lifted him up, then walked him to the squad car, placing him in the backseat.

After the police car drove away, the head guard turned to Welch. "I'm starving. You brought some pizzas?"

Welch nodded. "Yes, sir. Let me get them." He ran back over to where he'd dropped his boxes and retrieved them. "Sorry, they're probably not going to be hot after all that."

"How much do we owe you?"

"Thirty-nine dollars."

The head guard handed him a hundred-dollar bill. "Keep the change."

"Thank you."

He put out his hand. "My name is Patrick."

"David," Welch said.

The guard lifted the lid of the box. "You like this stuff?"

"The Monster Meat Lover?"

Patrick laughed. "No. Delivering your . . . meat lovers whatever."

"It's a job. I'm working my way through college."

"What are you studying?"

"Criminal science."

"With your build, you could play football."

"I did. Lost interest."

"What's your last name?"

"Welch. Like the jam."

Patrick smiled. "All right, Welch-like-the-jam. Looks like you can handle yourself in a jam. Do you want a real job?"

"Doing what?"

"Security detail here. You can work at night, go to school in the day. I guarantee it will pay a lot better than delivering pizzas."

"I meet girls delivering pizza," Welch said.

Patrick laughed. "But do you impress them?"

Welch didn't answer.

"You'll impress girls working here. Not that every girl doesn't want a . . . pizza delivery boy."

"Now you're mocking me."

"Am I right?"

"I can see how that would be true," Welch said.

"Good. Do you have class tomorrow?"

"Until three."

"Come at four; I'll take you in to HR and get you hired."

"Wait. What does it pay?"

"The position starts at fifty K a year. With benefits. Insurance. Christmas bonus and paid vacation after six months."

Welch had never even made half that. "Thank you."

"Don't mention it. The stars aligned tonight. I've got a feeling you're supposed to be here."

6

Lost Loves

Welch's childhood had been less than idyllic. His biological parents were drug addicts, and he had lived in and out of foster homes before, at the age of seven, he was permanently adopted by a family.

The adoption didn't go well. Welch was rebellious and had a violent temper. Part of his problem was that he had always been larger than the other children his age and subsequently hung out with older kids. He was with teenagers four years older than him when they were caught stealing a car from a Walmart parking lot.

After his arrest, his adopted family "un-adopted" him, and Welch was sent to juvenile detention for eight months. It was the best thing that ever happened to him.

One of the police officers at the facility, a rugged former Golden Gloves boxer, took an interest in Welch and became his mentor. That relationship changed everything. Welch stopped acting out and got

serious about school, where he learned, for the first time, he was not
dumb like many had told him, but rather he had an above-average
intelligence. He was also a gifted athlete. Much to his previous foster
families' surprise, Welch not only graduated from high school, but did so
with a 3.98 grade point average and an academic and sports scholarship.

That summer, Welch was in his third year of studying criminal
science. His scholarship only covered tuition and books, so he got a
job delivering pizzas. He'd worked for the pizzeria just three months
before the evening when he subdued the vandal at the Elgen building.

Patrick, the Elgen's head security guard, had been accused of hiring
his guards by the pound, and Welch was no exception. But it soon
became clear to him that Welch was more than muscle; he was a
quick learner and ambitious, and within just six months he was pro-
moted to head of the graveyard shift.

Welch liked the work and the pay but found it a little lonely.
He would patrol the dark, quiet halls of the Elgen building at night,
sometimes hoping someone would break in just to liven things up.
Oftentimes he would look in through the glass windows of the fifth-
floor laboratory and watch the scientists at work, wondering what
they were doing. He didn't know them, at least not personally, but he
knew the pecking order.

The main scientist was a man known as Dr. Coonradt. It seemed
to Welch that Coonradt had no life outside of his work, as he was
always there. Many times it was only the two of them in the building.

One night Coonradt called Welch over to the laboratory.

"Yes, sir?" Welch asked, wondering what the scientist wanted.

"Come in for a moment, please."

"Yes, sir." Welch stepped into the laboratory.

"What's your name?" Coonradt asked.

"Welch, sir."

Coonradt smiled. "I can read your name tag. What's your first name?"

"David."

"Well, David, have a drink with me."

"Thank you, sir, but I can't. I'm on the job."

Coonradt still poured two crystal glasses half full from a bottle of champagne. "I'm giving you permission. A sip of Dom Pérignon won't jeopardize our security. It's a special occasion. I'm celebrating a breakthrough." He extended the drink to Welch.

Welch just looked at the glass. "I'm really sorry, but I don't drink alcohol."

Coonradt looked at him in surprise. "A teetotaler, that's refreshing." He set down the glass, walked over to a refrigerator, and brought back a bottle. "Then have a Coke."

"Thank you, sir."

Both men sat down.

"Why don't you drink? You a Mormon?"

"No, sir. My biological father was an alcoholic. I figured I inherited his genes."

"You're a smart man," Coonradt said. He took a drink.

"What kind of breakthrough are we celebrating?" Welch asked.

"A big one. It has to do with a variation of the standard magnetic vector created when a polyatomic ion is covalently bonded—"

"Wait, wait, wait," Welch said, raising a hand. "You lost me way before polyatomic zions, or whatever you said."

Coonradt laughed. "Sorry. I get carried away sometimes."

Welch took a swig from his cola. "You're always here."

"It would seem that way. My work is my life. It's my wife, my family, my religion." His voice fell a little. "It's the only thing I have left." Welch thought he saw a flash of pain in the scientist's eyes. Coonradt sipped his champagne, then put his glass down. "What about you? Do you have anyone you can't live without?"

"I had a girlfriend for a while, but we broke up about six months ago."

"Was it mutual?"

"No. She dumped me for a med student."

"I'm sorry. Are you pining for her?"

"Pining?"

"Sorry, it's an old-fashioned word. Do you miss her?"

"Yes, sir."

Coonradt lifted his glass again. "Then we'll toast lost loves."

Welch lifted his drink. "To lost loves," he said as they clinked the glasses together.

Welch drank, then looked at the scientist. "Do you have lost loves?"

Coonradt looked down for a moment, finished his drink, then lifted the one he'd poured for Welch and took a drink from it as well. When he finally spoke, his voice was soft.

"Yes. Two loves. My mother when I was fourteen, my wife eleven years ago. I lost both of them to cancer. Technically, I lost three, I guess. My wife was three months pregnant when she died. I lost my child, too."

"I'm sorry."

Coonradt took another drink. "Me too."

"Did you ever consider marrying again?"

"No. Not seriously. I suppose that I feel cursed. I couldn't bear another loss. But life has a way of figuring itself out. It's why I'm where I am right now. I decided to dedicate my life to revenge."

"Revenge? On who?"

"On cancer. It's a living organism, and I am going to kill it, just as it killed my loved ones. Turnabout is fair play, right?" He took another drink.

Welch looked at him with admiration. "Yes, sir. I think that's pretty awesome."

"Thank you. And if I succeed, I will save millions of lives and make the Elgen Corporation billions upon billions of dollars." He sighed deeply. "Well, I better get back to work and let you get back to yours. Thank you for celebrating with me."

Welch quickly stood, taking the comment as his dismissal. "Thank you, sir. For the drink and the talk. Congratulations on your break-through. Maybe someday you'll win a Nobel Prize."

Coonradt smiled. "That would be nice. Not so much for the prize, but because it would mean that I had accomplished something." He stood. "And it's a pleasure to meet you, Mr. Welch. I wish you a long future and much success at Elgen Incorporated."

7

The First Meeting

Coonradt's breakthrough in magnetism didn't cure cancer or win a Nobel Prize, even though he was nominated for one. It did make the Elgen Corporation hundreds of millions of dollars.

During the apex of their growth, the Elgen's CEO, a man named Briton Hill, died unexpectedly, and the board immediately set to work searching for a new leader. They ended up hiring away the CEO of an upstart pharmaceutical company, an ambitious young MIT graduate named Charles James Hatch.

Eight months previous to the change in leadership, Welch's boss, Patrick, had retired and Welch became the acting head of Elgen security.

Welch never forgot the first day he met Hatch. He was called into the new Elgen CEO's office for an introduction.

"Come in. Sit down," Hatch said forcefully.

Welch sat down uncomfortably in one of the two leather chairs in front of the CEO's desk.

"So you're our head of security," Hatch said, staring at him intensely.

"Yes, sir."

"Do we need security?"

"Yes, sir."

Hatch smiled. "I would expect you to say that. In fact, I would have been disappointed if you'd answered to the contrary."

"Yes, sir."

"Would you like a drink?"

"No, sir. I don't drink."

"We'll fix that," Hatch said.

He stood and walked over to a decanter filled with an amber liquid and poured himself a glass. Then another. "And why is it that we need security? Industrial espionage?"

"Yes, sir."

"How long have you been here?"

"Seven years, sir."

"And during that time, Mr. Welch, have you stopped anyone from stealing our patents?"

"I don't know, sir. Deterrence can't always be measured."

"Good answer," Hatch said, smiling. "Good answer." He stood in front of Welch and stared at him for nearly a minute without speaking. Welch had never met anyone like Hatch before. He was already starting to dislike his new boss.

"David L. Welch. You've had a rocky childhood, in and out of foster homes, bad friends, delinquency and crime. Still, you somehow turned your life around and went to college to study criminal science. I can see why. We often become what we hate in order to take away our fear of it." He took a drink. "But then you dropped out to work here. Good career move?"

"I thought so at the time," Welch said.

"And you don't now?"

"That depends."

"On what?"

"On whether or not you're going to fire me."

Hatch looked at him for a moment, then laughed. "I'm not going to fire you. There'd be a mutiny. You're beloved here—practically an icon. And yes, of course, Elgen Inc. needs security. And, as we grow, that need will grow. And you, Mr. Welch, your salary and your future will grow with it." He leaned forward and looked intently into Welch's eyes. "*If* you are loyal." He held out the second drink. "Now drink with me, sir."

Welch just looked at the glass.

"It's not polite to turn down a gesture of friendship. That wouldn't be loyal, would it?"

Welch took the glass.

"To your future with the Elgen," Hatch said. "I've a feeling it's going to be a wild ride."

"To the future," Welch said. He lifted the glass, paused, then took a drink. The ride had begun.

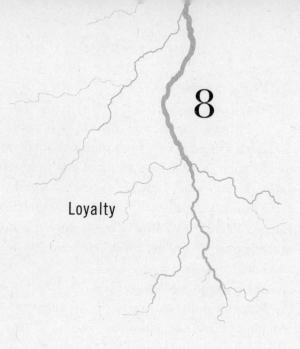

8

Loyalty

Hatch was an expert at manipulation. He was continually grooming Welch, testing his loyalty and rewarding or punishing him accordingly. After the disaster with the MEI, when Hatch was fired as CEO, Welch was the first person he called into his office.

"I want you to hear this from me first," Hatch said bitterly. "I've been removed as Elgen CEO. They've replaced me with an Italian jester named Giacomo Schema."

Welch was stunned by the news. "Why?"

"The malfunction of the MEI. The board is terrified that if the word gets out and the deaths are linked to us, it could cost us billions."

"Where will you go?" Welch asked.

"Nowhere. I'm staying here. As director."

Welch was even more surprised. "With all due respect, sir, they're not firing you?"

Hatch grinned. "Fire *me*?"

"That seems to be the standard corporate procedure."

"No," Hatch said. "They can't."

"Why is that?"

Hatch smiled. "Precisely *because* the board is terrified that if the word gets out and the deaths are linked to us, it could cost us billions. I let them know that if they fired me, there was a very good chance that word would get out. Not from me, of course. But via an anonymous source."

Hatch reached into his desk drawer and brought out a large manila envelope. He handed it across the desk to Welch. "Keep this somewhere safe. If anything happens to me, I want you to take this envelope to the *Wall Street Journal*. The precise contact information is inside. Can you do that for me?"

"Yes, sir."

"Thank you. I knew I could depend on you." He looked at Welch for a moment, then said, "Be assured, this is only a temporary setback. I will run this company again."

"I believe you, sir."

"I know. You've been loyal from the beginning, and trust me, your loyalty will be rewarded. Until then, I will see that you retain your position. However, I would like to broaden your responsibilities."

"How so, sir?"

"I want you to gather information on each member of the board, especially Schema. I want to know the skeletons in their closets, their loves, their affairs, their thought crimes, their every vulnerability. Everything. Can I count on you?"

"Yes, sir."

"I want you to forget what you know about corporate security and start running the Elgen guard like an army, with you its general."

Welch nodded, excited at the prospect. "I can do that."

"One more thing. And this must never leave this room. Schema is talking about silencing some of those who are potential leaks."

"By 'silencing,' you mean . . . *killing*?" Welch said.

"Exactly."

"Who in particular is he considering silencing?"

"Carl Vey, the research manager from the Pasadena Hospital; his assistant, Anna Ferguson; and our own head of research and development, Dr. Coonradt."

Welch's chest froze. "Dr. Coonradt?"

"Yes. Those are the main names. And if Schema's making a list, you can bet that I'm on it as well. That's why I gave you the envelope."

"Yes, sir." Welch looked down at the envelope, then back up at Hatch. "Do you think it will come to that?"

"I don't know," Hatch said. "But billions of dollars are at stake. You'd be surprised at what people will do for a little money."

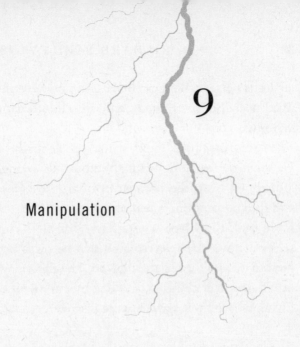

9

Manipulation

Everything Hatch predicted, with the exception of his own murder, came true. Carl Vey and, presumably, Coonradt, were terminated. Vey's assistant, Anna Ferguson, went into hiding.

It was only a few years after that that the existence of the electric children was revealed. It was Hatch who learned about them. He was looking into the children who had survived, to see if any of them had subsequently died of MEI complications, when he discovered, from confidential state and medical records, that the survivors had been affected in peculiar ways.

The first electric child discovered was Nichelle. She'd been in foster care from the time she was very young, and state records showed that she had been in and out of an unusually high number of homes—sometimes only lasting a day or two before being transferred to a new one. Foster families she'd stayed with reported that she was

an unusually challenging little girl, and several of the homes she'd
lived in had burned down, typically due to damage to the electrical
systems.

It was the note about damaged electrical systems that piqued
Hatch's interest. The next afternoon he arranged to have Nichelle
kidnapped from the backyard of her latest foster home, where she
was found uprooting a bed of flowers.

It took the Elgen a few days, but after running her through a
series of tests, they determined that she was essentially an electrical
ground wire. From that point on, Hatch was motivated to find the
other electrical children, and one by one they were brought into the
Elgen, where their powers were discovered and developed.

As Elgen director, Hatch continued to work as if he ran the company.
He also began steering the Elgen on a new course. Shortly before his
"death," Coonradt had demonstrated to the Elgen board how the
MEI could electrify rats. While initially Schema considered the dis-
covery nothing more than a curiosity, Hatch recognized the potential for a new source of electrical energy and, with board approval,
launched the Starxource Plant Initiative (SPI), turning the Elgen into
a massively profitable corporation and setting them on a trajectory to
someday become the richest company in the world.

Internally, Hatch took draconian measures to guarantee that his
mandates were followed and his power protected—measures that
included spying, wiretapping, murder, and extortion.

The first person Welch killed was a man named Paul Wang, a
former Elgen scientist who was caught trying to sell Elgen secrets.
Hatch convinced Welch to kill the man the same way he'd gotten
Welch to take that first drink of alcohol—a simple, quiet request.
After Welch had blood on his hands, he was much easier to manipu-
late. And no one was better at manipulation than Hatch.

Once the Elgen, under Schema's guidance, moved their operations
from the United States to international waters, it became relatively
easy for Hatch to launch his takeover of the Elgen by force. The

coup was organized and carried out on the command ship *Ampere* by Welch and his two senior Elgen commanders. By that time, Hatch had turned the Elgen security into an active personal army solely under his control.

Hatch and Welch together created the complex hierarchy of the Elgen guard. Hatch was named supreme commander, general, then admiral-general, while Welch became his chief EGG and right-hand man. That is, until Hatch sentenced his most loyal and enduring friend to death.

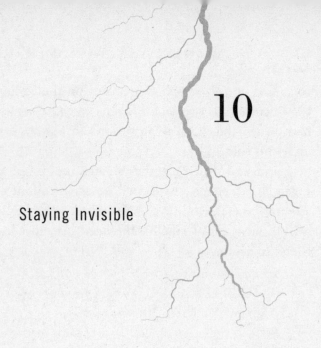

10

Staying Invisible

Kaohsiung, Taiwan
EGG Welch's Escape

Welch and the brig's guards were in a cab in the bustling center of downtown Kaohsiung, Taiwan, just three city blocks from the docked *Faraday*, when Tara's power wore off. Suddenly Welch looked like himself instead of the Taiwanese prisoner the guards thought they were escorting off the ship. The guard in the backseat with Welch was the first to notice.

"What the . . ."

Quentin had disarmed the guards before they left the boat, and Welch, who was waiting for the moment, lifted the guard's own gun on him. "Not who you expected?"

The guard looked at him in fear. "EGG Welch."

The guard in the front turned back, his eyes wide with surprise. "No. It's impossible."

"Enigmatic, perhaps, but clearly not impossible. Unfortunately, you've just aided the escape of Admiral-General Hatch's most prized prisoner. He's going to be so unhappy with you. I would wager good money that it's the rat bowl for both of you."

The guard next to Welch stammered, "But—but—we didn't know it was you."

"Come now, man. You really think that will matter to Hatch?"

The guards knew the answer.

"What are you going to do with us?" the backseat guard asked.

"Nothing," Welch said. "It's catch and release. You're no use to me now. In a few minutes I'll let one of you off; then I'll let the other one of you off a few miles later. Now empty your pockets. Give me all the money you have. Hurry."

The men pulled out their money and handed it to Welch. In all it was less than two thousand yuan, not as much as Welch hoped or needed, certainly not enough to get him out of the country.

Welch stuffed the guards' money into his shirt pocket. *"Sye, sye."*

"How do you know that we won't just turn you in to the Elgen?" the guard in front asked.

Welch shook his head. "Are you trying to convince me to just shoot you now?"

The man blanched. "No, sir."

"I'm probably giving you too much credit, but you won't turn me in because you're not that stupid. It would be a death warrant for either of you. Hatch is merciless. He never forgets and he never forgives. You broke three Elgen protocols in my escape, and now you're guilty of aiding an Elgen fugitive. Hoping for mercy from the admiral-general would be like waiting at a bus stop for an airplane. No matter your excuse, you'll be executed. Shot if you're lucky, but most likely fed to the rats, since that amuses him."

The guards were speechless. They knew Welch was right.

"And in case you're not as smart as I give you credit for and you're still thinking of taking a chance on turning me in, Quentin is waiting for you. He's already reported you as accomplices in my escape, so you'll be shot on sight, but if for some reason you're not, Torstyn will see to it that you never speak. He can fry your brains from a hundred yards out. Don't forget, his life is on the line too. Trust me, there's no going back. You'd better hide."

"Where?"

Welch's brow furrowed. "You ask me where? Do I have to do your thinking for you? This is one of the most populated cities in the world. Blend in."

"But we don't look Chinese," the front-seat guard said.

"And I don't speak Chinese," the other added.

"Wear a disguise," Welch said. "And how hard can it be to speak Chinese? Little children speak it."

"Where are you going?" the front-seat guard asked.

"If I told you that, I'd have to kill you."

"Let us come with you."

Welch shook his head. "No. Three Americans will stand out too much. Besides, it's only a matter of time before the temptation for one of you to turn me in would be too great." Welch leaned forward. *"Syan sheng, ching ni ting yi sya dzai nei byan."*

"Hau, hau," the driver said, his words sounding a little like laughter.

Welch turned to the guard at his side. "This is your stop. You have a new FOD; your mission is to survive. Because if the Elgen find you, they'll kill you."

The cab pulled up to the curb in front of a busy sidewalk before the crowded corridors of an open market. Welch leveled the gun at the driver. "And if I see you again, I'll kill you." The guard looked at him, then opened the door. The pungent smell of roasting tofu from a nearby food cart filled the air. "Get out."

"All right, all right." The guard climbed out of the car, looked both ways, then ran off into the thick of the market, quickly vanishing into the bustling crowds.

Welch reached over and pulled the door shut. *"Women dzou ba,"* he said to the driver.

"Dzai nali?"

"Jeng dzou."

The driver pulled away from the curb and back into the traffic like a fish thrown back into a slow-moving stream.

"What about me?" the other guard asked.

"A few more miles, then I'll let you off."

The man's head fell into his hands.

Welch said, "Don't worry too much about your predicament. It was probably only a matter of time before you were found guilty of something and Hatch had you executed. This way you at least have a fighting chance."

About fifteen minutes later Welch ordered the cab to stop again. They were near the wide, open ground of the Chiang Kai-shek Memorial.

The guard made one last appeal. "It's just the two of us now. We could protect each other."

"No," Welch said. "It doesn't work that way. Now get out. And shut the door behind you."

The guard unlatched the door, then climbed out. He furtively glanced back at Welch, hoping for a last-minute reprieve, then, not getting it, slammed the door shut, turned, and ran.

"Take me to the train station," Welch told the driver. *"Hwo che jan, chyu."*

The driver again pulled out into traffic. A few minutes later Welch changed his mind, scolding himself for his carelessness. The train station was the last place he should go, unless he wanted to be found.

No one knew the Elgen's routine of hunting AWOL guards better than Welch. As captain of the guard for more than fifteen years, he had led the majority of the Elgen's manhunts, capturing seventy-six of seventy-seven guards, a 98 percent success rate. All but one of the captured guards was executed.

Welch knew exactly what procedures the Elgen would follow. With luck, he figured that he had about five or six hours before he would be discovered missing. That's how much longer it would be before the changing of the *Faraday*'s guards.

Once Welch's absence was confirmed, Hatch would be informed and the EGGs would take over, unleashing everything in their arsenal. In addition to the Elgen guards and the elite Lung Li, the Taiwanese army and police would be looking for him as well.

Using advanced face-recognition software, they would meticulously search through every camera they could access, but especially those at the airports and train stations, where they'd suspect he'd go. They would find him. They would track down his ticket and his destination. For now he was still invisible. He intended to stay that way.

"*Deng yi sya!*" Welch said. *Wait a minute.* He needed a moment to think. As they parked at the curb, he watched two Muslim women passing them on the sidewalk, their heads covered in burkas. *That's the ticket*, he thought. He told the driver to take him to the Kaohsiung Lingya district, the Muslim section of the city.

Across the street from the Lingya mosque was a store with Muslim clothing. Welch purchased the largest burka he could find, then ducked into an alley and put it on. The garment wasn't as long as he needed, falling only to his ankles, but he doubted that the Elgen would notice. He walked back out to a busy street and hailed a new cab for the train station.

In his new disguise, Welch purchased a ticket for the small, southern town of Kangshan. He knew a woman there. Her name was Mei Li, which, in Chinese, means "beautiful." He thought that the name fit. He had met Mei Li when she was working as a waitress at the officers' lounge at the Dzwo Ying Starxource plant. When she was a child, Mei Li's parents had been Christian missionaries in Australia, so she had learned English, though through the years she had forgotten some of it.

There were three things the Elgen EGGs were strictly prohibited from: first, they could not belong to a religion; second, they could not contact their families; and third, they could not marry or even date. Welch had no trouble with the first two rules but failed the third. He had fallen in love with Mei Li. They started a secret romantic relationship. As their love deepened, Welch diverted a large sum of money to her—more than 6.5 million yuan, nearly one million American dollars—with the plan of someday running off together.

Welch was careful that they were never seen together, and after

Mei Li left the Elgen's employ, Welch erased all record of her employ-
ment. As far as the Elgen were concerned, she had never existed. No
one, not even Hatch, could trace him to her.

The train ride to Kangshan was less than an hour from the Kaohsiung
station. Welch disembarked with a dozen other passengers, then
walked outside the small, open-air station, slightly stooped in his
burka and shuffling his feet as he walked.

It took him nearly a half hour to hail a taxi, and it was dark when
it let him off three blocks from Mei Li's apartment. He gave the
driver most of the money he had left.

He waited a half hour until there was no one in sight; then he
climbed the stairs to a second-floor apartment and rang the doorbell.
After a moment a feminine voice answered from behind the door.
"Wei?"

"Mei Li, it's me. David."

"My David!" she exclaimed. "My love." She slid back the security
chain and threw open the door. "I thought you were—" She froze.
"Why are you wearing this . . . ?"

Without answering, he quickly stepped inside her apartment,
shutting the door behind them. Mei Li was in the middle of fixing
dinner, and the home smelled of curry and incense. With his hand on
his gun, Welch cautiously examined the apartment. "Are you alone?"

"Yes." She looked at him quizzically. "What is happening?"

"I've left the Elgen." He took off the burka, revealing his face and
sweat-stained clothing. "I'm being hunted. I need a place to stay for
the night. You're the only one I can trust."

Mei Li looked at him anxiously, then embraced him. "Of course
you can stay here." After a moment she looked into his eyes. "Why
are you being hunted?"

"I was arrested by Admiral-General Hatch. He condemned me to
death."

She gasped. "Death? For what reason?"

"It doesn't matter. I've missed you so much." Welch pulled her
in tighter and they kissed. After a moment Welch stepped back.

"What am I doing? I never should have come here. I've put you in danger."

"You came to the right place. I can help."

"No, I never should have involved you."

"I would not feel loved by you if you had not involved me. Especially if you had gone away without telling me. Tell me now, what do you need?"

Welch breathed out slowly. "I need help getting out of Taiwan. I need some of our money and a phone. A few of them."

"You can use my phone."

"No, they'll find you. I need for you to get me some prepaid phones."

"The stores are closed now. So is the bank."

"We can get everything in the morning. I'll leave tomorrow afternoon."

"Wherever you go, I will go with you."

Welch shook his head. "It's much too dangerous. The sooner we're apart, the better."

She sighed. "That would not be better. I would rather die than not see you again."

Welch kissed her forehead. "I'd rather neither of us die. After I'm safe, I'll send for you. Then we can be together."

"Then for now you will stay with me and I will be happy. Are you hungry?"

"I'm starving," he said. "I don't remember the last time I ate real food. In the brig they only serve Rabisk."

"What is Rabisk?"

"It's made from dead rats."

She shuddered. "Come eat."

Welch chained and bolted the door, then followed Mei Li across the room to the kitchen. The apartment had stone tile floors and an icon mounted to the wall, with a gold-framed picture of Mei Li's deceased parents between sticks of burning incense.

In the kitchen he sat down at the small table.

"I have made curry rice." She brought him a plate piled high with sticky rice covered with a yellow sauce and chunks of chicken meat and green pepper. Then she got a plate for herself and sat down across from him at the table. She let him eat for a moment, then asked, "Do you know where you will go from here?"

He finished chewing, then said, "No. But I wouldn't tell you if I did. It's too dangerous for you."

"I have a cousin who lives near Changhua. He owns a farm in the country. He cannot speak. What is that word?"

"He is *mute*."

"Yes. *Mute*. You can go there. They will never find you there. It is *remote*."

He shook his head. "I'll stand out too much in a country town."

"Not if you wear that clothing. Besides, the village people keep their own stories. It is their way. You can stay there while you make your plans to leave Taiwan."

Too tired to think of a better plan, Welch said, "All right. I'll consider it."

For the next few minutes he ate ravenously as Mei Li watched him, barely picking at her own meal. Then she said, "A week ago there was a story in the newspaper about the Starxource plant and the Elgen. The reporter wrote that in other countries the Elgen had grown so powerful, they had taken control of the government. Is that true?"

Welch looked up from his dinner and nodded. "Yes."

"Do they plan to take control of Taiwan's government?"

"They plan to take control of the whole world."

She looked upset. "Two days ago the newspaper building was . . . explosion. Twelve people were killed. Did the Elgen do that?"

"Probably," Welch said. "It wouldn't be the first time we . . ." He stopped himself. ". . . the *Elgen* has terrorized the media."

Mei Li quietly returned to her dinner. A few minutes later she asked, "If they find you, what will they do?"

"They will kill me. I don't think that they will bother to capture me alive."

"Then they must not find you."

"Not if I can help it."

"Is there anyone, besides me, who will help you?"

Welch finished his meal, then pushed his plate away. "Maybe." He looked at her full plate. "You didn't eat much."

"I'm not hungry. What else can I get you to eat?"

"Nothing. I just need to sleep."

"Yes, let's sleep."

Welch first went into Mei Li's bedroom and stacked pillows under the sheets so it looked as if someone was in the bed; then he led her to the back room. The bed was small but sufficient. He laid his gun under his pillow, then got in bed.

Mei Li climbed into the bed next to him, laying her head on his chest. She started to cry. "This could be our last night."

Welch kissed her forehead. "Not if I can help it."

As tired as he was, he didn't sleep well. He expected the Elgen to attack at any time, and he woke to every sound he heard, then stayed up, listening to the pattern of cars driving by, barking dogs, even the sound of Mei Li's breathing. He had trained the men looking for him in how to track down a fugitive. He now wished that he hadn't done such a good job.

The next morning Welch woke alone to the sound of the apartment's front door opening. He sat up and grabbed his gun and held it at the door. Then he heard soft footsteps coming toward him, and the back room door opened. Mei Li stood in the doorway holding a plastic grocery sack. "Don't shoot me," she said, half smiling.

"Sorry," Welch said, lowering his gun. "I didn't hear you leave. You should have woken me."

"You needed your sleep."

"Where have you been?"

She lifted the grocery bag. "The market. I brought you hot dumplings and soy milk. Get dressed and come eat." She walked back to the kitchen.

Welch put on his clothes, then came out. There was a *lung*, a woven bamboo steamer basket, on the table next to a shallow dish of soy sauce and chopsticks.

"You remembered that I like those," Welch said as he sat down. He lifted the lid off the basket, and a cloud of pungent steam filled the air. "Hmm."

"Yes, I remember."

He lifted his chopsticks and picked up a dumpling, dipped it into the soy sauce, and then took a large bite. "That's . . . remarkable."

"Mr. Tsai at the market makes a *mean* pork dumpling."

Welch laughed. He always laughed whenever Mei Li used an American idiom.

"Did I say that right? 'Mean,' it means *'Fei chang hau,'* like 'very good.'"

"Yes," he said, still smiling. "You used it perfectly."

"It is very strange that Americans sometimes say the opposite of what they mean."

Welch smiled. "Yes, they do. Often. Was the market busy?"

"The market is always busy in the morning. It is our way. We do not like the big supermarkets like in America."

"Did you see anything suspicious in town?"

"If you mean foreigners, no. Just some students."

"How about police?"

"You think the Taiwanese police will be hunting you?"

"I know they will be. And your military. The Elgen have arrangements with both."

"Are you sure?"

"Very. I helped make them. Hatch will tell them that I'm one of the terrorists involved with shutting down the Starxource plant. I'm certain that a picture of my face has already been circulated."

Mei Li frowned. "I saw nothing unusual."

"Is there an Internet café nearby?"

"I have Internet in my home."

"No, I don't want them to track us here."

"There is an Internet café at the end of the street near the phone store."

"Good. I can kill two birds with one stone."

She looked at him quizzically. "Why do you want to kill birds?"

"It's an American saying," he said. "It means I can do two things at once."

"*Multitask,*" she said.

Welch laughed again. "Where did you learn that?"

"American television channel. That's where I learn most of my English slang words."

Welch fumbled with his chopsticks and dropped one of the dumplings into the dish of soy sauce, spattering the brown liquid all over himself. Mei Li stifled a laugh. "Americans have more trouble with chopsticks than the Chinese language."

"We have trouble with both," Welch said.

She walked to his side. "I have a question. How are you to get out of Taiwan? If Hatch has reported you as a terrorist, you will not be able to use your passport or you will be caught."

"I'm thinking I could charter a small plane or even a boat. It's only six hundred nautical miles to the Philippines."

"I could find you a boat," Mei Li said. "But then what will you do?"

"I need to get back to America." He rubbed his chin. "I'm going to need inside help for that."

"Who will help you? Who can you trust besides me?"

"There is no one besides you. I don't know anyone who isn't Elgen or who the Elgen know about." He paused, then said, "Except Michael Vey."

"Who is Michael Vey?"

"He's a Glow."

"What is a glow?"

Her question reminded Welch of how little Mei Li actually knew about his world or the Elgen. "Michael Vey is part of a group who is fighting the Elgen."

"You mean the terrorists who attacked the Starxource plant in Zuoying?"

"Yes."

"They are bad people. You should not be with them. It is very dangerous."

"They weren't trying to shut down the plant. They were trying to rescue a little girl we had kidnapped."

Mei Li looked upset. "You kidnapped a little girl?"

"The Elgen did."

"I do not understand."

Welch leaned forward and kissed her on the forehead. "I know. There is much you don't understand. It's better that way." He held her for a moment, then said, "We don't have much time. The Elgen could already be on their way here. This morning I need you to get me money and phones."

"You need more than one?"

"I'll need six. I'll go out with you."

"Six phones? Why so many?"

"I can only use a phone once."

"You can use a phone more than once. You can use it many times. It is not . . . *disposable*."

"I'm saying, I should not use it more than once. The Elgen will be tracking all signals."

"How much money will you need?"

"Fifty thousand dollars," he said. "I'd take more, but that's already enough to raise attention."

"Are you going to wear the dress again when you go outside?"

"The burka? No. Not today."

"Then you should bathe. You smell like sweat."

Welch laughed. "Sorry, when you're running for your life, personal hygiene takes a backseat."

"Why a backseat?"

He waved his hand. "We'll go after I shower."

Forty-five minutes later Welch and Mei Li emerged from the apartment to the street below. Even though Welch was wearing a baseball cap and dark sunglasses, he still didn't dare walk with Mei Li. He wasn't willing to risk having her seen with him. She was in enough danger just knowing him, and in Taiwan, a country with a large population but little land, the Elgen had eyes everywhere.

They walked about a hundred yards to the phone store at the end of the road she lived on. While Mei Li purchased the cell phones, Welch waited for her in the Internet café next door.

The first thing he did was pull up the website for the Meridian, Idaho, newspaper's advertising department. He jotted down notes on a napkin someone had left at his table. He was careful not to access anything Elgen, as that's how he had found several of the electrics, including Michael and Taylor.

An hour and a half later, Mei Li walked past the café window. She glanced at Welch as if she didn't know him, then started back to her apartment. He let her walk for a minute until she was well ahead of him, then logged out of the computer, folded the napkin into his pocket, and walked back himself.

Mei Li was waiting for him at the door to her apartment. "Do you really think they're watching us?"

He walked inside before he answered. "I don't know, but it's possible. It's not worth the risk. Did you get everything?"

"Yes, six phones."

"And the money?"

"It took much time, but no problem."

"Good." He sat down at the kitchen table. "Do you have some writing paper?"

"Yes." She retrieved a spiral-bound notebook, and Welch began sketching.

"Why is it so important to the Elgen to find you?" Mei Li asked.

"Because I know too much. I know everything. Most of all, I know Hatch. He won't rest until he has my head on a pike."

"A pike is a fish?"

"It is, but that's not what I meant. A pike is also a stick with a sharp end."

"I am sorry. Sometimes my English . . ."

"Your English is excellent," Welch said quickly. "A lot better than my Chinese."

"Thank you," she said. She watched him continue his work. "What are you drawing?"

"An advertisement. Tonight I'll scan it and send it to the newspaper."

Mei Li looked at him quizzically. "What are you advertising?"

"For someone to rescue me. I'm sending a secret message to the Electroclan. I just hope someone is paying attention."

PART FOUR

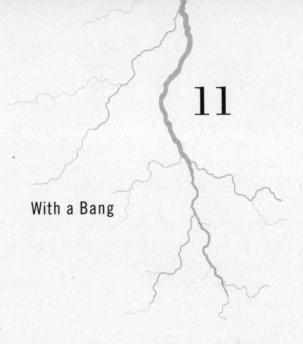

11

With a Bang

Hades Island (formerly Niutao), Tuvalu

Torstyn was tossing back and forth on his bed when he heard the pneumatic hiss of the lock on his cell door. He had been trying, unsuccessfully, to sleep for more than four hours—anything to escape the horror he felt. Making sleep even more difficult was his uncomfortable paper-fabric jumpsuit that made rustling sounds as he rolled in bed. That and the fact that the lights in his cell were always on as the cameras panned back and forth, scanning every inch of the room.

The Hades cells were patterned after the Purgatory in the academy, with some of Hatch's own "improvements." Worst of all, there was a flat-screen monitor built into the wall, and every fifteen minutes it would automatically turn on to a scene of the frenzied rats in the bowl ripping the flesh off some animal or human.

Torstyn knew the scene hadn't come from Tuvalu, as the rats were mostly being fed bulls or cows. On Tuvalu, like Taiwan, the rats were fed fish. Still, the video had the desired effect. The constant shrieks of the rats had broken him down emotionally until he could no longer eat, and he kept breaking out in uncontrolled fits of sobbing. Torstyn had tried to use his power to blow the screen, as well as the lights and cameras, but couldn't. He was powerless in this room. The cell had been designed for Glows.

He had no idea what time or day it was when the door opened and Hatch, escorted by two guards, walked into his cell.

"Stand up," Hatch said sharply.

Torstyn looked at him coolly, without moving. Hatch had already ordered him to be fed to the rats, so he didn't have much more to fear. Or so he thought.

"Stand," Hatch said. He pointed a handheld RESAT at Torstyn and pulled the trigger.

A powerful wave of pain shot through Torstyn's body, forcing him to gasp out.

"All right. You win. But I can't stand with that on."

Hatch turned off the machine. "The next time you disobey an order, I'll leave it on until you beg to be fed to the rats. Do you understand?"

"Yes, sir," Torstyn said, forcing himself to his feet.

As soon as he was standing, Hatch said, "Sit."

Torstyn did his best not to show his anger as he fell back down onto his bed. One of the guards set a chair down next to Hatch. Hatch slid it forward, then sat down across from Torstyn, his legs slightly spread.

"Leave us," Hatch said.

The guards turned and walked out. Now that Hatch was alone, Torstyn thought of physically attacking him but pushed the idea from his mind. Hatch held his RESAT with the trigger in hand. All he needed to do was flip his finger.

"So, you've had time to regret your decision," Hatch said softly.

"Yes, sir," he said eagerly. Was Hatch thinking of freeing him?

"Of course you're hoping that I have had a change of heart."

You'd have to have a heart first. "Yes, sir. I've learned my lesson."

"Hope can be such a cruel thing," Hatch said. "Camus was right. From Pandora's box, where all the ills of humanity swarmed, the Greeks drew out hope after all the others, as the most dreadful of all. . . ."

Torstyn just gazed at him, trying to decipher his meaning.

"Unfortunately, for you, at least, what is done is done." A bizarre frown twisted Hatch's mouth, and his voice fell. "*You* are done. It's already been announced to the troops that there will be a public feeding with you as the main course. They've already started the betting pools—you know the ones, you've participated in them. They'll wager on exactly how long you'll live before your heart stops, or how long your screams will last. I understand there is some wider speculation about this contest. Outside of Vey, we've never attempted to feed an electric to the rats before. But Vey was special, wasn't he? Unfortunately, you don't have the same power that he does. Unfortunate for you, at least. I'm actually fine with it."

Torstyn just blinked.

"So the only question that remains, really, is not *if* it will end for you, but *how* it will end for you. Will you fade off into oblivion peacefully?" He paused. "I mean, of course, *comparatively* peacefully? Or in prolonged, horrifying agony?"

Hatch leaned forward, his hair falling over his dark eyes. "I've come to make you a deal. For old times' sake. If you cooperate with me, I will see that you are anesthetized before going into the bowl. You will not feel those little mouths, bite by bite, eat away your life." He took a deep breath. "I can also promise you that if you don't cooperate, I will make sure that your vitals are well protected so that the furry little creatures will have to gnaw their way up your body cavity to end your life. Could you imagine what that would feel like? Rodents under your flesh? What could be more terrible?"

Torstyn tried not to show his fear but shuddered anyway.

"It was a medieval torture, you know. During the Inquisition, the torturer would place rats in a cage on top of a prisoner's body, then put hot coals on top of the cage. The rats would burrow through the body to escape the heat. I can't imagine how terrifying that would be. I've wondered what would be more painful, the rats or the horror itself. What do you think?"

Torstyn didn't answer.

"No, I don't suppose you'd care to conjecture. So I'll continue with my offer. If you fail to help me, you will be terrifyingly aware of every rat's bite. Your head and eyes will be caged, so you can see your own skeleton as the rodents strip the flesh from your legs and arms to the bones. You will witness your own slow consumption." He leaned back. "So, traitor, what will it be? Cooperation or untold agony?"

"What do you want?" Torstyn asked.

Hatch leaned in. "What I want is Welch. Where is he?"

Torstyn just looked at him. "I don't know."

Hatch gazed at him for a moment, then, with an audible sigh, stood. "I was afraid you'd say that."

"I'm telling the truth," Torstyn said frantically. "We helped him off the boat. He got into a taxi with two guards. That's all I know. I'm telling the truth."

Hatch looked at him sadly. "That's unfortunate for both of us, but especially for you." As he walked to the door, the guards opened it for him. Hatch turned back. "Tara was more creative. She made up a story. I knew she was lying, of course, but I don't fault her for trying. Fear is a powerful motivator." The guards stepped to Hatch's sides.

"If it makes you feel any better, in the words of Röhm, all revolutions devour their own children." A strange, infantile smile crossed his face. He sang sweetly:

"*Red of the morning, red of the morning,*
Thou lightest us to early death.
Yesterday mounted on a proud street,
Today a bullet through the breast."

Hatch stared into Torstyn's eyes. "You will be the first to go. You have fifteen days left to live. I suggest you use that time figuring out where Welch is." He walked out the door. The door hissed as the pneumatic lock sealed the cell after him. Torstyn fell over on the bed and sobbed.

After his visit to Tara and Torstyn, Hatch walked to the D corridor to visit Quentin, who had been released from Cell 25 just three days earlier.

Quentin was still in pain and was curled up in a fetal position on his cell's hard cot. His room was bare. He had no sheets, nothing he could hang himself with, not even his clothing, which, like Torstyn's and Tara's garb, was a pink, paper-fabric jumpsuit.

He had woken confused. He couldn't remember if it was the day he would be moved into the monkey cage. He thought he remembered a guard telling him that, but he couldn't remember or even be sure whether the guards were toying with him or not.

Ever since his stay in Cell 25 he had trouble keeping his thoughts together. Even with all the terror and humiliation of the monkey cage, he would still choose it over Cell 25. *How had Vey survived it?* Vey was a lot stronger than Quentin had given him credit for.

There was a loud burst of air, and Quentin looked up to see his door open. Hatch walked into Quentin's cell, leaving his guards outside.

"I came to see if you were ready to tell me about Welch."

Quentin looked away from him.

"I've been visiting with your partners in crime—the ones you've murdered by involving them in your plot. Not surprisingly, they are not doing well. It seems that they are afraid to die. Where you, on the other hand, would gladly die, wouldn't you?"

Quentin tightly closed his eyes.

"Cell 25 has that effect," Hatch said softly. "I went to see if they would tell me where Welch is. But they don't know, do they? Not that that would have spared them anything. Either way they will die a horrible and ignominious death." He walked closer to Quentin's cot. "I would ask if you knew where he was, but I know you don't—otherwise you would have told us in Cell 25. You have nothing to give me."

"Then what do you want?" Quentin asked.

"I just wanted to see you." Hatch sat down on the edge of Quentin's cot. "And enlighten you.

"You might be wondering, why the monkey cage? I did not invent this torture, you know. I wish I had, but someone beat me to it. There is precedence for this. You'll be glad to know you're in good company.

"At the end of World War II, the Americans established an army disciplinary camp in Pisa, Italy. Right next to the famous leaning tower. At that time, the greatest attraction in Pisa was not the tower. It was an American traitor named Ezra Loomis Pound. Pound wasn't just any American; he was one of the most famous poets in the world. He was a friend to Yeats. He collaborated with T. S. Eliot on his masterpiece 'The Waste Land'—in fact, the book is dedicated to Pound. He even hung around with Ernest Hemingway. He learned boxing from him.

"He was an absurd little man, the pride of the world's intelligentsia and the social elite. He was invited to all their fancy soirees. He once attended a London society party dressed in an all-green suit made from the felt of a billiard table.

"But none of that mattered after the war. He had betrayed his country. He, like you, was a traitor. To punish Pound for collaborating with the enemy, the Americans put him in a monkey cage. It didn't take long for it to crack his beautiful mind.

"The uncultured American soldiers would stand next to the cage and listen to the madman rant in English, Italian, Chinese, French, and even some languages he made up. They didn't realize that what he was ranting was the brilliant mental vomit of a genius, and what he said became some of the greatest poetry of his time:

"The enormous tragedy of the dream in the peasant's bent shoulders
Manes! Manes was tanned and stuffed,
Thus Ben and la Clara a Milano
*   by the heels at Milano*

. . .

yet say this to the Possum: a bang, not a whimper,
with a bang not with a whimper, . . .

"Ben and Clara were Benito Mussolini and his mistress, Clara, who were hung by their feet in Milano. The Possum was Pound's nickname for his old friend T. S. Eliot. He was mocking Eliot's poem 'The Hollow Men.'" Hatch sighed. "This is how the world ends, not with a bang but a whimper.

"Imagine the sight of it, this brilliant cracked mind throwing his pearls to the swine. It was Pound who later declared, 'All America is an insane asylum.'" Hatch looked at Quentin. "He was right, you know. Except he was too limited in his scope. The whole *world* is an asylum. And it needs a new director.

"Tomorrow you go to the cage. Perhaps there you too will find the insanity of genius." A cruel smile crossed his face. "Or, then again, maybe just insanity." Hatch walked to the door. "Eliot was right, not Pound. This is how the world ends, not with a bang, but a whimper."

"There will be a bang," Quentin said. "The sound of your fall after you're brought down and made to pay for your crimes."

"You're delusional," Hatch said. "Who can challenge me? Who can't I buy off?"

"Michael Vey," Quentin said. "He's the good guy. I can see that now. And in the end he's going to win."

For just a moment Hatch's arrogance flickered. Then his eyes narrowed. "Michael Vey is nothing. And in the end I will feed you his flesh." He turned and walked out of the cell.

Quentin curled back up into a fetal position.

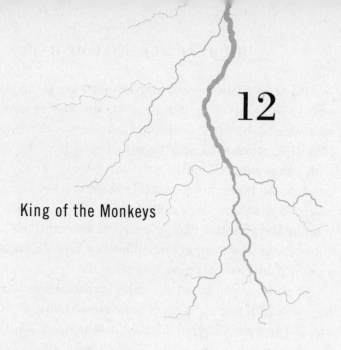

12

King of the Monkeys

Early the next morning the lights turned on in Quentin's cell, signaling the start of a new day. Actually, a new life. A terrible life. Quentin wondered how long he would survive it.

He forced himself from his bed and walked over to the sink. For reasons he didn't understand he desperately wanted to brush his teeth—a strange desire, considering what was to come. He was shaking so hard, he had trouble holding the brush.

His heart froze when he heard the sharp, synchronized clicks of heavy boot steps coming down the hall, followed by the hiss of his cell door's pneumatic lock.

The door swung open. Quentin turned to see a guard step inside his cell. He wore the scarlet armband of a Zone Captain, just one level down from an EGG. Behind him was a lower-ranked Squad Captain in the purple Elgen uniform. The men were followed by twelve guards.

Hatch was noticeably absent. Quentin guessed that he was making a point by not being there. He was also making a point by sending a dozen guards when two would have been sufficient. In Quentin's present, weakened condition, one would have been enough. The guards were wearing dress uniforms, which meant that his internment would be a ceremony of sorts. There would be an audience at his encagement.

The Zone Captain spoke. "Quentin, face me."

Quentin slowly turned around. Since Cell 25, all his movements seemed slow. He looked the captain in the eyes.

"For acts of treason against Admiral-General Hatch and the Elgen politic, you have been sentenced to life internment in the eastern primate cage of the Hatch Center Square. Guards, take the prisoner."

Six of the guards rushed past the captain and surrounded Quentin. The Squad Captain stepped forward. "You are commanded to disrobe."

Quentin crossed his arms. There was usually humiliation involved in Hatch's punishment, but he wasn't going to allow it if possible.

The man looked him over, then smiled darkly. "Defiant? You can undress yourself, or my men will undress you. One way will be painful for you, one won't, but the end result is the same. I don't care which you choose."

Quentin took another deep breath, then took off his bright pink jumpsuit. "I never liked pink, anyway," he said, throwing the garment to the floor.

"... And your underwear."

Quentin bristled. "He's keeping me naked like the prime minister?"

"The Prime *Monkey*," the Squad Captain corrected. "No, the general is being more merciful to you. He's sent you this." He lifted a loincloth—a simple square of thin brown fabric just slightly smaller than a washcloth. It had two leather straps to hold it to his waist. "Now undress."

Quentin pulled down his underwear. The Squad Captain tossed him the loincloth. Quentin caught it and tied it around his waist.

Then he looked back up, his gaze meeting his enemy's. "Someday I will punish you. You *and* Hatch."

The Squad Captain laughed. "*General* Hatch," he said. "And insanity usually sets in after you've been in the monkey cage, not before."

"You're the insane ones. And you're following a madman."

The Squad Captain's eyes narrowed. "If you don't think your general is merciful, consider that, unlike Prime Monkey Saluni, you still have your tongue. If you can't be more judicious with it, I will happily relieve you of its burden."

Quentin glared at him but kept his tongue. Literally. The Squad Captain nodded to the guards, who grabbed Quentin by the arms and cuffed his hands behind his back.

"Elgen guard, deliver the traitor to the square."

The Funafuti Central Square was a half mile from the prison, and Quentin walked it barefoot and mostly naked. He was glad of just one thing: it was still early morning and there were few out to view his march.

The plaza, now renamed Hatch Center Square, was five acres of smooth, round cobblestone. In the very center, next to a flagpole, workers were erecting a fifty-foot marble column, which would eventually hold a bronze heroic-size statue of General Hatch. The project was behind schedule, and the original project manager had been sent to the rat bowl for incompetence.

On each side of the column was a large metal cage. The first cage Quentin was well aware of, as he'd passed it many times before. In addition to its primate inhabitants, it held the former prime minister Saluni. Attached to the bars of the cage was a metal sign that read:

PRIME MONKEY

The procession marched in front of the cage. Saluni was quietly huddled in one corner. He already looked more animal than human. He was pale and ill and had lost enough weight that his ribs seemed to stretch his skin. He was covered with filth and fleas and blood, as he bore dozens of bite marks. He had been attacked by the monkeys, fighting for the alpha position of the cage. The prime minister appeared to have lost. Where he once led a nation, he was now subject to the cage's largest monkey.

Saluni watched the procession with dull, lifeless eyes, and Quentin quickly turned away from him. Quentin had once mocked the prime minister for his misfortune. Now Quentin could hear the echo of his cruelty returning to him.

As he passed, the tongueless leader let out a loud screech, and Quentin jumped. The pitiful, anguished cry filled him with terror. How long until he too was reduced to an animal?

The guard passed the marble column to a second cage, where a crowd of Tuvaluan natives was gathered. Baskets filled with rotted fruit and vegetables sat on the ground in front of them. It was a smaller crowd than Quentin expected, less than a hundred natives, and he thought they looked nearly as miserable as him. Many of them even looked away from the procession, as if they were embarrassed for him. Quentin had imagined that there would be a larger crowd, eager for revenge. But even those gathered didn't look as if they wanted to be there. It occurred to him that they'd been brought against their will.

The guards walked Quentin in front of the second cage and paused briefly for him to view it. The cage was filled with capuchin monkeys, who watched the parading humans with curiosity as they swung around on tree branches, whistling and screeching with excitement.

The cage stunk from the monkeys' droppings, which covered the cage floor. Quentin realized that he had been so worried about the cage itself that he had neglected to consider its occupants. He wondered, for the first time, if the monkeys would attack him.

The guards marched Quentin around to a large platform on the side of the cage. Quentin recognized the platform as the same one he had stood on as Hatch pronounced him king of the Hatch Islands. It was not a coincidence that the same platform was being

used, and Hatch would have been pleased that the irony was not
lost on Quentin.

There was a door on the side of the cage with a handwritten sign:

**QUENTIN THE TRAITOR
KING OF THE MONKEYS**

An especially large guard stood next to the cage door, with a chain
draped over his shoulder and a heavy padlock in his hand. One of the
guards unlocked Quentin's cuffs and took them off.

Then the large guard opened the cage door. "Welcome to your
new kingdom," he said solemnly, reciting the words he'd been
assigned. "Rule it well."

Quentin looked warily at the monkeys who were already gathering near the door. He wished that he had Torstyn's or even Tara's
powers. An EMP would do nothing to monkeys. For the first time
ever he wished that he were Michael Vey.

"Go," the guard said.

In the lunacy of the moment, Quentin's mind drifted to something he had studied back at the academy: Dante's *Inferno*, Canto III.

Through me you pass into the city of woe:
Through me you pass into eternal pain:
Through me among the people lost for aye.

. . .

All hope abandon, ye who enter here.

"All hope abandon," Quentin mumbled to himself, unable to make
himself go any farther.

"Step inside, or I'll throw you inside," the guard said gruffly.

Quentin took a deep breath, then walked up to the cage door
opening and stepped inside, his bare feet squishing in the monkeys'
feces.

"Your new *kingdom*," the guard said again, this time laughing. He
shut the door behind Quentin, wrapped the chain around the bars of

the gate, and then locked it, slipping the key into his pocket. "By the admiral-general's orders, though sick or dying, you will never set foot outside of this cage again."

The pronouncement sent chills through Quentin's body.

The guards, still in formation, stepped down from the platform, and the Zone Captain picked up a megaphone from the side of the cage. "Citizens of Hatch Islands. Before you is a traitor to your country. Show him your displeasure."

The natives showed no displeasure nor interest whatsoever, but just stood there staring.

The Zone Captain lowered the megaphone and shook his head. "Idiots." He turned to his side. "Squad Captain. Show them the fruit."

The Squad Captain approached the people. "There's fruit here."

Still no one moved.

The Zone Captain growled, "Show the people what they're supposed to do with the fruit."

"Yes, sir." The Squad Captain walked over to one of the baskets and picked up an overripe tomato. Speaking slowly, he said, "You throw the fruit at the traitor. Like this." He turned and lobbed the tomato at Quentin, though he missed by at least twelve feet and hit a large, silver-haired capuchin monkey that screeched, then jumped to the opposite side of the cage, climbing the bars to the top.

The Zone Captain shook his head again. "Maybe we should get someone with a better aim."

"Sorry, sir." The Squad Captain picked up a rotten guava and walked up next to the cage and threw it, hitting Quentin on the calf. Then he walked back to the group, who still showed no interest.

"Now *you* pick up the fruit and throw it."

One of the older men stepped forward and lifted a papaya. He looked around, then took a bite of it.

"No!" the Squad Captain shouted. "Don't eat it! Throw it!"

The man looked at him curiously as he took another bite.

"They're mocking you," the Zone Captain said. He grabbed a machine gun from one of the guards and fired it just a few feet above the crowd's heads. Everyone fell to the ground. "Next time," he shouted, "I will aim lower! Now throw."

The frightened natives immediately began picking the fruit from the baskets and throwing it at Quentin, who cowered at the back of the cage, covering his face with his arms. Still, only a few pieces of fruit hit their mark. Quentin couldn't understand why they weren't trying harder to hit him. *After how he'd treated them, why would they show him mercy?* Their lack of resentment was completely foreign to him.

After the baskets were empty, the Zone Captain angrily dismissed the crowd, which quickly vanished. All of the guards, except the one assigned to the cage, marched back to their posts. The ceremony was over. Only Admiral-General Hatch, who was watching the ceremony on a security screen in his office, and the monkeys found the event amusing.

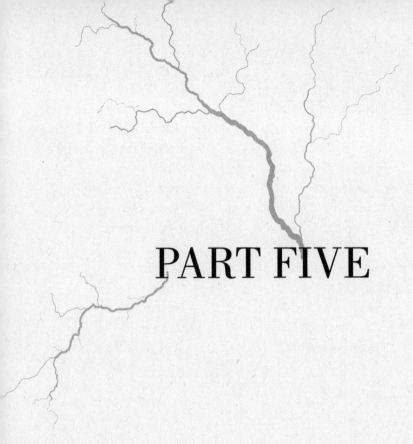

PART FIVE

13

ELGEN SOS

Christmas Ranch

It was a little after noon when Gervaso knocked on the door to Chairman Simon's office in the resistance's main ranch house.

"Who is it?"

"Gervaso. I need to talk to you."

"Come in," the chairman said.

Gervaso stepped into the small wood-paneled office.

The chairman looked up at him from his desk. "How are the kids?"

"Bored. Anxious. Exactly how they should be." Gervaso laid a piece of paper on the chairman's desk. It was a printed copy of a newspaper ad that had been cut out. "I think you should see this."

The chairman looked up. "Where did you get this?"

"Gabino, our mechanic up in Idaho, came across it in the *Idaho Statesman*. I had him e-mail it over."

The chairman looked back over the ad, then up again. "Is it a relative of Michael's?"

Gervaso shook his head. "There aren't any other Veys in Idaho. In fact, there's no such company as Vey Electric anywhere in the US."

"Then what is this?"

"It was the name 'Vey' that caught Gabino's eye, but there's something even more peculiar about this. Look at the phone number. The whole state of Idaho's area code is 208. This is an 886 number. I looked it up. Eight-eight-six is the country code for Taiwan."

"Taiwan?"

"I think someone might be trying to get in touch with us. But it's not just anyone. It's someone who knows that Michael Vey is electric, and that makes it a very short list." A more serious look crossed Gervaso's face. "And then I found the hidden message."

The chairman looked back down at the ad for a moment, then looked back up again. "I don't see it."

"Read the first letter of each line."

He looked back down, reading each letter aloud. "E.L.G.E.N. S.O.S." He looked up with wide eyes. "It's a call for help."

"I think it's Welch. He's trying to reach us."

"Or it could be a trap."

"It could be, but the Elgen aren't usually that subtle. They don't have to be. I think whoever did this only wanted the right eyes to find it."

"Have you tried the number?"

"Not yet. I wanted to make sure that you were on board and ready to send a team to bring Welch back."

The chairman thought a moment, then said, "There's a good chance the Elgen have found this as well."

"That is a risk. Still, it's one I think we should take."

The chairman took a deep breath, then said, "Call the number."

Gervaso walked a hundred yards up the hill behind the main house to the water tower. He climbed the ladder to the top to make the call. The ringing had a far away, tinny sound.

"Vey Electric."

The voice answering was low and coarse. Gervaso thought it was a strange thing to hear the voice of his enemy.

"I found your message," Gervaso said.

"Whom am I speaking with?"

"A friend of Michael's. I presume you are Welch."

There was a brief pause; then the voice said, "We cannot speak long. I need your help getting out of Taiwan."

"Why would we help you?" Gervaso asked.

"Don't play this game. We both know I have information you need to bring down Hatch."

"How do we know we can trust you?"

"Just go online. You can see for yourself that Hatch has put a million-dollar bounty on my head. That's not something he can fake."

"We'll send a team to get you out of the country. Where are you?"

"Obviously I can't say that over the phone. Create an e-mail address, and I will send you information. I'll give you more information after you arrive on the island. I need to be careful for both of us."

"Understood."

"I'm going to give you another phone number. Do not lose it. It's the only number where you will be able to reach me. Do you have something to write with?"

"Yes. Go ahead."

Welch gave him the number, then asked, "Is this number one I can reach you at later?"

"Yes. This is my personal number."

"I'll be in touch tomorrow."

"I'll wait to hear from you. Good-bye."

Welch hung up. Gervaso put the phone back into his pocket, then looked out over the sprawling ranch. The wind blew softly, and the tapping sound of a woodpecker echoed in the distance like a telegraph. Everything was so peaceful. *Not for long*, he thought. *Not for long.*

PART SIX

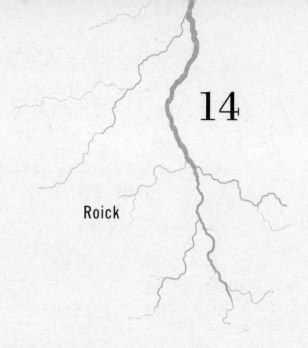

14

Roick

Nike, Tuvalu

"**A**dmiral-General, sir, I have something to report."

"Come in, Roick," Hatch said. Dawid Roick was the first Polish recruit to the Elgen force and had risen quickly to the rank of Zone Captain. He was loyal, smart, and a fanatic for the Elgen cause, all qualities Hatch admired.

"Our spiders picked this up," Roick said.

VEY ELECTRIC
Your Full-Service Electrical Experts
• Emergency Installations
• Lighting Designs
• Generator Systems
• Electric Water Heaters
• New House Wiring

Hatch's eyes slowly panned over the ad. "Mr. Vey, what are you up to?"

"We don't believe it's Vey," Roick said.

Hatch looked up. "No?"

"We believe it's from someone trying to reach Vey. It's a code." Roick ran his finger along the bulleted line. "ELGEN SOS," he said. "The phone number listed isn't an Idaho number. It's the country code for Taiwan."

"Welch!" Hatch said. "It's Welch."

"That's what we're thinking."

"That means he has a phone. And if he has a phone, we can track him."

"Exactly. We wait until he uses it, triangulate it, and capture him. We've already begun. He's in central Taiwan near the city of Changhua."

"Does EGG Daines know about this?"

"Yes, sir. He's already assembled a team to capture him. We're just waiting for Welch to use the phone again to pinpoint his exact location."

Hatch sat back. "Tell Daines I want to be briefed in real time about his mission."

"Yes, sir."

"Well done, Roick. After Welch is captured, I'll see that you are amply rewarded. We do have a vacancy among the EGGs."

"Thank you, sir. It's my pleasure to be of assistance, sir."

As Roick walked out of the office, Hatch smiled. "I've got you, Welch. You fool. I knew I'd get you. Once again, you've failed."

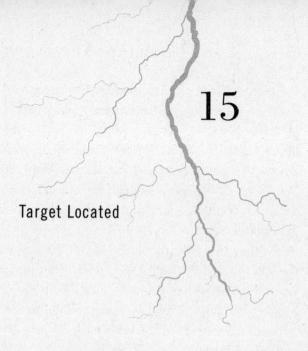

15

Target Located

The Elgen's cellular triangulation revealed that Welch was hiding out at a farm in the small Taiwanese farming village of Dazhu, along Taiwan's western coast. The village was built near a hilly valley stepped with rice patties. It was a remote location, primitive, about five miles outside of the main city of Changhua.

For Daines, it was a perfect place to attack. The only possible escape route was a small bamboo forest to the east, which was where the Elgen would create their line. If Welch chose to run, he'd be forced out into the open and gunned down.

Hatch wasn't taking any chances with losing Welch again. He personally alerted the Taiwanese army that he had located one of the terrorists who had brought down the Taiwanese Starxource plant. He also arranged for the Taiwanese Coast Guard to patrol the coast and supply a guard unit of a hundred men to supplement the eight squads of guards under the command of EGG Daines.

Those were only precautions. Hatch had complete confidence in Daines—he was as efficient as he was ruthless and had proven himself a skilled hunter of beast and men. Daines had been born in South Africa and, as a child, had learned the Zulu method of hunting lions. The native warriors would fan out in a large V formation armed with only leather-capped drums, which they pounded fiercely as they marched forward.

As they moved through the brush, the lion would run away from the sound to where hunters would be waiting with spears or, in later years, high-powered rifles. Daines's plan for catching Welch was roughly the same. The Taiwanese soldiers would, in a V formation, advance on one side of the farmhouse, forcing Welch into the waiting ambush of heavily armed Elgen guards.

The key was to make him run. A man holed up in a fortification can dig in for days, but a man on the run is exposed, vulnerable, and more likely to make rash, poor decisions.

Daines's force moved quickly as it surrounded the farmhouse. Drones, snipers, and men with high-powered binoculars watched every inch of the farm. Welch couldn't go anywhere without being seen. In addition, they were tracking his phone. Daines, who was positioned in a jeep at a vantage point a hundred yards away, was watching a monitor with a green dot designating Welch's phone's location. It was currently moving from side to side inside the farmhouse.

Daines said to Hatch over his handheld radio, "Sir, we've got the target located and surrounded. We're ready to move."

"Then move," Hatch said. "Bring me his head."

"Roger that," Daines said. He set down his radio and turned to his lieutenant. "Move in."

"Yes, sir." He spoke into his radio. "The guard will advance."

The staggered line of Taiwanese soldiers began closing in on the farmhouse.

After a minute Daines radioed his advance team. "Can you see any movement from the house?"

"Nothing," a voice replied. "A couple dogs just ran out of the house."

"They must have heard us." Daines looked down at his monitor. "Are you sure you see nothing? There's target movement on my monitor."

"No, sir."

"Could there be an underground tunnel?"

"No, sir. We're surrounded by rice paddies."

"We need to move in faster. Secure the facility. Let no one past you."

"Yes, sir."

As Daines watched his troops close in around the farmhouse, the green dot on his monitor suddenly passed through the army's line.

"Captain!" Daines shouted into the radio. "Welch has just crossed your lines and moved outside your circle. He's behind you."

"Unless he's invisible, that's impossible. Give me coordinates."

"Five, two-three-four, seven. Is he disguised as a soldier?"

"There is no human at those coordinates."

"Well, something just walked through your lines." Daines pulled out his gun and turned to his driver. "Go!"

The driver followed Daines's directions until he shouted again, "There! He's stopped in that clearing." Daines jumped out of the truck, holding out his gun. "Cover me."

"Yes, sir."

Daines walked around the brush, expecting to surprise Welch. Instead, all he found was a small, underfed dog lapping at the water in the rice paddy. It docilely looked up at him as he approached. The dog had silver duct tape wrapped around its torso.

"What have you got there?" Daines said, squatting down next to the animal. There was a rectangular, boxlike lump under the tape. Daines ran his hand over it, then let out a deep breath. "Welch, you clever devil."

Welch's cell phone was strapped to the dog's back. Unbeknownst to them, Welch was already in the center of Changhua.

16

Lying Low

By the time the Elgen had reached Changhua, Welch had used four of the six cell phones Mei Li had purchased for him. He would use each phone only once, then discard it, usually attaching it to a random vehicle or animal. One he had placed inside the bumper of a bus headed north to Taipei, another on a frozen-fish delivery truck. His first phone he had taped to the dog in Changhua.

It was the same phone that Gervaso had called to contact him. For the time being, Welch had taken the batteries from the last two phones. He wouldn't need them for a few more days—not until the Electroclan arrived in Taiwan. Until then he would lay low in a small apartment Mei Li had found and stocked with food and water.

Still, he was anxious. He just hoped the Electroclan found him before the Elgen did.

PART SEVEN

17

Unseen Currents

Michael Vey at Christmas Ranch

My life has taught me that nothing in this world stays the same. Nothing. Not me. Not even you. The sooner you accept this, the sooner you can figure out how to live your life. Maybe even enjoy it.

Two things I know about change. First, sometimes it seems like we're just bobbing up and down in the ocean trying to keep our heads above water, when really we are being moved along by unseen currents, imperceptibly being dragged to some distant shore.

Second, it pretty much always hurts.

I keep reminding myself of this, because while the world we live in is changing, so are our hearts and minds. Things that are important now won't be important later. And things that aren't important now will be super-important later. It's true for everyone. You start out thinking you're going to be some kind of person and that life is laid out and as predictable as a video game. Then you realize that the rules have changed. There are characters in your game you didn't plan on. There are things you have to do that you never wanted to do. And sometimes the purpose of the game seems to change. I suppose it's like that for everyone. Everyone must come to the realization that the life they have and the life they thought they'd have aren't ever the same thing. And then the question is, what are they going to do about it?

I suppose that's what Hatch and the Elgen are about. Change. Evolution. Or de-evolution. Oh, I guess there's one more thing I know about change. Not everything changes for the better.

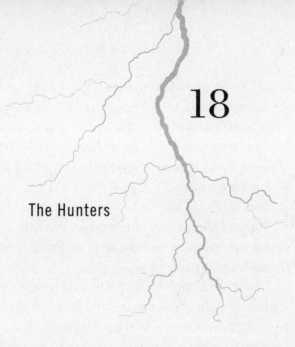

18

The Hunters

It was a Sunday, I think. I wasn't sure. Since arriving at the ranch, it had been hard to keep track of what day it was. The sun was setting over the western hills of Kane County, casting the ranch in a rose-gold hue, which, in spite of all the fear I carried, was still beautiful.

After dinner, Taylor and I grabbed a couple of quilts from my bunkhouse and walked down to the pond. We lay the blankets flat on the wooden dock that hung out over water that had been dyed blue-green so it looked more like water from the Bahamas than a cow pond.

The sun had fallen during our short walk, and the canyons to the east were bright pink with the sun's last offering. We lay down next to each other.

"It's so beautiful," Taylor said.

I pointed toward a large stone outcrop. "See that ridge right there, that juts out? It's called Queen's Throne."

"How do you know that?"

"Ostin," I said.

"Ostin," she repeated. "Of course Ostin knew."

"Just past that is the city of Kanab. They used to shoot a lot of old Western movies there. They call it 'Little Hollywood.'"

"Ostin again?"

I nodded. "He knows everything."

We looked out over the horizon in silence. The canyons changed as the sun fell more and shadows crept up from the plateau's jagged foothills like a rising hand.

I swatted at a moth that was fluttering in front of my face. Being outside at night at the ranch was a problem. As the sun set, the insects were attracted to our glows, but especially mine, which now seemed to be getting brighter almost daily. I felt like a glowstick. Or, more accurately, a bug zapper. (An Electrical Discharge Insect Control System, as Ostin would call it.) The truth is, I didn't need to swat at the bugs. They'd disintegrate as soon as they landed on my skin. I just didn't like the powder marks and the smell of burning insects on my body.

"Your glow is getting brighter," Taylor said.

"I'm still getting more electric."

"Does that worry you?"

"I don't know. I'm not sure what it means." I looked at Taylor. "I find myself still worrying about that lie Hatch told me at the academy about some of the electric children dying of cancer."

"He uses fear and lies to control people."

"The thing is, I know it's a lie. So why do I still think about it?"

"A lie can exist in your mind even when you know it's a lie. That's why you should never stop challenging your beliefs."

I looked out over the pond. A fish jumped. "You're right."

"It's so peaceful out here," Taylor said. She was tracing the fernlike scars on my arm with her fingernail.

"They're weird, aren't they?" I said.

"I like them. I always have." She was quiet a moment more, then said, "I'm afraid of this mission. I have a bad feeling about it." She looked up into my eyes. "Are you afraid?"

I took a deep breath. "Yeah. Like out of my skull afraid."

"Then why are we doing this? Why don't we just stay here?"

"Because eventually the Dark Lord will reach the Shire," I said. Taylor looked at me peculiarly. "I mean the battle will come here, too."

"Then let it," she said. "Let them come to us."

"By the time it reaches us, it will be too late. We'll have no chance at all."

She sighed. "You're right. I don't like it, but I know you're right." She went back to tracing on my arm. "Is everyone coming?"

"So far."

"Even Grace?"

"No. She'll be helping from back here. She'd just be another person we'd have to watch out for."

"My parents are freaking out about this. My father doesn't want me to go."

"When did he say that?"

"Last night. He said we just got back together and he'll never let me out of his sight again."

A part of me was glad to hear this. The protective part of me didn't want her to go, even though I honestly didn't think we could succeed without her.

"This morning I heard him telling the chairman that this was a suicide mission and he couldn't believe the chairman would send a bunch of kids to their deaths."

"What did the chairman say?"

"He said that we aren't just a bunch of kids. That we're not only gifted, we're smart."

"That describes us," I said sardonically.

"Then he said he knew it was dangerous, but these are dangerous times." She hesitated. "No, he said *desperate* times. And desperate times require desperate measures."

"So we're a desperate measure," I said.

"Apparently." She frowned. "You know what's really weird? My brothers in college have no idea what's going on. My father hadn't even told them that my mother was arrested."

"How would you even begin to explain things to them?"

"I have no clue. Especially since they probably think our parents are dead." She shook her head. "They don't even know I'm electric." Taylor's frown deepened. "Do you think that the Elgen would hunt down my brothers?"

I didn't want to tell her what I really thought. The truth was, I was surprised that the Elgen hadn't found them already. "I don't know," I finally said. "So what are you going to do about the mission?"

"What do *you* want me to do?"

I thought for a moment, then breathed out slowly. "I want you to be safe. I want you to be a million miles away from Hatch and the Elgen."

"That would put me on the sun."

I grinned. "The sun is ninety-three million miles from the Earth."

She grinned back. "Really, Ostin?"

"Sorry. I am starting to sound like him."

"One Ostin's enough." She laughed. "Actually, one is *more* than enough."

"My point is, I don't care how far you are from Hatch, just as long as he can't find you."

"So you don't want me to go?"

I again hesitated. "I want you to be safe. But I don't know if we can do it without you. I know I can't. You saved my butt at least ten times."

"You've saved mine, too," Taylor said softly. "Don't worry. I know you need me. And I'm not a kid asking my mommy and daddy for permission anymore. I left all that back in Idaho. My dad still doesn't understand the big picture. He still believes that things can go back to the way they were and we can be a cozy, innocent little family. What he wants right now doesn't matter. The only thing that matters is whether or not it's the right thing." She touched my face. "You taught me that."

"If we don't stop the Elgen, they'll just grow more powerful. The longer we wait, the more dangerous they become. Like python eggs."

"Exactly. Easy to crush, but let them hatch and grow, and they'll crush you."

Let them Hatch, I thought.

"There's something else I don't know what to do about. . . . I mean, in case we don't make it back," Taylor said.

"What's that?"

"I know what Jade Dragon knows. I mean, I don't understand it, but I could recite it all. Should I tell them?"

I swatted at another moth. "I don't think so."

"You don't trust the resistance?"

"I don't know if I trust them with *that*."

"But we've trusted them with our lives."

"It's not the same. Even if they weren't our friends, our lives are important to them. But this is different. Some information is too tempting. It's like, I've never stolen anything before, but if you told me that there's a million dollars, unguarded, in a box behind the school, I might consider taking it. You know what I mean?"

"Yeah."

"What if someone decides that it's a good idea to beat Hatch at his own game by creating their own electric civilization?"

"Someone? You mean, the resistance?"

I nodded. "We don't really know much about the voice, do we? What I do know is that that much power in one person's hands is too much. Besides, they know where to find Jade Dragon." I kissed the top of Taylor's head. "There will be time to figure this out after we come back."

She nodded. "*After* we come back." She cuddled back into me. We lay there quietly on the quilt with my arms around her, and her head on my chest. She felt so good. So warm and soft. In spite of the mess of my life, I still felt lucky. If my electricity had brought me nothing but Taylor, it was worth it. I couldn't imagine loving anyone more than I loved her.

Then Taylor lifted her head and looked at me. "There's something else I want to tell you. But I'm afraid."

I leaned up on one elbow. "Why would you be afraid?"

"I don't want you to think I'm crazy."

"I know you're crazy," I said.

She punched my shoulder. "No, I'm serious. It's weird."

"So? I'm weird. Tell me."

She took a deep breath. "How do I begin?" She hesitated a moment, then said, "I read something the other day that said we only use ten percent of our brains. Except, like Ostin, he probably uses like ninety percent, but this article said that if we could use all of our brains, we would not only be able to read minds, but we'd be able to see the future." She looked at me intensely. "I thought it was interesting that they made the connection of mind reading to seeing the future. What do you think of that?"

I shrugged. "I don't know how you could know something that hasn't happened. But I don't know if time is really the way we think it is. Ostin once tried to explain to me Einstein's theory of relativity and how time warps. I didn't get it. He also said that Stephen Hawking said that he couldn't understand why we couldn't remember the future, so maybe if our brains were powerful enough, we could."

"So you think that it might be possible to tell the future?"

"Yes. I mean, people have made predictions before, like prophets and Nostradamus and stuff." I looked into her eyes. "Why?"

"Something is happening to me. I keep having dreams. But they don't feel like dreams, they feel real. Almost like memories. And they come true. At least they have so far."

"What kind of dreams?"

She sat up, pulling back from me a little. "Like, right after we escaped the Starxource plant in Taiwan, I had a dream that all these black dragons were flying over Timepiece Ranch and then they started breathing fire over it until everything was burned to ashes. After it was over, there was one dead dragon on the ground.

"And when we got there, that's what we saw—the ranch was completely burned up and there was one crashed helicopter on the ground."

"Why didn't you tell me about your dream?" I sat up too.

"I didn't think it mattered then. I mean, we were facing real nightmares in Taiwan. But then I had another dream. The night after we met up with Gervaso in the Gadsden, I had a dream that my mother was in a cage and my father was walking around it dressed in his police uniform. I asked him why he didn't let her out, and he said, 'Because she stole you.' I said, 'How could she steal me, I'm right here?' and he said, 'No one can see you, so the police won't let her go.'" Taylor exhaled slowly. "Then, just a few days later, we find out that my mother had been arrested by the Boise police and charged with my disappearance."

"That's weird," I said, not sure what to say. Taylor looked upset.

"I don't know what to make of it." She looked me in the eyes. "Am I, like, psychic?"

"Maybe we should talk to Ostin about this. I'm sure he'll know something about this."

Taylor put her hand on my arm. "I don't want anyone else to know. At least not yet."

"Okay," I said. "Anyway, if it's true, then it's a good thing. We'll have an idea of what's going on."

"Yeah, if we knew what my dreams meant. Like, last night I had a dream that my father grew antlers like a deer and was running around the ranch being chased by hunters. Then one of them shot him."

"Were they Elgen?"

"I don't think so. I mean, it was like they were just . . . hunters."

Just then the serenity was broken by the sound of three gunshots— the sharp recoil echoing through the surrounding hills.

"What was that?" Taylor asked.

"Gunshots." My worst fear flooded in. *What if the Elgen has found us?*

"We'd better go see," I said. I looked to the hill south of us, where the water tower and sentry were. "It came from over there."

Leaving our blankets, we ran up the north bank of the hill toward the water tower. It wasn't easy in the dark, as our path was lit only by a rising moon.

We had run nearly two hundred yards from the pond when we reached the top of the hill. We were both out of breath, and my face was ticking like crazy. We stopped next to the water tower to rest.

The water tower was nearly thirty feet high, with a three-thousand-gallon water tank and an observation deck on top that was usually manned by a lookout, but wasn't now.

"Isn't there supposed to be someone—"

"Shh," I said, raising my hand. I could hear voices below us. "They're down there," I whispered, looking toward the base of the southern slope.

The hill was cast in dark shadows and covered with cedar and juniper, which gave us good cover as we hurried down. We pulled our sleeves over our hands so the only visible glow was on our faces.

At the base of the hill, on the dirt road that paralleled the corral leading to the main house, was a group of five or six men.

"Are they Elgen?" Taylor asked.

"I can't tell. Let's get closer."

As we neared the road, I could see that the two men with their backs to the ranch were Chairman Simon and Taylor's father. In front of them were four men with rifles.

"That's my dad," Taylor said, starting to stand. I grabbed her.

"Stay down. They aren't Elgen, but they've got guns."

"They're hunters," Taylor said. "What are they doing out so late?"

"Let's get closer."

About twenty feet from the road there was a fallen juniper with its roots extending high enough that we could hide behind it. We crept the final few feet, carefully picking our steps to not make any sound. As we reached the tree, we could clearly see the chairman and Mr. Ridley and the four men dressed in hunting gear. The hunters looked angry, and there was obvious tension. Mr. Ridley also looked angry. The chairman was speaking.

"I don't *care* where the elk ran. This is private property. You need to turn around and go back to where you came from."

One of the hunters laughed, then mumbled something. It sounded to me like he had been drinking.

"Listen, joker," one of the hunters said. "I got a shot on that elk, and I'm claiming it."

The chairman crossed his arms. "You can claim all you want, but this is private property. You can't trespass."

Another one of the men spoke, his words slightly slurred. "We chased it here. If we're in chase, we can continue. It's the law."

"That's only a law for police in pursuit," Mr. Ridley said. "I'm a cop. And I'm giving you ten seconds to turn around and get your hairy hides out of here."

The men looked at each other; then two of them leveled their guns at Ridley. "What kinda stupid are you? We're in the middle of nowhere, you got four men with guns, and you're telling them to leave? Maybe I'll just bag—" The man suddenly stopped, and his rifle drooped until it was pointing at the ground.

I looked over. Taylor was reaching toward him, rebooting him. Then he reached up and grabbed his forehead. Actually, it looked more like he was clawing it, as if there was something inside it that he was trying to get out.

Seeing the man's helplessness, Mr. Ridley rushed him, grabbing the barrel of the rifle. One of the other hunters pulled a large bowie knife from a sheath on his belt, and the other two lifted their guns.

"Stop it!" I shouted.

There was a rifle blast, and Mr. Ridley fell to the ground.

"They shot my father!" Taylor shouted, jumping up and running toward the men. One of the hunters, startled, wheeled around toward us with his gun.

"Taylor!" I shouted again. Before the hunter could pull the trigger, I pulsed, and a massive blue-gold wave of electricity exploded, knocking Taylor, the chairman, and all four of the hunters to the ground.

I ran to Taylor while the chairman crawled over next to Mr. Ridley. In the dark I could see something black around Mr. Ridley's stomach. I froze. It was like Wade all over again. Even in the dark I could see that Taylor's eyes were wild.

"Get help!" the chairman shouted to me, pulling up Mr. Ridley's shirt and pressing down on his torso. "Get Dr. Benton. Tell Gervaso we need the helicopter. Fast."

Taylor was still dazed but got up onto her knees. "Get my mom."

"All right," I said. "You're going to have to keep rebooting these hunters until I get back. Can you do that?"

"Yes."

"I'll be right back." As I ran down the hill toward the house, Jack, Ian, and Zeus came running out the back. Jack and Zeus carried flashlights.

"Over here!" I shouted, though Ian had already seen me.

"We need Dr. Benton and the helicopter," I shouted again. "Where's Gervaso?"

"I'll get both of them," Zeus said, heading back into the house.

"Get Abigail too," I shouted after him.

Jack and Ian ran past me up the road.

Just then Mrs. Ridley rushed out of the house with my mother.

"What happened?" my mother asked.

"Mr. Ridley's been shot!" I shouted.

Mrs. Ridley looked at me with panic.

"Where is he?" Mom asked.

"Up the road a hundred yards. Follow me."

I turned and ran back, suddenly worried about Taylor being alone with the hunters. Somewhere in the distance I could hear the sound of a helicopter powering up.

When I got back, Jack and Ian were kneeling on the ground next to Mr. Ridley and the chairman. Behind them the hunters were all on the ground rolling around, moaning in pain. I don't know what Taylor was doing to their brains—I'm not sure that she did either—but I'd never seen her more focused or intense. Then two of them started screaming, "Stop, please!"

"Taylor," I said.

She didn't respond.

"Taylor! Back off!"

She turned and looked at me. Her eyes were crazy and angry.

"Back off," I said, panting. "You're hurting them."

"I know."

I took her arm. "Come on." We both turned toward her father. He was now shaking. "Jack, can you watch the hunters?"

Jack nodded. He handed Taylor his flashlight and picked up one of the men's guns, checked its chamber, and then held the gun on them. "Which one of you scumbags shot Chuck?"

"That one," Taylor said, pointing the flashlight at one of the men on the ground.

Jack leveled the gun at the man's chest. "No one messes with family. Any of you try anything, pig-face goes first. Then I shoot the rest of you."

I doubt the men even knew what Jack was saying, as they were still too disoriented to even speak. Taylor had really messed with their brains.

Mrs. Ridley reached us, followed by my mom, Zeus, and Abigail. Mrs. Ridley was crying. "What happened? Is he okay?"

"He's lost a lot of blood," the chairman said. "I think he's going into shock. Taylor, can you shine your light over here?"

Mrs. Ridley knelt down next to her husband. "Chuck. Stay with us. Don't leave us."

Abigail knelt down and put her hand on Mr. Ridley's shoulder. His shaking body suddenly calmed.

"That's good," the chairman said. "It will slow his heart rate. Ian, what do you see?"

"Not good. There's a lot of blood. It's filling his stomach."

About a hundred feet from us the helicopter began to lower into the corral.

My mother, the chairman, and Ian moved between the corral and Mr. Ridley to block the dust being kicked up by the helicopter's rotors. Dr. Benton ran up and knelt down next to Mr. Ridley. "What happened?"

"He was shot in the stomach."

"It's filling with blood," Ian said.

Dr. Benton took Mr. Ridley's wrist to check his pulse. "We need to stop the bleeding and get him to the hospital."

"Maybe McKenna could cauterize it," Mrs. Ridley said.

"McKenna's at the other house," Ian said. "She's too far away."

"Michael could do it," my mother said.

"What do I do?" I asked.

"I can guide you," Ian said. "Stick your finger into the bullet hole and burn it shut."

"My fingers are dirty."

"The heat of your electricity will kill the germs," the doctor said. "Infection is the least of our worries right now."

Mr. Ridley groaned.

"We've just got to buy him enough time to get him to the hospital in Kanab."

"The helicopter is ready," Gervaso said, running up to us.

The chairman moved aside, and I knelt down next to Ridley. "Abi?"

"I got him." She closed her eyes. I could see her begin to tremble from the pain. I looked down at the mass of blood. The bullet wound was about the diameter of a dime and slightly ragged. I grimaced as I shoved my finger into the hole.

"How far?" I asked Ian.

"More. Push harder."

I pushed in, my knuckles pressing into his abdomen. I could feel the blood, thick and sticky around my finger.

"Now," Ian said.

I pulsed. Mr. Ridley's body tensed, and in spite of Abigail's help he still groaned out. I could feel his blood boil against my finger. The pungent stink of burning blood filled the air.

"I think it's working," Ian said. "I think it stopped."

I pulled my finger out and leaned back.

"Yeah, it stopped," Ian said.

"Let's get him to the helicopter," Gervaso said.

Gervaso, Dr. Benton, and Ian lifted Mr. Ridley and carried him to the helicopter.

"Can I go with him?" Mrs. Ridley asked.

The chairman said, "The chopper can carry two passengers. You and . . ." He looked at Abigail. "Abigail should go."

The two women ran toward the helicopter.

"What about me?" Taylor asked.

"Gervaso will drive," the chairman said. "It will only take twenty minutes."

"I'll go with you," I said.

"What about these clowns?" Jack asked, waving the gun at the hunters.

The chairman looked at them with disdain. "Blindfold them; then take them down to the lower barn and handcuff them to the wall. We'll deal with them after we get back from the hospital." His eyes narrowed. "If they try to escape, shoot them."

"I'll fry them first," Zeus said. "Extra crispy." He walked over to them. "Stand up, losers."

I took Taylor's hand. "C'mon, let's get to the hospital."

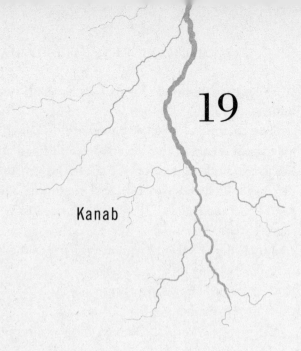

19

Kanab

The city of Kanab is a little more than twenty-five miles from Christmas Ranch, though with Gervaso's driving, it seemed closer. Because of the hour there was little traffic, and Gervaso instructed Ian to keep a sharp lookout for deer so he could drive insanely fast. At one point I looked at the speedometer, and he was going a hundred and twenty-seven, faster than I thought the truck could even go.

We passed a highway patrolman a few miles from the junction, but even before Gervaso could say anything, Taylor took care of it. The cars lights turned off and the car rolled to a stop. She was at least a hundred yards away from the vehicle when she did it. My first thought was that she was getting better at rebooting. More likely her power was enhanced by the intensity of her emotions.

Taylor didn't say a word the whole way, and as we got closer to the hospital, the mood in the car just got more and more tense. We all knew that there was a chance that Mr. Ridley hadn't made it to the hospital alive. I couldn't stop gulping.

Gervaso screeched to a stop in front of the hospital's emergency entrance, and Taylor jumped out and ran inside. I ran out after her. The large admitting room was mostly vacant. Abigail was reclined in a chair next to the door. Her armpits were wet, and blood was spattered all over her blouse. She looked so exhausted, I doubted she could stand.

"What's going on?" Taylor asked.

"They're still in there," Abigail said.

"Then he made it alive," Taylor said.

Gervaso and Ian walked in, looking around anxiously.

"He's alive," I said. Gervaso breathed out in relief.

For the next twenty minutes the five of us sat in silence. I began looking through a magazine about farm and ranch implements, but I couldn't focus on the pages. Then an actual rancher walked into the room. He was holding his arm as if it had been broken, but he didn't look overly concerned. He even took off his hat and nodded to the ladies.

A few minutes later, my mother, McKenna, Ostin, and both of his parents hurried in. "How is he?" my mother asked.

"We're still waiting," I said. "But he made it here."

Ostin shook his head. "I can't believe this happened. It wasn't even the Elgen."

"What's going on with the hunters?" I asked.

"Jack called the Kane County police. If the hunters try anything, Jack and Zeus will take them out like Elgen guards."

It was another half hour before Mrs. Ridley emerged from the swinging emergency room doors. Her expression was grave, but she wasn't crying, which I took to be a good sign. Taylor ran to her.

"He's going to be okay," Mrs. Ridley said. They embraced. "It was close. He lost a lot of blood."

Taylor broke down crying.

I walked over. "He's okay?"

Mrs. Ridley looked into my eyes. "Yes. Thank you. The doctor said that whoever cauterized the artery saved his life." She put her arms around me. "You saved his life."

Taylor also hugged me. "Thank you, Michael."

"I'm just glad," I said.

"I need to sit down," Mrs. Ridley said.

Mrs. Liss walked over to help Mrs. Ridley to a chair. "Come here, dear."

Taylor asked, "How long will Dad be here?"

"They want to keep him a few days. He's still low on blood, and they're worried about infection. They say I can stay in the room." She said to the rest of us, "The doctor said no visitors. You might as well go back. Thank you for coming."

My mother joined us. "You sure you don't need us?"

"I'm sure," she replied.

My mother hugged her. "You'll be in our prayers."

"I'll stay with you," Taylor said to her mom.

"I can stay too," I said.

Taylor took my hand. "I'll stay with my mother." She looked me in the eyes. "I'd like to be alone with my family."

"I understand," I said, feeling a little hurt. She must have seen it, because she kissed me on the cheek.

"I love you. I'll see you back at the ranch."

"Okay. I'll see you soon. Call if you need anything."

"I will. Bye."

As I turned to go, she said, "Michael."

"Yes?"

"It's just like my dream, isn't it?"

I nodded. "Exactly like your dream."

20

Always Been Together

I rode back to the ranch with my mother and the Lisses, leaving Taylor and her parents behind with Gervaso to watch over them. It was well past midnight when we got back. As we were entering the ranch's dirt road entryway, we passed two Kane County police trucks carrying the four hunters.

As we passed each other on the narrow road, one of the hunters glanced over at me. Electricity snapped between my fingers. I wanted to shock him.

The lights at the main house were still on as we pulled up the gravel driveway, and even though we had already phoned back the news, most everyone was still awake and waiting for us. I suppose they wanted to hear what was going on in person.

The chairman walked out to our car as we drove up. "How is he?"

"He's stable," I said, getting out of the car. "We didn't get to see him, but Mrs. Ridley filled us in."

"Is Gervaso staying with him?"

I nodded. "And Mrs. Ridley and Taylor are spending the night."

Jack, Zeus, and Tanner walked up. Jack and I man hugged. "You okay?" he asked.

"Yeah. What's going on back here?"

"We took care of the hunters," Zeus said.

Tanner grinned. "Every time they tried to move, Zeus shocked them."

I looked at Zeus. "You're not afraid they'll tell someone?"

"No one would believe them if they did," Tanner said. "They were so drunk, they couldn't even speak. It's like they were crazy."

"What do you mean?"

"They were morons," Jack said. "They just babbled. It was like they were speaking a foreign language. I didn't hear one real word out of them."

"They weren't babbling when I saw them," I said. I wondered if Taylor had broken their minds.

"Well, they were seriously messed-up dudes," Tanner said. "The police couldn't make sense of them."

"What will happen to the hunters?" I asked the chairman.

"For now the police will probably put them in the drunk tank, then keep them in jail until someone posts bail." The chairman's voice was slow, and he had dark rings under his eyes. I couldn't tell if he was worried or weary, or, most likely, both. "We'd better get some sleep. We just got new intelligence from the voice that I'll share with you tomorrow. We've got a lot to prepare for."

I said good night to my mother and the Lisses. Then Jack, Ostin, Zeus, Tanner, and I walked back to the bunkhouse. We didn't joke around like we usually did. Not even Tanner, who pretty much joked about everything.

I don't remember falling asleep, but I do remember the nightmare I had. Taylor, Jack, and I were being hunted in the dark by the four hunters. They cornered me, and I tried to use my electricity against them, but it didn't work. Then one of them came closer. His face was blurred but somehow familiar.

"Who are you?" I asked.

"I'm the voice," he said.

Then the hunter next to him said, "You know who I am." It was Hatch.

"Why are you together?" I asked fearfully.

Hatch put his arm around the voice and laughed. "Don't you know? We've always been together."

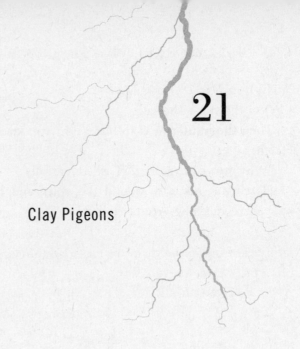

21

Clay Pigeons

The next morning my mood was as gloomy as the weather—gray and threatening. Most everyone was still asleep, so I went for a ride on one of the ATVs, then came back for breakfast. I went over to the girls' bunkhouse to see if Taylor had come back in the night, but Tessa said she hadn't.

I walked into the kitchen to find Ostin, Zeus, Jack, and Tanner already eating. None of the girls were at the main house yet except Nichelle, who rarely ate breakfast.

For breakfast they were serving French toast with powdered sugar and sliced bananas, link sausage, and banana smoothies. It had been a while since anyone had tried to push bananas on us. I sat down next to Ostin.

"Hey, where've you been?" he asked with a full mouth.

"Out riding."

"Taylor back?"

"Not yet."

"Hey, Michael," Tanner said. "We're going to shoot clay pigeons after breakfast. Want to come?"

"Never done it before."

"I'll teach you," Jack said.

Then Chairman Simon walked into the dining room. He looked about as bad as he had last night. He lifted a glass and tapped it with a fork to get our attention. The room quieted. "There will be a mandatory meeting in the main room at one thirty, right after lunch," he said gruffly. "Any questions?"

"Any word on Mr. Ridley?" I asked.

"Not yet. I'm sure we'll hear something by this afternoon."

After breakfast, Tanner checked out two twelve-gauge shotguns, and he, Jack, Zeus, and I drove one of the golf carts out near the pond to shoot clay pigeons. On the western side of the pond there was an automatic trap that flung bright orange disks into the air for us to shoot at.

I had seen trap shooting in a movie before but had never shot at clays, or even fired a shotgun, for that matter. Jack had done it a million times before, and he gave me a few tips before I tried. I missed the first four and hit the next two. Tanner was a pretty good shot, hitting six out of seven. Zeus was an even worse shot than I was. He finally got frustrated and ended up just shooting the clay pigeons with lightning bolts. It looked pretty cool.

The lunch bell rang at noon, and we packed up the guns and clay pigeons and drove back up to the main house. Lunch was corned beef sandwiches, pasta salad, and banana pudding. I asked the chairman again if he'd heard anything about Mr. Ridley.

"I spoke to him a half hour ago," he replied. "He's still recovering, but, all things considered, he sounded well. He says they may release him tomorrow."

"That's good," I said, wondering when Taylor would be back.

"Yes, we were lucky. I'd say we dodged a bullet, except we didn't." He stood. "Remember, we'll be meeting right after lunch." He walked out of the room.

I immediately started blinking. Something about the tone of his voice filled me with fear. It was clear that our time on the ranch was drawing to a close. Who knows, maybe even our time on earth. I was looking forward to the meeting about as much as a guilty murder suspect looks forward to the jury's verdict.

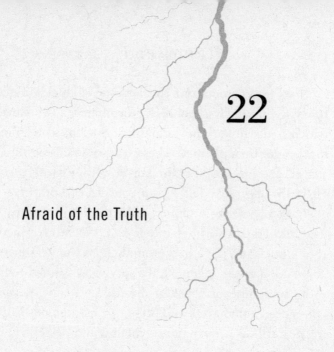

22

Afraid of the Truth

I figured that it was probably the most serious meeting we'd had at the ranch. Guards were posted outside the house and all the outside help had been sent off the property.

About twenty of us gathered in the big room of the main house. The mood was as solemn as a funeral. I sat down next to Jack, Abi, and my mother—who forced a smile when she saw me but couldn't hide her nervousness. I must have been shrugging a lot, because she reached out and rested her hands on my shoulders.

Gervaso was back from Kanab, and even he was acting different. There was still no sign of Taylor, which made me sad. We always sat next to each other at these meetings.

The chairman cleared his throat as he walked to the front of the room. "Before we begin, we have a report on Charles." He nodded at Gervaso, who stood.

"I've just come from the hospital. Chuck's hematocrit level is thirty-five, which is good. Unfortunately, he's developed a fever, which is usually an indication of infection, so they're going to keep him longer than planned. There was some talk about airlifting him to the St. George hospital, but for now they think they can handle it. He sends his gratitude for your concern and prayers.

"I also spoke to a deputy with the Kane County sheriff's office. The hunters are still being detained. We've identified the man who shot Chuck and ran a background check. As we suspected, he has no connection to the Elgen. He's a survivalist trained to live off the land, so he sometimes is gone for months at a time. Because of this, he's considered a flight risk and the judge has denied bail. He'll be sitting in jail until his arraignment, which could be several weeks. We'll be gone before then."

Chairman Simon nodded. "Thank you." He walked to the side of the room to a large map of the South Seas. "Now to the heart of our discussion—defeating the Elgen by stealing the *Joule*." He looked us over. "The only hard timeline we face is to strike before Hatch starts executing his Glows. Our sources tell us that he plans on doing this on the Elgen's sixteen-year anniversary of the MEI. That gives us very little time to prepare. Which leads to the next conversation.

"There's been a change to our original plan, one that we hope will give us an advantage. As you know, EGG Welch was sentenced to the rat bowl but, with Quentin, Tara, and Torstyn's help, escaped. Since then he's been on the run in Taiwan."

"How do you know he's in Taiwan?" Ostin asked.

"We've been in contact with him." There was an audible gasp in the room. "Needless to say, this changes things. So before attacking Tuvalu, we need you to fly back over to Taiwan to rescue Welch."

"We're rescuing an EGG?" Jack asked incredulously. "Why not just rescue Hatch while we're at it?"

The chairman ignored Jack's sarcasm. "He's not just any EGG. Welch was Hatch's right-hand man. And he's reached out to us for help. Without our help he's in trouble, and he knows it. He also knows more about the Elgen's procedures and plans than anyone but Hatch himself. A defector this high up is a godsend.

"That being said, you'll take the jet from Las Vegas to Taiwan, where you will meet up with Welch and take him with you to Tuvalu to rescue the Glows and steal the *Joule*."

"He agreed to this?" I asked.

"No," Chairman Simon said. "But we're not giving him a choice."

"This is going to be fun," Tessa said.

"What if he won't help?" Ostin asked.

"Then we leave him in Taiwan." The chairman walked back to the map. "From Taiwan, you will fly to Sydney, Australia, where you will take a commercial seaplane into Fiji. The Elgen have been using Fiji's port to transport food and necessities. You will be smuggled into Tuvalu on a supply boat."

"That sounds risky," Ostin said. "Why don't we just sail our own boat?"

The chairman frowned. "That would be far more risky. The Elgen are patrolling the waters around the island by sea and air. If an unknown vessel comes within twelve nautical miles of Tuvalu, it's engaged. The Elgen are jamming their radios, and the boats are being boarded and sometimes sunk. Last week they sunk a Filipino fishing boat that trespassed in their waters. There were no survivors."

Ostin nodded. "All right, smuggled it is."

"The boat you'll sail on is a supply ship called, ironically, *Risky Business*." The chairman slowly panned the room. "Now comes the difficult part."

"Because the rest of it was so easy," Jack whispered to me.

I shook my head.

"Your first mission is to rescue Quentin, Tara, and Torstyn. As far as we know, Quentin was being held in Cell 25 on the island of Funafuti. Now he's been sentenced to life in the monkey cage next to the previous Tuvaluan prime minister. Tara and Torstyn have been moved to the island of Niutao, or, as Hatch has renamed it, Hades. It's the Elgen's prison island. Right now it's mostly dorms and barb-wire fences, but they're nearing completion of their construction on a rehabilitation center. Tara and Torstyn are being kept inside the completed section of the prison building."

"Why do we need to save them first?" I asked. "Why not steal the *Joule*, and then, if things are going well, save them?"

"Why save them at all?" Nichelle asked. "They've got this coming."

"Because to steal the *Joule*, we'll need their powers," the chairman said. "Tara has the ability to make herself look like other people, including Hatch. We'll need her to get onboard the *Joule*."

"Why would we trust her?" I asked. "Or any of them?"

"Hatch has Tara and Torstyn scheduled for the rat bowl," the chairman answered. "If that hasn't shaken their loyalty, I don't know what will."

"What if they think they can earn it back?" Nichelle asked.

"It's a possibility, which is why we should free Quentin first. Tara and Torstyn will do what Quentin says."

Zeus nodded in agreement. "That's true."

The chairman walked back to the board. "So here's the rundown. The *Risky Business* has permission to sail directly to the Elgen's island headquarters of Funafuti, which Hatch has renamed Nike. This is uncommon, as most of the supply ships are only authorized to sail to Demeter, the third-northernmost island, which Hatch has designated for agriculture and livestock.

"Once on Nike you'll need to disembark without being seen. The dock is about a quarter mile from the town square where Quentin is being kept. It should not be too difficult to get to him, as the cage is in the center of the square. Unfortunately, accessibility isn't the problem. The problem is that it is *too* accessible. There may be people around, and there are cameras everywhere. There are two full-time guards stationed in the square, one at each cage. In addition, we'll need a way to get into the cage. Hopefully, one of the guards will have a key."

"Hope isn't a strategy," Ostin said.

"No. It's not. So if there's not a key, McKenna will need to melt through the bars."

"What if the metal is an alloy too strong to melt?" Ostin asked.

"It won't be, with Tessa's help."

McKenna nodded. "I can do it."

"We'll have to bring a lot of drinking water," Ostin said, looking at McKenna. "For after."

"Yes, of course," the chairman continued. "After Quentin has been liberated, you'll need to get back onto the boat and sail to Hades. That's where you'll find Torstyn and Tara."

"What about Kylee and Bryan?" Zeus asked.

"Bryan could burn through the bars," Ostin said.

"Bryan and Kylee are currently being held at the Nike Starxource plant. Unlike the others, they're scheduled to be released. As far as we know, they're still loyal to Hatch."

"We land on Hades, then what?" I asked.

"Once on Hades you'll break into the prison and free Tara and Torstyn. After you have them, you'll make your attempt to steal the *Joule*. I don't have details on that plan, since it would be best if you devise that plan with Welch's help." He breathed out heavily. "Any questions?"

"Only a thousand of them," Ostin said softly.

The chairman looked concerned. "I'm not going to soft-pedal this. You're going in like lambs among wolves. It's not impossible, but it's going to be difficult. We've got one shot at this. Remember, at any sign of trouble the *Joule* will submerge, stranding you on the islands—which means you would come under attack from the entire Elgen army."

Jack slowly shook his head. "We're so screwed."

"I have a question," I said. "How are we going to get onto the boat in Fiji undetected?"

"I can speak to that," Gervaso said. "The captain is a friend of mine from the Gulf War. He lost a leg saving my life. I trust him with my life."

"Do you trust him with ours?" Tessa asked.

Gervaso looked incredulous. "Do you think I would consider this if I didn't?"

No one said anything else, so Chairman Simon said, "That's a lot to digest for now. Please don't discuss any of this outside this room, especially near any staff. We can't afford any leaks. You're dismissed."

We all slowly got up to leave. My mother hugged me. "Are you okay?" she asked.

I nodded. "Are you?"

"I don't know." She hugged me again; then I turned to walk out with the rest of the Electroclan.

On the house's front porch Tanner said to me, "We're going to die. You know that, don't you?"

I turned to him. "No. I don't know that. And neither do you. So don't say that again."

"Why? Afraid of the truth?"

"I'm afraid of you making it *your* truth. And then ours." I walked away from him, followed by Ostin.

After a moment Ostin said, "Statistically speaking, he's probably right."

I looked at him for a moment, then turned and walked the other way.

23

The Right Time

I suppose that the real reason I was so upset by Tanner and Ostin was that deep inside I was afraid that they were right. I guess that's usually how it goes, right? If someone says something that has no basis in truth, it doesn't bother us much. It's the things we fear they might be right about that hurt.

It seemed to me that the closer we got to leaving on the mission, the more uncertain I felt about the whole thing—and the more unlikely I thought it was that we'd succeed. It didn't help that Taylor hadn't been at the meeting. She somehow made things feel better to me. Or at least she made me feel better about them.

I took one of the ranch's mountain bikes and went out alone for a ride to clear my head. I think that I must have ridden at least ten miles on the dirt, washboard road before coming back. I kept to myself for the rest of the afternoon, only joining the others at dinner.

Ostin was waiting for me as I walked into the dining room. He looked sad, like someone who had just lost his best friend. He hadn't, but he looked like that.

"Hey," he said, walking up to me. "I'm sorry about what I said."

I really wasn't in the mood to talk about it. "Don't worry about it."

"That's all I've done since you left. Besides, I found another logical way of looking at this. It's more positive."

"How's that?"

"So far we've faced six life-threatening missions and we've beaten them all. So, statistically speaking, we're more likely to beat bad odds than not. So the more unlikely the odds, the better our odds."

I squinted. "Isn't that a paradox? Because if they're now good odds, they're not."

"No sense overthinking it," Ostin said.

I couldn't help but grin. "Whatever works. Let's eat."

Ostin looked relieved. "Great. 'Cause I'm starving, man. I'm starving."

Taylor and her mother didn't return to the ranch until after dark, about two hours after dinner. I was sitting on the front porch talking to Jack as their car pulled up and Taylor got out. She looked as if she hadn't slept for days. I remember how messed up I was when I lost my father, so I wasn't surprised. I walked over to her. "How's your dad?"

"He's doing okay," she said. "He's come down with a fever, so they've got him on antibiotics, but they're still hopeful that they can release him soon." She looked at me. "I hear I missed an important meeting."

I took her hand and we walked a little ways off.

"Yeah. Before we steal the *Joule*, we're going to fly to Taiwan and rescue Welch."

"I'm not going," she said.

I looked at her. "What?"

"I'm sorry. I wasn't going to tell you tonight. . . . I just can't." She looked at me. "I'm sorry to let you down."

I had no idea what to say. Even though part of me had wanted her to stay, my heart felt like a bag of concrete had just dropped on it. Finally I said, "You'd just get in the way, anyway."

She didn't respond. She didn't need to. We both knew what I was saying was absurd. Ridiculously absurd. Then she looked at me in a way she never had before. Her eyes welled up with tears and her chin started quivering. "Michael, I think we need to break up."

If the last announcement had hit me like a bag of concrete, this one was the entire concrete truck. "What?"

"I've been thinking a lot about this. I think it's the right thing to do."

When I could speak, I asked, "Did I do something wrong?"

She wiped her eyes. "No, it's not you. It's not even us."

"If it's not us, then what is it?"

Tears fell down her face. "It's just . . . it's just not the right time for us."

Now my eyes began to well up. "Please don't do this. Not now."

"I'm sorry. *Now* is the time to do this."

I didn't know what to say. I couldn't have said it anyway. There was a lump in my throat the size of a basketball.

Finally she said, "I'm going to bed. I just want this day to end." Without saying good night, she turned and walked away.

I hadn't felt that awful since my father died.

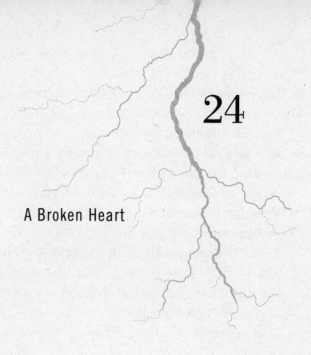

24

A Broken Heart

When I woke the next day, it felt like that concrete truck was still parked on my chest. I didn't want to get out of bed. I didn't want to do anything except disappear. Taylor was my first girlfriend. I'd never had my heart broken by a girl before. It sucked.

That afternoon Jack came to find me. "Hey, dude," he said. "It's, like, past noon. You missed breakfast and lunch. Aren't you hungry?"

"No."

"No?" Jack paused for a moment, then said, "You okay?"

"Taylor broke up with me last night."

"What?"

"Let's face it, it was only a matter of time. She was always out of my league."

Jack glared. "That's totally messed up, man. She's the one out of her league. And if she's too stupid to see that, then she doesn't deserve you."

"She's not stupid," I said.

"See? She treats you like crap, and you're still loyal. You're too good for her, man. Way too good for her. I've always thought that."

I know he was trying to make me feel better, but it wasn't working. I felt like defending her. I felt like crying. Mostly I just felt stupid. I'd been shot at, beaten, tortured, and fed to rats—and none of those things hurt as much as this. Why did I feel the same sense of panic I had in Cell 25? This was new territory for me and it sucked big-time.

"I'm not too good for her," I said. "It's just a hard time."

"When has it been otherwise?" Jack said.

I rolled over. I couldn't answer his question.

I spent most of the day in bed. I was twitching and sparking like crazy. I had no appetite. I wouldn't have eaten, anyway. I wouldn't have gone into the dining room. I didn't want to take the chance of seeing *her*. I couldn't stand the pain of that. *How could she just dump me like that?*

That night my mother came and got me for dinner. I was still lying in my bunk staring mindlessly at the bottom of Ostin's bunk when she walked into my dorm.

"Hey," she said.

I looked over. "Hey."

"You okay?"

I didn't answer. I'm sure she already knew the answer. That's why she was there, right? She sat down at the foot of my bed. "Jack told me what happened." She slightly grinned. "Then Ostin did, then Zeus and Nichelle and Tessa and Tanner . . ."

"Great," I said. "Everyone knows I'm a loser."

"You're not a loser. They just care about you." She rubbed her hand along my leg. "I'm sorry, honey. There's nothing worse than a broken heart. Except maybe being eaten by rats. That would be pretty awful too."

I knew she was trying to get me to smile, but it didn't work.

"I wish I could take your pain away."

"How could she just drop me like that?" I said. "How does that even work? How do you just stop loving someone?"

My mother frowned. "Hearts are complicated machines."

I closed my eyes.

"She still loves you, you know."

"No, I don't know that."

"She does."

"She has a bizarre way of showing it."

"Maybe. But she's hurting too."

"How do you know?"

My mother hesitated. "Because I talked to her."

I rose up on my elbow. "You talked to her? That's none of your business."

"You're my business. I care about you. And I care about Taylor, too."

I lay back down. Finally I asked, "What did she say?"

"Not a whole lot, really. She mostly just cried. She also told me that you're her best friend and how much she needs you."

"Then why did she break up with me?"

"I think that's maybe why. *Because* she needs you so much."

"That doesn't make any sense."

"Who said that love is supposed to make sense?"

I breathed out heavily. After a full minute I said, "What should I do, Mom?"

"Have a little faith," she said.

"In what?"

"In love."

"You just said it doesn't make sense."

"No, not always. But it does have a way of coming around to itself. You know I told your father that I wouldn't marry him for a million dollars?"

"When did you say that?"

"A month before we got engaged." She leaned closer to me. "Just give her some time. It's when we feel desperate and try to force things that permanent damage is done. Just let go. Let her find her way back."

"What if she doesn't come back?"

She smiled at me sadly, then said, "Then some other girl will thank her lucky stars." She leaned over and kissed me on the cheek, then sat back. "Now come eat. It's a broken heart, not a hunger strike."

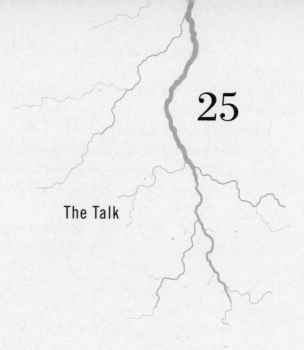

25

The Talk

The next few days I didn't see Taylor at all. Not just because of us breaking up, but because her father had finally returned and she stayed at his side to take care of him.

In spite of my friends' efforts to the contrary, I kept to myself. I slept a lot. I told myself it was because I was storing up for the mission ahead, but I'm pretty sure that everyone knew the truth—I was seriously depressed. And nothing saps the energy out of you like depression. That and RESATs, I guess. RESATs, at least, can be turned off.

When I wasn't sleeping, I was looking for things to do by myself. Finally, one afternoon of my "post-Taylor" life, I took one of the golf carts and drove out to see Matthew, the guy who was in charge of running the ranch—the cattle, farming, all the ranching stuff. I had met him before but had never really talked to him. He was with the resistance, but he was also a real rancher, the kind who wears cowboy boots and a hat to church and is like sixty years old but can still wrestle a cow to the ground.

As I walked in, Matthew was fiddling with the black hoses on the back of a tractor. I cleared my throat and he looked up. "Mr. Vey," he said slowly with a Western twang. "Didn't hear you come in. To what do I owe the pleasure?"

"I was bored. Is there anything I can do to help out around here?"

"Well, I thought of puttin' you kids to work, but Mr. Simon said to let you get your rest. Lord knows you'll be needin' it."

"I know. But I'm going crazy."

He thought a moment, then said, "Well, you could cut some firewood. That's always good when you got a little excess energy to work out. It's as therapeutic as a punchin' bag. You ever use a chain saw?"

"No, sir."

"Have you ever seen one?"

"Just in a horror movie."

He laughed. "Well, it ain't horror and it ain't rocket science. It ain't even tractor science. I'll show you." He walked to the side of the garage and brought down an orange-handled saw. He checked it for gas, then set it on the ground.

"You take it by this safety handle. To start, you put it on the ground, prime it by pushing this little bubble, then pull this rope." He pulled the rope and the saw fired up. He lifted it, shouting over the sound of its whine.

"This lever right here engages the chain." He pulled it back, and the chain started spinning. Then he released it and the motor stopped. "It's got this safety. If you drop it, it will turn off." He handed me the saw. "Think you can handle it?"

"Yes, sir."

"I know you can. There's two ol' cedar trees just west of the RV shed that I cut down yesterday. Go ahead and cut them into two-foot logs and pile them up. I'll send someone by later to pick 'em up."

"All right. Thank you."

"No, thank you. And wear these." He handed me some safety glasses.

"Start by cuttin' the smaller branches off the trees, then cut the trunks. Just be careful. That saw will cut through your leg as slick as snot."

I had never heard that phrase before. I hoped I'd never hear it again.

I drove the golf cart back around to the RV shed. The trees Matthew had told me about were on their sides next to the base of their freshly cut trunks.

I dragged one of the trees away from the other and put on my glasses and started the saw. I began cutting off the smaller branches at the top of the tree. I can see why Matthew thought it was therapy. It felt good just cutting, the air filling with the fresh smell of sap and sawdust.

It was hot work, and after twenty minutes I took off my shirt. I had completely stripped the first tree and was starting on its trunk when I noticed Mrs. Ridley standing about ten yards from me. I turned off the saw and took off my glasses.

"Sorry, I didn't hear you."

"Hi, Michael. I'm sorry to interrupt you. When you get a chance, Chuck would like to talk to you."

I couldn't imagine what he wanted. "Is he up walking already?"

"No. Not yet."

"Let me finish cutting this tree; then I'll come up."

"Thank you." She turned and walked away. I watched her for a moment, then fired up the saw and went back to cutting up the trunk. I wondered what he wanted. Honestly, I didn't look forward to seeing him. He was almost always abrasive. Some guys are just gruff that way. Especially about their daughters. Not that that mattered anymore. I wondered if I would see Taylor. I hoped so because I still loved her; I hoped not for the exact same reason.

About twenty minutes later I put on my shirt, got into the golf cart, and drove down to the small house where Mr. Ridley was recovering.

Mrs. Ridley met me at the door. "Thank you for coming, Michael."

I furtively glanced around for Taylor, but she wasn't there. I wondered where she was hiding. "No problem."

"Chuck's in here," she said, leading me to the main bedroom.

Mr. Ridley was sitting up in bed, propped up by pillows. It was the first time I'd seen him since he'd been shot. Not surprisingly, he looked a lot better. "Michael, come in. Please."

I stepped inside, and Mrs. Ridley stepped out and shut the door behind me.

"What can I do for you?" I asked.

"It's what you already did. Simon told me how you saved my life."

"It was nothing."

"My life's nothing?"

Inside I groaned. This guy could even make thanking you for saving his life painful. "I didn't mean that."

"You did something heroic. Accept it."

"I was just trying to help."

"Well, you did. Take a seat." He motioned to a stool next to a small writing desk. I sat down facing him, waiting for what he was going to say. "Taylor said you two broke up." He made it sound as if it had been a mutual decision.

"She dumped me."

"Do you know why?"

"I guess she doesn't love me anymore."

He just looked at me for a moment, then shook his head. "If she didn't love you, she wouldn't have been in her room crying for the last few days."

"Then I guess I don't know why."

"It's because she cares *too much* about you."

I shook my head. I wondered if this was a line all adults used. "She didn't seem to care too much about breaking my heart."

He frowned. "I know." He carefully shifted his legs. "The first thing any police officer learns on duty is that people are strange animals. They often do the exact opposite of what you'd expect. For instance, they're so afraid of failure that they embrace it. Do you know what I mean?"

"No, sir."

"Let's say you meet someone you think is attractive. You think to yourself, *I'd like to meet her*. But then that other voice in your head, you know the one, the voice that tells you how stupid or how ugly you are, says, *Are you crazy? She'd never be interested in you.* So you never introduce yourself, and the result is, you never meet her. You have embraced failure."

"Why are you telling me this?"

"Because I owe you. Truth is, I owed you before you saved my life. And I've been a jerk." He sat up a little more, grimacing with the action. "It's no secret that I love my daughter. And I know her. She's miserable. She's terrified of losing you. She's so afraid that she broke up with you."

"That doesn't make sense."

"I know it doesn't. At least not to us. That's because you and I are straightforward kind of guys. We call a spade a spade, you know?" He paused. "I've had a lot of time to think over everything the last few days, and here's the truth of the situation. If you go on this hare-brained mission—and I'm pretty sure you're going to—and you don't come back, Taylor will never forgive herself. She'll wonder if she could have saved you. The unknown will kill her."

"And there's more on the line. She told me about her sister being fed to rats. I know there's not a lot of love there, but blood is blood. And they share the same DNA. I don't know how that will play out either, but I don't think Taylor can stay back and respect herself.

"Truth is, it's a crappy situation all around. You're a good kid, Michael. No, you're a good man. You've made choices fully grown men aren't strong enough to make. And Taylor is a good woman. She's made those same hard choices. Her experiences have put her way beyond her years. Way beyond me. She's experienced enough to make this decision by herself. That's a hard thing for a parent, to trust their children to make decisions that could have dangerous repercussions—perhaps more difficult than you can understand right now." I noticed that his eyes were actually welling up. "I love Taylor more than I can say, and this is an awful dilemma for me to be in. But I'm not a fool. If I let her go, I could lose her. If I make her stay, I could lose her. So how do I choose? I suppose the bigger question is, is it even my decision to make?"

"I think she's already made her decision," I said.

"It would appear so, but she didn't. I manipulated the situation. When your parent almost dies and then makes a request . . . well, that's more pressure than a child should have to face. Look at what you were willing to do to save your own mother, going to Peru and all that.

"And that leads me to another revelation I've had lying here. Here I am in one of the safest places on the planet, guarded by enough weaponry to have won the Civil War, and I was still almost killed.

"The truth is, life is a house of cards. Taylor could stay back and be killed in a car accident next week. She could get cancer. Heck, she could catch the flu and die. Safety is an illusion." He leaned slightly forward, and I saw him grimace with pain. Then he said, "So I'm going to ask you a very important question, and I want your completely honest answer. No matter how painful it is for either of us. Can you do that for me?"

"Yes, sir."

"In your opinion, how important is Taylor to this mission?"

I took a deep breath. "She's been important to every mission."

"And this one?"

"There's no way of knowing that."

"You're right, but what does your gut tell you? Can you succeed without her?"

I looked down for a moment, then said, "I don't know. We haven't tried. But looking back over Peru and Taiwan, we wouldn't have succeeded there without her."

He was quiet a moment, then said, "I thought so." He rubbed his chin. "I appreciate your honesty. I'm going to have a talk with her. Thanks for coming by."

"Don't mention it."

"Michael."

"Yes?"

"Thanks for being so good to my daughter. I'd be proud to call you my son. Not anytime soon, but maybe one day."

"Thank you." I turned and walked out.

Mrs. Ridley stood as I came out of the room. "How was it?"

"Surprising," I said.

She looked at me curiously. "Surprising good or bad?"

"I guess we'll find out," I said, and walked out of the house.

I wondered what Mr. Ridley planned on saying to Taylor. More interesting, I wondered what she'd say back.

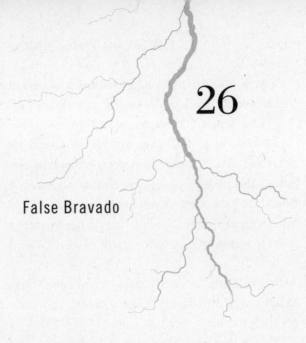

26

False Bravado

The following afternoon around three o'clock the dinner bell rang. Ostin, McKenna, and I were just east of the horse corral watching Eric and Peggy, our beekeepers, check the hives. They were dressed in white, full-body bee suits and looked a little bit like space people as they walked between the rows of white boxes.

When we first got there, they had sprayed the area with smoke to calm the bees, but the bees still weren't happy with them poking around and kept swarming them. I was glad it wasn't me, but it was still kind of cool to watch.

I did notice something peculiar. The bees were more attracted to me and McKenna than Ostin. Actually, more to me than McKenna. It didn't bother me that much, except that I kept killing bees. I'd gotten so electric that anytime they got too close, my electricity would zap them. McKenna purposely made herself too hot to land on, which kept the bees from stinging her.

Ostin noticed the phenomenon too and immediately created a hypothesis. "I think we're seeing an example of electroreception."

"What's that?" McKenna asked.

"When bees fly, they collect atmospheric electricity in their antennas. When it visits a flower, it deposits that electricity. Bees can detect the pattern of electric fields on flowers and use that information to tell whether or not other bees have already visited the flower. You both probably look like very large flowers to them."

"How disappointing for them," I said.

A few minutes later the dinner bell rang. Ostin checked his watch. "That's weird. It's only three o'clock. Too early for dinner. Not that it's ever too early to eat."

"Must be a special meeting," McKenna said.

We said good-bye to Peggy and Eric and walked up the hill to the house.

Chairman Simon, my mother, and Gervaso were standing on the porch near the front door. They all had somber expressions—not freaked out or anything, just really serious. I also noticed that two of our vans were parked near the side of the house and things were being carried out to them.

"What's up?" I asked.

"Just go into the meeting room," Gervaso said. "We have an announcement."

I looked at my mother. She hugged me but offered no explanation.

Only Zeus and Tessa were inside, so Ostin, McKenna, and I sat down next to them and waited for everyone else to arrive.

Within ten minutes everyone came, even Grace, whom none of us ever saw much of.

Abi and Jack came in with wet hair. They had been swimming in the pond.

After everyone had arrived, my mother came in looking around for me. I waved to her, and she walked over and sat down by my side.

I should say that everyone came except Taylor. She wasn't there, but I guess that I didn't really expect her to be. She seemed to have checked out, not just from my life but the Electroclan as well. I can't say that I was happy or sad about her being absent; seeing her, not seeing her, both were painful. Hearts are weird that way.

We quieted as Gervaso and the chairman entered the room. Gervaso shut the door behind them.

"Thanks for coming," the chairman said. "I'll cut right to the chase. We've just got our orders. It's time to go."

Even though we knew it was coming, the actual announcement still knocked the collective wind out of us. Not one of us said a word. Gervaso let the announcement settle, then said, "We're leaving tomorrow morning at nine. We'll drive to Las Vegas and spend the day, then fly out early the next morning."

"Yeah, Vegas," Zeus said, slapping hands with Jack.

"Why Vegas?" McKenna asked.

"That's where the plane is right now. We also thought it might be nice for you to have some fun before you go."

"You mean the mission isn't going to be fun?" Tessa mumbled.

"There will be twelve of us going on this mission," Gervaso said. "Michael, Taylor, Ostin, McKenna, Zeus, Tessa, Abi, Jack, Tanner, Ian, Nichelle, and me. Grace will be helping from here. If all goes well, we'll be coming back with sixteen."

"Excuse me," I said, raising my hand. "But Taylor won't be going."

"Yes, I will," Taylor said.

I looked over. Taylor was standing next to the door.

Gervaso slightly nodded to her, then turned back to us. "So we've got an even dozen. Bring your bags with you to breakfast tomorrow. We're traveling light, so take only what you need. Breakfast will be ready at eight and we'll be leaving at nine sharp, so say your long good-byes tonight. Everyone get some good sleep. We need you sharp and well rested, and over the next two weeks that's not a luxury you're going to get enough of." He took a deep breath. "All right, Electroclan. You're dismissed."

I looked back over to where Taylor had been, but she was already gone.

I turned to my mother. Her eyes were filled with tears.

"You knew it was time?" I asked.

"They just told me." She brushed a tear from her cheek.

"It's going to be okay," I said. "We'll be back in a few weeks."

I think we both knew it was false bravado, but she nodded. "Of course. Just a few weeks." She gave me a hug. "Just be careful."

I looked at her for a moment, then forced a smile. "I'm always careful. Besides, what could go wrong?"

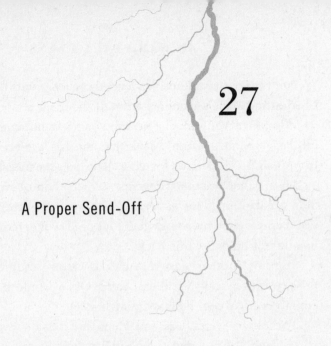

27

A Proper Send-Off

In spite of Gervaso's counsel, none of us slept much. Jack, Zeus, and I played Texas Hold'em until three in the morning. Five hours later we carried our bags up to the house. As we trudged up the hill with our packs slung over our shoulders, we could smell the wafting sweetness of bacon and syrup.

"Waffles," Ostin said with religious fervor.

"A proper send-off," I said.

"How far is Vegas from here, anyway?" Jack asked.

"I think it is about three hours," I said.

"I can't wait," Ostin said. "I've been studying how to count cards. I'm going to bring down the house."

"You're too young to gamble," Jack said.

Ostin thought a moment, then said, "That's okay. I'll just tell some adult how to play."

*   *   *

We ate breakfast while others loaded our bags into the vans. We finished eating, then walked out front of the main house, where the cars were waiting. Pretty much everyone on the ranch came out to see us off. Peggy handed Ostin, McKenna, and me a piece of honeycomb from their previous day's foraging. "The bees send their love," she said.

My mother was pretty weepy, which didn't surprise me, but it didn't make things any easier. She held me for a long time. The truth was, I was feeling more sad than I let on. I wondered how she would handle it if I didn't come back.

Still, my mother wasn't as bad as Ostin's mother, who, no surprise, was practically wailing. I think Ostin would have been super-embarrassed, except he was crying himself.

The others weren't as bad. Zeus and Tessa showed no emotion whatsoever. It's not that they had attachment disorder or anything. It's just that, outside of the Electroclan, they lacked anyone to be attached to.

Taylor hadn't come up for breakfast and only showed up with her parents a few minutes before we were to leave. Mrs. Ridley's eyes were red and puffy, and Mr. Ridley looked sad but was walking for the first time even though he was leaning against a tall wooden walking stick.

Taylor climbed into the van I wasn't in, which didn't surprise me but still made me kind of mad. I wondered what was going through her head. I think it's the first time I wished that I could have her power instead of mine.

Gervaso took roll call, then climbed into the passenger seat of the other van. "Adios!" he shouted out the window. The vans pulled out, kicking up gravel and dust as we left the ranch.

My mother blew me a kiss, then covered her eyes with her hands. I had to look away.

28

The Bad Banana

Maybe Vegas was kind of like a last meal before being executed, but I wasn't about to complain. We arrived a little after noon and checked in at the Bellagio hotel. I had never stayed anyplace so luxurious before. The closest I'd come was that hotel in Taiwan. Of course the Gadsden, that place in Douglas, Arizona, used to be nice. But now it was just haunted.

Zeus, Nichelle, and Tessa had stayed at the Bellagio before, but in a suite roughly the size of Idaho, so they weren't as impressed as the rest of us, but they were also still glad for the break.

Gervaso gave us a thousand dollars each and sent us off with a stern warning not to talk to strangers.

Ostin, McKenna, Taylor, Ian, and I went to the David Copperfield magic show, something Ostin had always wanted to do. I didn't sit next to Taylor. It felt strange to not touch her or hold her hand. It was as strange to have lost that privilege as it had been to initially have it granted.

Ian kind of ruined the show for us because he kept telling us how the tricks were done. We had to leave the show early because someone noticed us glowing and pointed at us. Everyone thought that we were part of the show. David Copperfield even took a bow for it.

Afterward, we ran into Gervaso in the casino, and Ostin gave him five hundred dollars and got him to play cards for him. They kept playing until Gervaso had won more than five thousand dollars and quit because he was drawing too much attention.

Ostin took his winnings and bought a gold bracelet for McKenna, and still had enough left to stop in M&M's World and load up on a couple of hundred dollars of chocolate for the ride to Taiwan.

Still, Taylor stayed close to McKenna. I caught her looking at me several times. I knew she wanted to talk, but I wasn't ready. Frankly, my emotions had shifted. I was less sad than mad. I know it sounds weird, but people are wired that way. It's like when a parent loses their kid. They get all frantic and upset, afraid that something has happened to them, but after the kid finally turns up, the parent wants to beat them. I guess that's how I was feeling. Like my mom said, "Who says love is supposed to make sense?"

Jack told us that before the marines went to war, the guys would go to town and get tattoos—mostly ones they hoped that they would live to regret. Jack wanted to get tattoos on his arms that looked like my lightning scars, if it was okay by me, which it was, but I had to go with him so the tattoo artist could copy them.

McKenna and Taylor wanted to hang out by the pool before it got too late, so Ostin came with us. As we were leaving the hotel, we ran into Nichelle. When she found out we were going to a tattoo parlor, she wanted to come even though she already had like twenty of them. Actually, it probably was because she had twenty of them.

"I should get one that says 'Death to Hatch,'" she said. "With a lightning bolt through a skull."

"Maybe after he's dead," I said. "Otherwise he might not take kindly to it."

"You're right," she said. "Are you going to Sin City Tattoo? It's

famous. It even has its own reality TV show. I got this one there."
She lifted her shirt just above her belly button to show the words in
black, Gothic letters:

Not all who wander are lost

Nichelle actually had a pretty great stomach, something you'd
never notice with the loose clothes she always wore.

Jack looked up. "No, I'm taking this guy's recommendation. He
had killer ink."

"What guy?" she asked.

"One of the hotel's security guards. I ran into him in the gym. He
looked like he eats nails for breakfast."

Ostin's brows fell. "You mean he had no teeth?"

Jack just shook his head.

We took a taxi about four miles from the hotel to the tattoo parlor that
was down a side street, then down an alley the car couldn't fit through.
The place was called the Bad Banana, which I thought was a stupid
name, but once I met the owner, it kind of made sense. He looked wrin-
kly and overly tanned like an old banana. He also looked like he hadn't
bathed since Bush was president, and he had like seven teeth.

He noticed Nichelle first and commenced to hit on her.

"What do you need, babe? I've got a special for the ladies as long
as it's on lady parts."

"Save it," she said. "We're here for the marine wannabe."

"I want my arms to look like his," Jack said, pointing to my arms.
"Can you do that?"

The dude stared at my arms. "Those are some nasty tats. Where'd
you get that ink?"

"Mexico," I said.

"Mexico," he repeated. "The only thing I get from Mexico is the
runs."

Nichelle slowly shook her head. "Wow, you've got class written all
over you."

"In ink," the man replied, mistaking what she said as a compliment.

"Well?" Jack said. "Can you?"

"Yeah, I can do it."

The guy was creepy, but I had to admit that he was pretty good at what he did. It took about two hours, but after it was done, Jack's arms looked exactly like mine, though with a lot bigger muscles.

The tattoo parlor was in a pretty dodgy part of town, and as we walked out of the shop, a man wearing a hoodie approached us and pulled out a gun. A revolver. It looked ancient compared to what the Elgen were carrying these days.

"Give me your money," he said. "All of it."

Jack just looked at him. "Man, did you ever pick the wrong guys to stick up."

"What kind of a gun is that?" I asked.

"A .38 Special," Ostin said. "Practically a dinosaur. Smith and Wesson started making them more than a hundred years ago. I mean, they were using those things in World War I. I wouldn't use one if I was mugging someone. I mean, pretty good chance someone like Jack is going to survive it and beat you senseless. Of course, Michael would survive anything, but with this gun, even I've got a chance."

The mugger looked at us with a bewildered expression. "Just give me your money."

I looked at our would-be mugger. "Okay, Mr. .38 Special. You clearly don't know much about guns. Do you know anything about electricity?"

He just blinked. "What?"

"Electricity. Did you go to school?"

"Do I look like I went to school?"

"A school for losers," Ostin said.

"He looks like he crawled out from under a rock," Nichelle said.

The man's face turned red. "You're dissing a man holding a gun at you, and you think I'm dumb? I'm about to blow a hole through one of you. Then we'll see how smart you are."

"That doesn't even make sense," Ostin said.

"That's not going to happen," I said. "Normally I'd give you the chance to walk away, but then you'll probably just do the same thing to someone else, so you can either give me the gun or I'm going to have to take it from you."

He looked at me incredulously. "You guys high?"

"On life," Ostin said.

Nichelle rolled her eyes. "That was really lame, dude."

"Just give me the gun," I said again.

"Take it," he said, his finger moving a little on the trigger.

I shrugged. "If you say so."

I blasted him up against the wall of the building behind him. His gun went off from the pressure of my pulse, but the strength of my pulse stopped the bullet in midair. The man fell to the ground.

After everything had settled, Ostin reached over and picked the bullet up off the ground. "He wasn't as dumb as we thought. Hollow points. That could have done some damage."

"Still dumb," Nichelle said.

Jack squatted down and checked the guy's pulse. "He's still breathing."

I picked up his gun. I held it by its barrel and focused my energy to the palm of my hand. The barrel bent like rubber. "That's not going to work again." I tossed it back down onto the ground next to the mugger, who was still unconscious.

"You just melted it," Jack said.

"Holy crap," Ostin said. "That's a high alloy chromium-molybdenum steel. You melted it like ice cream. I didn't know you could do that."

"Neither did I."

"You know what that means?"

I turned and looked at him. "Yeah. It means I'm still getting more electric."

29

Real Love

After the tattoo place we stopped for ice cream at a Cold Stone. Then I went back to my room to take a nap. About an hour later Ostin woke me as he came back into our room. I think there had been quieter entries at Walmart stores on Black Friday. I groaned out in frustration. "Really, man? I was sleeping."

"Sorry, dude. Didn't know you were sleeping."

"What time is it?" I asked, rubbing my eyes.

"A little after eight. Almost time for dinner."

"Where have you been?"

"Just hanging down at the pool with McKenna and Taylor." He walked over next to me. "Are you ever going to talk to Taylor again?"

"I don't know. Ever's a long time."

"She's really upset."

"Yeah," I said. "Been there."

Ostin suddenly nodded. "Oh, I get it. It's payback. Let her stew in her own juices. Awesome."

I glared at him. "I'm not letting her 'stew in her own juices.' I'm not trying to hurt her."

"Oh," he said, looking confused. "Well, you're still doing a good job of it." He went into the bathroom and turned on the shower. For the first time since Taylor broke up with me, I felt like I was the mean one.

Ostin and I met up with everyone for dinner at Prime, an expensive steak house in the Bellagio. It had large floor-to-ceiling windows that opened to the fountains outside. Gervaso told us to not worry about the price and just go crazy with our orders, so we all did. I ordered a caviar appetizer (I didn't like it, but I've always wanted to know what the big deal was with eating raw fish eggs); the dry-aged, bone-in rib eye steak; truffle mashed potatoes; and a crème brûlée for dessert.

Ostin, Zeus, and Jack had even more than I did. I looked at the prices on the menu, and just my meal alone was more than two hundred dollars. I figured that we wouldn't be eating much for a while and if this was going to be our last real meal, it might as well be epic.

Taylor was quiet throughout dinner. At one point we made eye contact. As we looked into each other's eyes, I suddenly saw my friend again. And the thing is, you can't hurt a friend without hurting yourself. I wanted to take her pain away. Most of all, I finally wanted to be with her more than I wanted to punish her for hurting me. I guess that's a sign of love. Maybe it's a sign of maturity too.

After dinner Taylor got up to leave. I stopped her outside the restaurant's front door.

"Taylor."

She stopped and turned to me. She looked anxious.

"Would you like to go for a walk?"

She didn't speak but nodded her head.

"All right. Let's go."

I didn't take her hand. At least not at first. Things were still awkward.

We walked out to the main Vegas drag. Even though it was night, we didn't have to worry about our glows, as it was practically like day, bright with the million-watt jungle of Vegas casino signs. Without speaking, we walked on the long sidewalk that ran along the outside of the Bellagio's fountains. I wasn't sure what to say.

Taylor broke the silence. "I'm so full."

"Yeah, I ate way too much. It felt kind of good."

"I know, right?"

Silence.

"How was the pool?" I asked. "It looked kind of crowded."

"Good. Mostly good. There was this creepy guy in the hot tub hitting on us, so McKenna heated the water up to like a hundred and thirty degrees until he fled. It was funny watching him squirm as it got hotter. He didn't want to act like it was too hot for him, because we were just sitting there."

"How did you stand the heat?"

"Abigail took away the pain. It was cool. I mean, I kind of got burned, but it was totally worth it."

"You could have just rebooted him and told him to leave."

"I don't think there was much there to reboot."

I smiled, and she said, "I heard you had a little excitement."

"A little," I said. "Who told you?"

"Jack told Abi, Abi told McKenna, McKenna told me. The usual network."

"Yeah, some dude pulled a gun on us. I melted it."

"It's kind of amazing. A year ago that experience would have been traumatic. Now it's practically boring you. Do you think Superman gets bored beating up bad guys?"

We both leaned against the stone ledge separating the sidewalk from the fountain. "I'm not Superman."

"No, because there's no such thing as Superman. But there is such a thing as you. Think about it. The whole world is obsessed with superheroes, and you're the real thing. How does that feel?"

"*We're* the real thing," I said. "And it feels heavy."

"You're right. Life is heavy."

"Did you see Jack's tattoos?"

Taylor smiled and nodded. "I told you that your Lichtenberg things were cool. Jack wanted to look just like you."

"I don't know why."

"I do. You're his hero. He wants to be just like you."

I looked at her. "Jack? Yeah, right."

"Of course he does. He looks up to you. We all do." Her expression turned more serious. "Especially me."

I just looked at her.

"Michael, I'm really sorry." She looked into my eyes. "Will you please forgive me? Please?"

I turned away from her toward the fountain. "I'd rather not talk about it."

"I know." She started to cry. "I don't blame you for being mad."

"Are you reading my mind?"

"No," she said. "I can see it."

I took a deep breath, then turned back. "I've never been in love before. I didn't know how to handle that kind of rejection. It was painful. Like when my dad died painful."

"I'm so sorry."

"My heart isn't like a light I can just turn on and off."

She wiped a tear from her cheek. "You think mine is? You think I wasn't hurting too? I cried almost the whole time we were apart. I wasn't rejecting you. I didn't love you less. I never stopped loving you. Not for a second."

Taylor wiped both of her eyes. "I once read something about love—that real love isn't that 'can't live without you, sweaty palm' thing. Real love is caring about someone else more than yourself. I know it sounds stupid, but the only way I could let go of you was because I love you so much."

"You're right," I said. I looked deeply into her eyes. "It does sound stupid."

She punched me on the arm. "I was stupid to think I could live without you."

"Don't ever leave me again," I said.

"I won't."

"Promise?"

"I promise. Will you?"

I looked at her for a moment, then replied, "Ditto."

30

The Impossible Dream

They say that what happens in Vegas stays in Vegas, and in our case, with the exception of Jack's tattoos, and Taylor's and my reunion, that's probably true. They also say that Vegas is a desert mirage, and I think that's true too, because by the time we were on the plane, it already seemed like a dream. A dream headed into a nightmare.

We left early in the morning, like five thirty, which meant that none of us got much sleep. In fact, Tessa, Zeus, Tanner, Ian, Nichelle, and Jack never went to sleep at all. They figured that with a twelve-hour flight they could sleep on the way. Pretty smart, really.

When Ostin and I got to the lobby, Gervaso and two white shuttle buses were waiting for us. The all-nighters were already inside and, with the exception of Zeus, were asleep. Zeus had consumed three Red Bulls.

Our plane was a few miles from the hotel at a small executive airport. Scott and Boyd, our pilot and copilot, walked out to meet us. I hadn't seen either of them since we had separated in Douglas. It was good to see them again. Scott went to hug me but jumped back.

"You shocked me."

Another reminder that I was getting more electric. "Sorry. I can't always help it."

Boyd just gave me a salute from a safe distance. "Good to see you, Michael."

We helped the pilots load the plane, and we were in the air in less than a half hour. Everyone was kind of grumpy, but I couldn't blame them. First, we were tired. Second, it's like we were just given the shortest vacation in history and it had already ended. Third, well, we were going to visit Hatch. Not exactly a joyfest.

Taylor fell asleep lying against my shoulder. It was good to be back together.

I couldn't help but wonder if we were doing the right thing or if there was a better way of defeating the Elgen. I couldn't think of a better way. Still, I felt like we were marching into hell. That's actually a line from a song my father used to like. Ironically, maybe appropriately, the song was—is—called "The Impossible Dream."

It's a really old song, but still a pretty cool one. It's about doing what's right no matter the consequences. I don't remember the whole song, but I do remember watching my father as he listened to it. Sometimes he would get teary-eyed when it played. I remember that. My father wasn't one to cry. He was a tough guy. But like those pictures of muscle-bound dudes holding kittens, he had a soft side. He was a good father. I remember that, too. I know that. I wonder how different my life would have been if he hadn't died.

And the world will be better for this,
That one man, scorned and covered with scars,
Still strove with his last ounce of courage . . .

I suppose I was living out my father's impossible dream.

The truth was, my heart hurt. Something told me that I wasn't going to come back from this trip. That's the main reason why I couldn't let Taylor read my thoughts, and why I finally learned how to stop her from reading my mind. It's a kind of pulse I focus around my temples, like jamming a radio signal. Still, it takes effort and concentration, and I was just too tired to worry about that kind of crap right then. I had too many other things to occupy my mind. Way too many things.

Lately I've been wondering where Wade is—you know, the whole death thing. Life after life. Where do we go after we die?

Or is this it and when we're done, we're done? I don't know. It's possible that Wade and my father are hanging out right now, watching us. Cheering us on. Maybe. It's weird to think about that. But it's possible. I guess one day everyone finds out what death is about.

The way things were looking, I might be finding out sooner than I hoped.

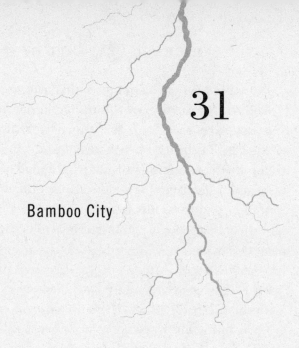

31

Bamboo City

Our plane stopped in Tokyo on our way to Taiwan. Tanner and Tessa tried to talk Gervaso into letting us stay for a few hours to get some decent sushi. Their favorite restaurant sends sushi around on a conveyor belt. It sounded kind of fun, but Gervaso wasn't going for it. He said we had a strict schedule to keep and we needed to be ready for Welch.

Gervaso said, "It's like this: imagine a group of hunters on horseback with dogs chasing a fox. We're going to ride in and scoop up the fox. Best we're not eating sushi in Tokyo when the dogs tree it."

Pretty good story, I thought.

The sun was setting as we landed in Taiwan. It wasn't the same place we'd landed before. This time we were north in Taipei. As we got off the plane, we saw a familiar face.

"Ben!" Taylor shouted.

"Hwan ying, Peng youmen," he said. "Welcome, my friends."

We took turns embracing him. He looked surprisingly well considering all he'd been through since we'd last seen him—mainly evading the Taiwanese police and military.

"I was so pleased to learn your mother and friends were safe at the ranch," he said to me.

"So were we," I said. "The . . ." I hesitated. I remembered that we weren't supposed to speak the word "Elgen" in public. "*They* destroyed the ranch. It was burned to the ground."

"Yes. I was told. But our friends were saved."

"Yes. They were saved."

"Now you have a new mission. There are many of the enemy in Taiwan right now. Too many. They are working with the Taiwanese army and the Taiwanese police to find the man."

"Do you know where he is?" I asked.

"He is south of us. I do not know exactly where, but we know the city. Tomorrow he will contact us and we will rescue him and get him out of Taiwan."

"What city?" Ostin asked.

"It is near the city of Changhua."

"Changhua," Ostin repeated. "Also called Bamboo City and the county seat of Changhua County. Well known for its landmark, an eighty-five-foot-tall statue of Buddha. It was once home to the Babuza aboriginal tribe and was owned by the Dutch East India Company."

Ben looked at me. "How does he know these things?"

I shrugged. "He's Ostin."

"Yes. He is awesome."

I didn't correct him. "When do we go to Changhua?"

"I will drive you there tonight."

There were more of us now than the previous time we'd been in Taiwan, and anytime we moved, we required two vans. Ben drove one, Gervaso the other. We kept together, with Ben in front leading the way.

The drive to Changhua was about two and a half hours along the western coast, and it was late at night when we arrived.

"What hotel are we staying at?" McKenna asked.

"No hotel," Ben said. "House."

The house Ben took us to was on the outskirts of Changhua and surrounded by rice paddies. It looked more like a building than a residence, which is common in Taiwan. It was three stories high and made of concrete covered with tile. It was part of a complex of a dozen similar structures, though only two of the buildings looked occupied.

"We are here," Ben said. "Please be quiet. We do not want neighbors to notice so many people. Especially foreigners."

Without talking we got our bags and went inside. Ben switched on just one light on the main floor, leaving most of the room dark. The place didn't really look lived in. The only furniture on the first floor was a table with four chairs, a computer desk, and a file cabinet.

"Girls on second floor, boys on third floor," Ben said. "Gervaso, there is a room there for you and me."

"Thank you," Gervaso said.

We all walked up one flight to where the girls were staying. I kissed Taylor good night, then went up to the third floor with the rest of the guys. Unlike the girls' level there were no beds, just thin, woven bamboo mats laid over the marble tile floor.

"Nice," Tanner said. "Nothing like sleeping on a rock floor."

"Beats Cell 25," Zeus said.

"Hell beats Cell 25," I said.

Tanner frowned. "How is that supposed to make me feel better about sleeping on a rock floor?"

Like the safe house we'd stayed at in Kaohsiung, there was a stairway that led to the roof. I guess that's pretty common in Taiwan. People don't hang out on their roofs in America so much. I'm not sure that they do in Taiwan, either, but at least you have that option.

I claimed a mat by throwing my bag onto it. Then Jack and I went up onto the roof to look around. The night air was cool and moist, and even though it was dark, we could see the silhouette of the eighty-five-foot Buddha sitting on a mountain in the distance.

Neither of us spoke for a while. Then Jack said, "I can't believe we're back here."

I continued looking out into the horizon. "Fight the Elgen, see the world."

Jack turned to me. "You're really glowing."

"I know. I just keep getting more electric."

"I've tried to imagine what that must feel like."

"It's bizarre. Sometimes I can feel electricity crackle inside me."

He looked at me quizzically. "That must feel really weird."

"Yeah." I took a deep breath. "So you've been pretty quiet about things. What do you think about this mission?"

He hesitated for a moment, then said, "I think that if you have something hard to do, it's better to focus on the task at hand than the outcome."

"Sounds like something Coach Dibble would say."

"Dibble was always saying junk like that. 'Don't beat them, Vranes, just sink the basket you're shooting.' He said that my freshman year before he cut me from the team." Jack looked me in the eyes, and his voice turned softer. "Speaking of shooting, you know I would take a bullet for you."

His words shook me. "I'd rather you didn't."

"I'd rather not either, but if it comes to that . . ."

"If it comes to that, I'll deflect it," I said. "I can't lose another friend."

Even in the darkness I could see a shadow cross his face. "Like Wade."

"He was a hero," I said.

"I prefer my heroes alive," Jack said.

"Sometimes it's dying that makes them a hero."

"No," Jack said. "It's acting courageously in the face of death that makes someone a hero. Dying is *superfluous*."

I looked at him for a moment; then we suddenly both grinned.

"That's a pretty good word," I said.

"Yeah. I heard Ostin say it. I have no idea if I used it right."

We both laughed. "Come on," I said. "Let's get some sleep."

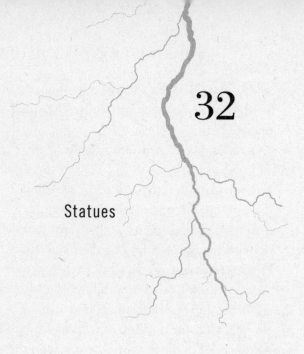

32

Statues

We got to sleep in the next morning, which was good because it took me like three hours to fall asleep. Around ten o'clock Ben brought us breakfast: sweet sesame-seed biscuits with honey inside and hot soy milk. It probably doesn't sound that good, but it was. Or, as the Taiwanese like to say, *Fei chang bu tswo*. Extremely not bad.

Ben said there were a lot of Elgen in the area, so Gervaso didn't want us wandering around. After breakfast Taylor and I went up to the roof. It reminded me of our last night in Taiwan—the night we were told Timepiece Ranch had been attacked by the Elgen.

The city's traffic was ridiculously loud, as if constantly honking your horn was a requirement. I'd been through some seriously dangerous things, but driving in Taiwan would probably rate high on that list.

I tore apart a cardboard box and laid it down on the gravel roof floor for Taylor and me to sit on. Taylor pulled her knees in to her chest. She was quiet, as if she had a lot on her mind.

"What are you thinking about?" I finally asked.

"I don't want to tell you."

"Us again?" I hesitantly asked.

She reached over and touched me. "No, it's just . . . I had another one of my bizarre dreams last night." She looked back down at her feet. "As usual, I have no idea what it means."

"Tell me about it."

"We were in Taiwan. All of us were standing in front of a school."

"What kind of school?"

"I don't know, like a high school or something. All the students were Chinese and wearing, like, sailor uniforms, you know? The weird thing is, so was McKenna. She looked just like them. And there was some American guy I didn't know; I think it might have been Welch. Then there was an Elgen army. They were about to get us, but suddenly everyone turned into statues. No one was moving." She looked into my eyes. "Except you and some girl. The two of you were just walking around between us."

"A Taiwanese girl?"

"No, she was American. She was our age, pretty, with short blond hair. And she liked you."

"How did you know that?"

"I always know when girls like you. It's the curse of my power." She sighed. "What do you think it means?"

I shrugged. "I have no idea."

"It scares me. Maybe it means that everyone's going to die except for you. You and some mystery chick you're going to run off with."

"That's not going to happen."

Taylor looked back down at her feet. "I wish I'd stop having these dreams. It's not like they're helping. I get just enough information to freak me out."

Just then Nichelle walked up the stairs. "Hey, there you are. Ian said you guys were up here."

"There's no such thing as privacy with Ian," Taylor said.

"I think of that every time I shower," Nichelle said.

"It doesn't matter if you're showering," I said. "He can see through your clothes, anyway."

"That makes me feel a lot better," Nichelle said sardonically.

"So what's up?" I asked.

"Gervaso says to hurry down. It's almost time to go for Welch."

"How far do we have to go?" Taylor asked.

"I don't know." As we walked to the stairway, Nichelle turned back and said, "All Gervaso told us is that we're meeting Welch in front of a school."

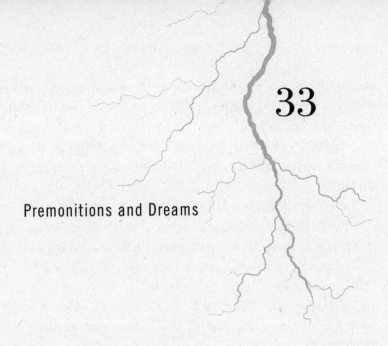

33

Premonitions and Dreams

By the time we got down to the first floor, everyone else was already gathered. Gervaso and Ben stood next to each other on one side of the room, looking at a map. They both looked up as we came down.

"We're here," Nichelle said.

"That is everyone," Ben said.

"All right," Gervaso said, looking around the room. "Everyone listen up. I just got off the phone with Welch. He's ready to surrender to us. This might be tricky. We know that the Elgen are in the area. Ben has seen them, and Welch said they've been tracking him for some time now and they're getting close.

"Keep this in mind. Our number one priority isn't rescuing Welch. It's to make sure that this isn't a trap. That's why we're meeting in a public place.

"The plan is to meet in front of the Cheng Gung High School

near the center of town. As soon as the bell rings, the students will flood the front of the school to go home. Welch will be hiding some- where near the school. Once there is a crowd, he will walk out with the students." He turned toward McKenna. "McKenna, we have a high school uniform for you. You will blend in with the rest of the students."

Taylor shook her head. "It's just like my dream."

I frowned. "Exactly like your dream. I need to tell Gervaso about it."

Ostin said proudly, "The part about McKenna was my idea!"

McKenna dramatically crossed her arms and turned back to him. "Why, because we Chinese all look alike?"

"Well, you do," Ostin said. "Genetically speaking, you have the same hue of hair color, dark-pigment irises, an unusual relativity of height and . . ."

McKenna glared at him.

"But not you," he said. "You are one in a billion."

McKenna smiled.

"He's getting so much better," Taylor said softly.

Gervaso continued. "McKenna, you will find Welch and lead him back to where we are waiting. That way we are in charge of the situation. If Ian, or any of us, sees anything suspicious, we'll call off the mission and leave Welch to himself." He looked at his watch. "We have one hour and forty-eight minutes until the bell rings. McKenna's uniform is on its way. We leave in one hour.

"We won't be coming back here, so get your things packed up and have them waiting by the door. Once we have Welch, we'll be going directly back to the airport to leave the country. Any ques- tions?"

Tanner raised his hand. "If we don't rescue Welch, are we still going to try to steal the *Joule*?"

Gervaso looked at him. "As of now, the plan is to steal the *Joule* no matter what."

"Even if it's impossible?"

Gervaso looked angry. "Of course not. None of us has a death wish. Now go get your things. You're dismissed."

As we turned to walk away, Ostin said, "I wish Tanner would keep his mouth shut."

Tanner overheard him. "Maybe I'm trying to save your little life, Einstein."

"Knock it off," I said.

"Why did you even come?" Zeus asked.

"Yeah," Tessa said. "If you're already chickening out, you should just go home to your family."

Tanner looked at us all sadly, then said softly, "You guys are my family." He turned and went up the stairs alone.

None of us knew what to say to that.

An hour later we all met back downstairs. McKenna was dressed in a schoolgirl uniform that looked like a sailor outfit: a navy-blue skirt, knee-high white stockings, and a white blouse with a broad blue-and-white collar, with a matching navy tie. There were Chinese characters above her left breast, presumably the name of the high school. She didn't look happy about being in uniform.

"If anyone says anything, I'll melt you," she said.

Ostin shrugged. "I think you look cute."

I walked up to Gervaso. "I need to tell you something. Alone."

"All right." We walked into his bedroom and he shut the door. "What's up?"

"This is going to sound a little weird, but Taylor's been having these premonitions that come true."

"What kind of premonitions?"

"Like she had a dream that Timepiece Ranch was attacked by fire-breathing dragons just before the Elgen torched it. She also dreamed that her father was shot by deer hunters the day before it happened."

Gervaso looked at me with concern. "Did she have a dream about what we're doing today?"

"Yeah. She dreamed that we went for Welch in front of a school and that McKenna was dressed up like one of the students."

". . . Just like we are planning."

"Yeah."

"Did she see anything else?"

"The Elgen found us."

Gervaso looked even more concerned. "How did her dream end?"

"This is the part that was most weird. She said that suddenly everyone was frozen like statues. Everyone but me."

"Frozen? As in dead?"

"She didn't say 'dead.'"

Gervaso looked down a moment to think. When he looked back up, he asked, "What do you think we should do?"

"I don't know. We need Welch."

"Yeah, we do."

Neither of us spoke for a moment. Then I said, "I just wanted to warn you that we need to be careful. If her dream is real, we're going to run into Elgen."

He slowly nodded. "All right. Thank you. I'll keep Ian especially close." He took a deep breath. "Now we better go. We're running out of time."

We climbed back into the same vans we had arrived in and quickly drove off.

"How far to the school?" I asked.

"Not far," Ben said. "Maybe just fifteen minutes."

"Fifteen minutes," I repeated. I wondered if we were driving into a trap.

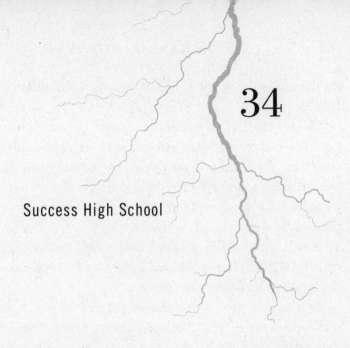

34

Success High School

The traffic was relatively light as we made our way downtown. When we were a block from the school, Ben said, "There is the school ahead of us. We are going to first drive pass the school . . ." He hesitated. "No, *past* the school, then drive around the block and park the van on the north side of the school. Gervaso will park across the street near the Yin Hang."

"The what?" I asked.

"The bank," Ostin said.

As we continued ahead, I looked back to see Gervaso turn left into the bank's parking lot. A moment later we passed a four-story, ivory-colored stone-facade building in the middle of the block.

"That is the Cheng Gung Gau Sywe," Ben said. "Success High School."

"I hope it is," McKenna said.

I looked around but saw no one other than the people walking on the sidewalk in front of the school. I turned to Taylor. "Look familiar?"

She frowned. "This is the same place."

"Ian sees nothing," Gervaso said over our radio.

"Okay," Ben said. We drove past the school, then took a right on the next street, drove to the corner, then took another right, driving past the back of the school. The grounds were empty. No sign of Elgen, at least.

A moment later Ben pulled the van up to the north side of the school. He killed the engine and looked back. "McKenna, the bell will ring in just six minutes. Are you ready?"

"Yes, sir."

"Welch is tall and the only American, I think. He will stand next to the flagpole. It is pass that food truck." He pointed to a large white truck parked to the north of the school's front doors. It had Chinese writing on it. "He is wearing a light blue shirt. When you see him, do not look at him, just walk pass him and tell him to follow you."

"Wait, we're not sending her alone," I said.

"Yes, that is the plan. It is most safe that way."

"It's not safest for her," Ostin said.

"That's not going to work for me, either," Taylor said. "I'm going with her."

"But they will see you," Ben said, his voice rising. "That is why we have McKenna in a uniform."

"We won't be with her," I said. "We'll just keep in the background."

"You are not Chinese. You will stand out." Ben glanced at his watch. "We are almost out of time."

I slid open the van door. "Ben, it's okay. I promise."

Ben looked frustrated but helpless. "I do not like this. Do not get caught. You have thirty seconds until bell. Twenty seconds. Ten seconds." The school bell rang. "McKenna, go now!"

McKenna glanced at Ostin. "Wish me luck."

"Good luck," Ostin said to her.

* * *

The front doors of the school opened, and students dressed in matching uniforms poured out like water. McKenna was dressed exactly like them, and we quickly lost track of her, which, I suppose, was the point.

We continued walking toward the flagpole. I felt like a salmon trying to swim upstream against the current of kids. Ben was right, we didn't look like them. Still we were lost in the sheer number of bodies.

As we got closer to the school, I saw a tall American man walking out from the shadow of the school. I don't know where he came from, but seeing him gave me chills. He was taller than I expected, more powerfully built. He wore slacks and a light blue, short-sleeved linen shirt.

He fell in with a stream of students that were walking toward an aluminum flagpole with a Taiwanese flag. He suddenly stopped, casually looked around, and then began walking toward us.

"There's McKenna," Ostin said. "They must have connected. She's about ten feet in front of him."

"Keep your eye on her," I said.

"Look at him," Taylor said. "It's like looking at the devil."

"Hatch is the devil," I said. "Welch is just his henchman."

"His *chief* henchman," Ostin said. "The right hand of the devil." He turned to me. "Do you think it's a trap?"

"I wouldn't be here if it was," I said. "Taylor, does any of this seem familiar?"

"Something's not right," she said.

"What's that?"

"Where are the Elgen?"

Suddenly McKenna froze. She clutched her chest, then fell to the ground.

"Do you feel that?" I asked.

Taylor was trembling. "Yes. How can they do that?"

"What is it?" Ostin asked.

Taylor looked at him with pain in her eyes. "RESATs."

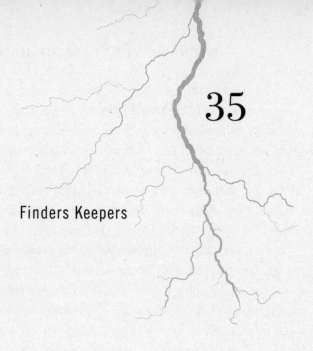

35

Finders Keepers

Apparently, the Elgen had developed a new way to RESAT us without darts or boxes. "This just keeps getting better," I mumbled.

McKenna dropped to her knees, then fell to her side on the asphalt, moaning and clutching her ribs. Three Taiwanese policemen walked up behind her and Welch.

"Cops!" Ostin said.

I'm pretty sure that Welch didn't see the police as he stopped to help McKenna.

"They're after them," Ostin said. "We've got to help her."

"We're walking into RESATs," Taylor said. "We'll be worthless."

"They won't affect me," Ostin said.

"I think I can do it," I said. "I'm getting so electric. Go tell Ben to call Gervaso."

"Okay." As Taylor ran back toward our van, Gervaso and his group began moving toward Welch as well.

"Ian must have already spotted them," Ostin said.

"We'll need help," I said. "Especially Jack's and Gervaso's. Let's go."

Ostin and I ran toward McKenna. When we were about twenty yards away from her, the back door of the food truck we were hiding behind slid open. More than a dozen Elgen guards jumped out the back.

"This way," I said. We dropped to our hands and knees, and Ostin and I crawled under the truck toward McKenna.

"Déjà vu," Ostin said. "Just like Peru."

We stopped at the back of the truck just a few yards from the Elgen guards.

Then two other guards, one of them in the uniform of an EGG and wearing a mind helmet, walked up from a different direction. He took out a gun and held it to Welch's head.

"Did you really think you could escape us?"

Welch said nothing.

The other Elgen guard was dressed in the uniform of a Zone Captain and also wore a mind helmet. He pointed a gun at McKenna. "Tell your friends to give themselves up."

In spite of her pain McKenna said, "Tell them yourself, loser."

The guard took a small control from his pocket and turned a knob. McKenna screamed out.

"I can make it worse," he said.

Ostin started crawling forward.

"What are you doing?" I whispered.

"I've got to stop them." He stood and ran toward them, waving his arms. "Stop it! Leave her alone."

"That was stupid," I said.

The guard, with an amused expression, pointed his gun at Ostin. "You must be Ostin."

"Let her go!" Ostin shouted.

"This isn't catch and release," he said. "It's finders keepers. Now kneel down next to her, or I'll kill you both."

"Yes, sir," Ostin said as he knelt on the ground.

I watched the rest of our group slowly creep forward. I had no way to warn them about the RESATs.

"They're coming, sir," one of the guards said.

"We've got them covered," the first guard replied.

That's when I saw the full regiment of guards coming from outside the school grounds. There were at least a hundred of them. It *was* a trap, and we'd walked right into it.

When Gervaso's group was within thirty yards all the electrics fell to their knees. I could feel a wave of RESAT wash over me, powerful enough to jolt me, like a slipped dental drill. But just for a second. It didn't stop me.

"You are completely surrounded!" a Squad Captain shouted. "Don't try to escape or we'll kill your friends. Hands on your heads. You there!" he shouted at Gervaso. He pointed his gun at McKenna. "Bring everyone in, or I start shooting."

Gervaso looked furious but obeyed. "Come on, everyone. Put your hands up."

Everyone had been captured except for me, Taylor, and Ben. The EGG looked pleased. "Look at this. I swung for a base hit and got a grand slam. The general will be celebrating tonight."

It *was* a trap, only Welch wasn't a part of it. They had set the trap for him, and we had foolishly rushed into it.

"Let them go," Welch said. "I'm the one you want."

"Yeah, I'm not going to do that," Daines said.

"How did you find me?" Welch asked.

The EGG looked at Welch with disdain. "It wasn't easy, after you sent us on all those goose chases with your different phones. But in the end it was your cleverness that was your undoing. It occurred to me that you might still have more phones.

"We traced the phone we captured back to the shop in Kangshan where you purchased them, and with a little persuasion, we got all the phone numbers you had. Then I programmed our systems to look for the ones you hadn't used yet. The very second you activated one, we were notified. It still took a while to find you, since you don't stay in the same place long, but this time we were close, just patiently waiting."

"So now what?" Welch asked.

"General Hatch will be so happy to see you." He looked around. "All of you."

"I thought there was a death order," Welch said.

"There is. But I couldn't exactly open fire around all these schoolchildren. We might accidentally hit a few of them, and you know what kind of negative press that would generate. So we're going to take you back alive, and I'm going to give the general the pleasure of—"

Daines froze midsentence. Actually, everyone around him froze: Welch, the students, the guards, everyone on the entire street. A car driving by slammed into a stopped car, and cars began stacking up behind them. A stuck car horn blared.

Everyone was frozen except for me. My electricity just amplified. It took me a moment to realize that I wasn't the only one unaffected.

A young, blond woman about my age walked confidently through the midst of the people, looking as calm as if she were walking through a museum's statuary.

As I climbed out from under the truck, she turned and looked at me. She wore a large smile on her face. "Michael Vey, I presume. I wondered if it would work on you."

I intensified my electricity. "Who are you?"

"Don't shock me," she said. "We're on the same team."

"I know my team. I don't know you."

"But I know you. And I'm a huge fan. My name is Cassy. The voice sent me."

36

Cassy

"We've got to turn off the RESATs," I said.

"It's coming from those two," Cassy said, pointing at the EGG and the Zone Captain.

I walked over and pried the RESAT devices from their frozen hands as they just stared at me helplessly. I pulsed hard enough to make the RESATs blow, then tossed them onto the ground.

"Where's Tessa?" Cassy asked.

I looked around. Tessa was frozen next to Zeus. "She's over there," I said, pointing to her.

"I'm holding a lot of people right now. I could use a little help."

"She's the one with the light red hair."

"Of course," Cassy said. "I've only seen pictures of her. But she was a lot younger in them." Cassy reached out toward Tessa, who suddenly moved, falling over.

"Okay, that hurt," Tessa said, getting to her feet.

"I'm sorry. I just froze everyone until I could figure out who was who. Could you give me a hand?"

Tessa's eyes narrowed. "Who are you? And how do you know what I can do?"

"I'm with the voice. Electroclan 101. I know everything about all of you." She looked back at me. "We need to hurry this up. People are watching."

I glanced at the buildings around us. People were hanging out their windows pointing.

"Okay," I said. I looked in EGG Daines's frightened face. He could only move his eyes. I lifted my hand in front of him and let my electricity spark loudly.

"I could just electrocute you," I said. "And be done with you. That's what you or Hatch or the rest of you Elgen losers would do. Isn't it?"

He blinked.

". . . But there are better ways of dealing with Elgen." I turned back to Cassy. "Unfreeze the rest of my people."

"No problem."

Suddenly everyone started moving again. Ostin groaned out as he fell over to the ground next to McKenna. I helped them both up.

"Are you okay?" I asked McKenna.

She looked to still be in pain but nodded. "It just took the wind out of me."

Cassy said, "Michael, is that . . . Taylor?"

I looked behind me as Taylor and Ben ran up to us.

"Yes. And Ben."

"I know Ben," she said.

When Taylor was at my side, Cassy extended her hand. "It's nice to meet you, Taylor. I'm Cassy. I'm with the voice."

"Hi," Taylor said, looking at her warily.

"Hello, Cassy," Ben said.

"Benjamin, what's up?"

"Same old crazy."

She laughed. It's like she had forgotten we were in the middle of a crisis.

"Taylor, I need your help," I said. I removed Daines's and the Zone Captain's mind helmets. Not surprisingly, neither of the men seemed very happy about this. I think they would have bitten me if they could. Definitely would have.

I turned back to Taylor. "Remember what you did to the hunters?"

"Yes."

"Do it again. Scramble them. Permanently."

"With pleasure."

Taylor looked at Daines, then reached her hand out until it was an inch from his forehead, and concentrated. In spite of his still being frozen, he began to tremble. When Taylor finished, the look in Daines's eyes was different. Vacant.

Taylor touched his shoulder, then turned back to me. "We don't need to worry about him anymore. He doesn't even know his own name."

"As long as we've got a blank slate here, you might as well program him," I said.

"For what?"

"Something peaceful."

She nodded, putting her hand back out. "After you are free, you will buy all the men in these black uniforms an ice cream, then take them to the beach to play volleyball. It's a lot of fun."

". . . Fun," he said, sounding like a robot.

"Now him," I said, looking at the Zone Captain.

The Zone Captain looked terrified. Somehow he got a word out. "Freak."

"That's not nice," Taylor said. "I'm not a freak. But I used to be a cheerleader. That was kind of freaky." She put her hand just an inch from the Elgen's forehead. "This is for what you did to McKenna." She closed her eyes, and the man began shaking. When she stopped, he had the same blank expression on his face as the EGG.

Suddenly Jack walked up to the man and punched him, knocking him over.

"Scumbag Elgen," he said. Then he walked around punching each of the terrified frozen guards.

"Is someone going to stop him?" Tessa asked.

"Why?" Zeus replied.

"Hmm," Tessa said. "Hadn't thought of it that way."

Taylor looked down at Welch. "What about him?"

Welch, who was still frozen, just stared at her without emotion.

"I need you to lie detector him," I said.

Taylor touched Welch's forehead. "Go ahead."

I said to Welch, "Did you have anything to do with this trap?"

"No."

"He's telling the truth," Taylor said. "He's glad to see us."

"Especially with the Elgen here," Jack said as he walked back to us, rubbing his red knuckles. "I should have used a stick or something."

I turned to Cassy. "You can release him. We can go."

Welch's shoulders dropped, and he breathed in deeply. "Thank you." He looked at me. "The last time I saw you, you were embarrassing my forces at the Taiwan Starxource plant."

"You were at the plant?"

"I was in charge of protecting the plant and catching you. Why do you think Hatch had me arrested?"

"Really, guys. We've got to go," Cassy said. "I can't do this much longer."

"Let's go!" I shouted to everyone. I turned to Cassy. "Are you alone?"

"Just little me."

"Come on, we're this way."

"Wait," Gervaso said. "Michael, I want you, Taylor, and . . ."

"Cassy," Cassy said. "Can we please hurry this up?"

"Cassy, come with us. We need to talk to Welch. Zeus and Tessa, go with Ben."

"Got it," Tessa said. "Come on, lightning bolt."

"I don't want to be in the same car as Welch, anyway," Zeus said.

"Can we go with you?" Ostin asked.

"We're full," Gervaso said.

"It's good," Jack said. "Abi and I can switch cars."

"All right," Gervaso said. He turned to Welch. "Come with me."

We followed him back across the street to their van, which was still parked at the bank. Gervaso unlocked the doors, then said to Welch, "Do you have any weapons?"

He reached into his pocket and pulled out a gun. He offered it to Gervaso. "Just this."

Gervaso took the gun. "Anything else?"

"No."

Gervaso looked at Ian.

"No, that was it," Ian said.

"Okay. Ride up front with me," Gervaso said to Welch. Welch got into the front passenger seat.

"Taylor." Gervaso leaned forward to whisper to her. "I want you to sit behind Welch and monitor him. We don't know what's going through his head, but I suspect he's volatile."

"Yes, sir."

He walked back to the driver seat. Nichelle opened the side door, and Cassy climbed in first and slid down the first seat of the van. I got in after her, with Taylor next to me and directly behind Welch.

Ostin, McKenna, Nichelle, and Ian sat in the middle and backseats.

"Are we all here?" Gervaso asked from the front.

"Everyone's here," Ian said. "Jack, Abi, Zeus, Tanner, and Tessa went with Ben."

Sweat was streaming down Cassy's face. "Seriously, I'm losing it. We've got to go."

"Shut the doors," Gervaso said, starting the van. "Let's get out of here."

Ian slid the side door shut, and Gervaso jerked the van forward out of the bank parking lot into traffic, eliciting a few horns. As he did so, Cassy let out a loud gasp. "I'm done."

After we were away, Ostin said, "Your power is really amazing."

Cassy took a deep breath in and out. "Thank you. It's exhausting."

"McKenna, how are you?" Taylor asked.

"I'm feeling better. That was a little terrifying."

"Thank goodness Cassy showed up," Ostin said. He turned back to Cassy. "How far can you keep someone frozen?"

"Just one person?"

"Yes."

"About two kilometers. A little more than a mile. If it's a lot of people, it depends."

"That was a lot of people today," I said.

"Tell me about it," Cassy replied.

"It depends on what?" Ostin asked.

"Different variables. The weather. Obstacles. Mostly the people. Some people are just more susceptible than others."

"It makes sense," Ostin said. "Electricity affects people in different ways. Some people get struck by lightning and live, some die."

"Where are we going?" Welch asked. It was weird hearing his voice.

"Taipei," Gervaso said.

"When do we fly to America?"

"As soon as we can," Gervaso said. "There are some important things we need to attend to first."

"What things?" Welch asked.

"*Important* things," Gervaso said.

Welch leaned back in his seat.

"He doesn't know about Tuvalu," Taylor said softly. "Why didn't Gervaso say something?"

"It's not the time," I said. "Welch needs to digest things."

Taylor asked Cassy, "How did you get to Taiwan?"

"I flew commercially. It's not the luxury of a private jet like you guys had, but at least it was first class."

"I guess with your power the resistance doesn't worry too much about protecting you," I said.

"No. I've never met anyone I couldn't freeze. Except you."

"Where did you come from?" I asked.

Cassy glanced up to the front toward Welch, then back at us. She asked in a hushed voice, "You mean, where was I born?"

"No, where did you fly here from?"

"I can't tell you. It's one of our secrets."

"The voice keeps a lot of secrets," Taylor said.

"Which is why the voice is still alive."

"Then you've seen the voice?"

Cassy again glanced suspiciously at Welch, then said, "We need to keep our voices down."

"All right," Taylor whispered. "So have you seen him?"

"I see him every day. He's my boss."

"Who is he?"

"I can't tell you."

"Can't or won't?" Taylor asked.

"Won't. Can't. Both. Especially with Mr. Elgen sitting six feet from me." She looked at Taylor. "I know you could read my mind if you wanted to, but trust me, you don't want to. For your own safety. If the Elgen knew that you knew who the voice was, they'd stop at nothing to get that information out of you." She glanced at me. "Including killing everyone you love."

"I get it," Taylor said.

"After we steal the . . ." She hesitated. "I mean, after we complete our mission, I've been instructed to tell you everything." She paused. "Well, *almost* everything. There are things the voice wants to tell you himself."

Ostin asked, "How long have you been with the voice?"

"Since I was four. He's pretty much like my father. The Elgen killed my parents, but when they tried to kidnap me, the voice and his people intervened. They were both looking for me at the same time."

"How long ago did the voice start the resistance?" I asked.

"The voice didn't—" She stopped herself and again nervously glanced toward the front. "I've said too much."

"There's someone above the voice?" I whispered.

Cassy hesitated. "No."

Taylor glanced at me.

"I've said too much," Cassy said again. "We can talk later." She leaned back against the side of the van.

The rest of the trip was mostly quiet except for Ostin, who kept grilling Cassy about her power. Ostin can think up more questions than anyone else I know. I suppose that's one of the reasons he knows so much—he asks so much.

Gervaso drove us to a hotel called the Hotel Midtown Taipei, which, I figure, must have been in the middle of Taipei City to get that name. Ben must have known a shorter route to our destination, because he was already there when we arrived, and the van was empty. Gervaso parked next to the van, then turned back to us. "Dinner in the ballroom at eight."

Ben walked up to Gervaso's window.

"Where is everyone?" Gervaso asked.

"They have gone to their rooms," Ben said. "I have your room keys."

"Where are our bags?" Taylor asked.

"Your bags will be in your rooms," he said.

Ben walked around to the curb while one of the bell captains opened the door for Welch, then the side door. As we got out, Ben handed us our keys. He said to Cassy, "You are alone."

"No worries," she said. "I'm used to it."

As usual Ostin and I were together, as were Taylor and McKenna. Cassy got off on the floor before the rest of ours. The tenth.

We rode to our floor, then got off. As we walked up the hall to our room, I said to Taylor, "Is Cassy the girl you saw in your dream?"

"Yes. And she was lying."

"About what?"

"About there being someone else besides the voice. There's someone above him."

"You shouldn't read her mind."

"I wasn't trying to. Her lie was so obvious that I couldn't not. I'm surprised you didn't see it."

"I knew she was lying," I said. "But if there's someone above the voice, I can see why she wouldn't want to share that."

"I think she would share everything with *you.*"

"What do you mean by that?"

"I told you, it's just like my dream. She likes you."

"No, she doesn't."

Taylor's eyes narrowed. "I'm not being a jealous, crazy girlfriend; I'm telling you what I know." Her brow furrowed. "Or maybe I am being crazy jealous, but I'm still telling the truth. If it wasn't the truth, why would I be jealous?"

"I don't know why you would be jealous."

"Because she's pretty and cool and powerful, and she thinks you're a rock star. Even Ostin was slobbering all over her."

I stopped walking and turned toward her. "I didn't notice she was pretty."

Taylor rolled her eyes. "Really. You didn't notice."

"I really didn't."

"How could you not notice?"

"Because I wasn't looking. Someone already owns my heart."

Her expression changed with my response. "Who would that be?"

"Do I need to say it?"

Taylor took my hand. "Yes. I kind of need to hear it right now."

"You, Taylor Ridley, own my heart. Forever."

Taylor leaned forward and kissed me. "Sorry, Michael. I'm just feeling really insecure."

"I know."

"You own my heart, too," she said. "You always will. No matter what happens."

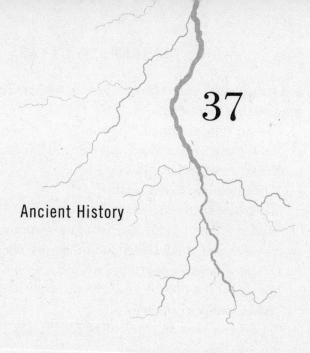

37

Ancient History

Ostin and McKenna were going for a walk in the city, and Taylor wanted to take a shower, so I went to my room to rest. It was dark when Ostin returned to get me for dinner. He had McKenna and Taylor with him. I splashed some water onto my face; then we met up with the rest of the Electroclan on the hotel's fourteenth floor for dinner.

The dining room was modern and clean and took more than half of the entire floor. Against the wall was a massive buffet. Fortunately, we didn't look out of place, because there were as many foreigners as there were Chinese. More, in fact.

Even though we blended in, we still kept separated in small groups just to be safe. Taylor and I got in line together at the back of the entrée line. The food was mostly Chinese. There was duck, chicken, pork, noodles, *bao dz*, egg drop soup, and hot-and-sour soup with curdled pig's blood. (I'm told that's the only way to eat it.) They also had *syau lung bao* dumplings, one of the foods I liked and remembered from our last visit to Taiwan.

"You love those things," Taylor said.

"Love them," I said. "So does Ostin. I'll have to tell him."

"Look, they also have swamp eel."

"I just threw up in my mouth."

She grinned. "Just kidding."

While I was lifting dumplings onto my plate, a redheaded American woman on my right side leaned toward me and pointed at the *syau lung bao*. "What do you suppose those are?"

I looked at her. "They're called *syau lung bao*. They're dumplings."

"What's inside them?"

"They have pork and kind of a broth inside. They sometimes call them soup dumplings."

"That sounds interesting. Are they good?"

Considering that my plate was full of them, it was a dumb question. *No, they're sculpted vomit. That's why I filled my plate with them.* "Yes, ma'am. I like them."

"Then I guess I'll just have to try some. Thank you."

I started to move down the line when she asked, "Are you American?"

Another dumb question. "Yes, ma'am."

"Me too. Where are you from?"

"Idaho," I said.

"No way! I'm from Idaho. What city?"

Now I was feeling a little nervous. "Meridian."

"I'm from Eagle! We're practically neighbors. We might have met before. What a small world."

Taylor glanced at me anxiously.

"Sometimes it is," I said.

"What brings you to Taiwan?"

"I'm just visiting," I said. "I'm with a school group. . . ."

"Which school?"

I hesitated. "It's just a little private school. You probably haven't heard of it."

"My son went to a private school in Meridian. Which one is it?"

I swallowed. ". . . The Liss Academy."

Her brow furrowed. "I don't think I've heard of that one."

Before she could ask another question, I said, "What are you doing here?"

"My husband's here on business. His company manufactures steam turbines for electric plants. There's a really large power plant in the southern part of Taiwan that just broke down. We're headed there to . . ." Her eyes suddenly went blank. Then she pointed at the *syau lung bao* and said, "Excuse me, do you know what these are?"

I looked over at Taylor. She slightly nodded.

"They're called *syau lung bao* dumplings," I said. "They have pork and soup in them. They're really good. You should have some."

"That does sound good. I guess I'll have to try some."

"Great, have a good dinner," I said. Taylor and I quickly slipped away.

After dinner we all gathered in Gervaso and Jack's room on the seventh floor. Jack and Gervaso still hadn't eaten, as they were talking with Welch, and Ostin and McKenna brought them boxes of food.

Taylor, Tessa, and I sat next to Welch on the edge of the bed.

Again, Gervaso wanted Taylor to monitor Welch's thoughts without him knowing it. The room was pretty crowded, and so it didn't seem weird that Taylor was slightly touching him.

Tanner was sitting by himself against the wall by the closet. He'd been pretty quiet since his last outburst. I felt bad for him. Also, I noticed that Cassy wasn't there, but I didn't say anything. I figured it would only bother Taylor that I noticed.

"Mr. Welch has been telling us what he knows about the Elgen movement," Gervaso said. "Especially after they attacked the ranch."

"Call me David," Welch said. "The Elgen thought they had destroyed the resistance."

"They came close," Gervaso said. "Fortunately, we were tipped off. The ranch was deserted before the Elgen forces arrived."

Welch looked ashamed. "That was fortunate."

"It was more than fortunate. It was prepared for," Gervaso said. "We are careful."

"Of course." Welch looked around the room. "Thank you again for rescuing me. When will we head back to the States?"

Gervaso looked around as if to make sure we were all prepared for Welch's reaction. Then he said, "We're not going back to the States. We're headed to Tuvalu."

Welch made no attempt to conceal his feelings. "You're not serious . . ."

"As a heart attack," Zeus said. He looked like he was relishing Welch's pain.

"I'm not going to Tuvalu," Welch said. "It's a death trap. The entire Elgen guard is there right now. No one gets in or out of Tuvalu without Hatch's permission. No one."

"No one gets in or out of the Elgen Academy, the Peruvian compound, the *Ampere*, or the Taiwan Starxource plant, either," Jack said. "But we did."

"Notwithstanding, I can't go back. They have a price on my head."

"We all have prices on our heads," Gervaso said. "You know that. You put them there."

"Only a few of you," Welch said, furtively glancing at me.

"What a chicken," Zeus said.

I hadn't realized until then just how much Zeus hated Welch. There was clearly bad history between them.

"Watch your tongue, *Frank*," Welch said.

"What are you going to do to me, *Davey*?" Zeus retorted.

"Stop it," I said. "Both of you. Whatever history you two have is past. We're on the same team now." I turned to Welch. "We're going back to Tuvalu because of you."

He looked at me, then Gervaso, then back at me. "I don't understand."

Jack said, "If it wasn't for you, they wouldn't be getting ready to execute Tara, Torstyn, and Quentin."

Welch looked as if Jack had just slugged him in the stomach. "What?"

Gervaso said, "Hatch found out that the three of them helped you escape, and he has them locked up. He originally put Quentin in Cell 25. After that Quentin was locked in the monkey cage in the city square, where he'll stay for the rest of his life. Tara and Torstyn are scheduled for the rat bowl."

Welch's head dropped into his hands. When he looked up, his eyes were fierce. "I didn't know. I had no way of knowing."

"You do now," Zeus said. "Still want to run away?"

I glared at Zeus. "Not helpful, man."

Welch took a deep breath, then said, "What do you need from me?"

"We need your help rescuing them," I said. I purposely didn't tell him about the *Joule*.

"Then I'm with you."

Gervaso glanced at Taylor for confirmation. Taylor nodded in the affirmative. "We'll fly out early tomorrow morning," Gervaso said. "We leave here at oh-five-hundred hours. We'll fly to Sydney, then Fiji."

"You have a plane, then?"

"We have a jet."

Welch nodded. "Good."

"From Fiji we've arranged to stow away on one of the supply boats. We'll free Quentin first, then the others."

"Be aware that the Elgen have spies all around Fiji. Are you sure you can trust everyone on the boat?"

"We can trust the captain," Gervaso said. "He's a friend of mine."

"All right. I'll help however I can."

Gervaso glanced at Taylor, and she nodded again. I was glad that Welch was telling the truth. It would be good to have someone on our side who knew everything about our enemy. It was still hard to believe that a month ago he *was* the enemy.

"All right, then," Gervaso said. "We leave first thing in the morning. Try to get some sleep. You're going to need it."

38

Sleeping in the Hallway

Again, I didn't sleep well. I had dreams. Nightmares. To make it worse Ostin was snoring like a chain saw. At two in the morning I got up and walked out into the hall. To my surprise Taylor was standing there in the dark.

"What are you doing out here?" I asked.

"I heard you say you were coming out."

"I didn't say I was coming out."

"You thought it. Loudly."

"You could hear me?"

She nodded. "I think it has to do with how electric you've become. Do you want to go for a walk?"

I shook my head. "Not really. I'm exhausted. It's bizarre. I can't sleep but I'm exhausted."

"I know what you mean. Do you want to hang out for a while?"

"Yes."

We sat down on the floor outside my door, and I lay my head back on her shoulder.

"You're afraid," she said.

"Yeah."

"Me too." She ran her hand over my cheek. "Do you think we'll ever come back?"

I didn't answer. At least not vocally.

After a moment she said softly, sadly, "Yeah. Me too." She took a deep breath. "You know, part of me doesn't care anymore."

I looked at her. "What do you mean?"

"When my father was shot and I thought he might die, I was freaked out, but I realized that part of me was happy for him. All I could think of was how lucky he was that he didn't have to worry anymore about the Elgen or Hatch . . . or the end of the free world."

I closed my eyes.

After a minute she said, "Me too."

"You too what?" I asked.

"I don't want to lose you."

I sighed. "Sometimes I think you're the only reason I want to keep living."

"Maybe love is really the only reason we have to live."

"That's profound," I said.

"Maybe," Taylor said.

The two of us fell asleep in the hall.

I woke to some Chinese guy dragging his luggage over my foot as he walked by us. He didn't bother to say "excuse me" or whatever they say in Chinese; he just ran his bag over me like I was carpet lice. I made a lightning ball, then caught myself and threw it against the wall in front of me instead of at him.

I could see from the glowing curtained window at the far end of the corridor that the sun was beginning to rise. We would be leaving soon.

Taylor was lying on her side next to me. I leaned over and kissed her, then whispered into her ear, "We need to get ready."

She lightly groaned. Then her eyes fluttered open. "Is it time to go?"

"Soon," I said.

"Just hold me a little longer."

I lay back down and pulled her head onto my chest, and she quickly fell back asleep. I didn't sleep. I couldn't. Actually, I didn't want to. I wanted to feel every second of her next to me. What I had said in the night was true. If something happened to her, I didn't know if I would be able to go on.

As I looked at her sleeping, I said softly, "I love you." I gently slid my hand up her neck under her hair. "I would die for you."

Taylor sighed a little. Then she said in a half-asleep voice, "What?"

I pulled her in close. "Nothing," I said. "Nothing."

39

The Monster's Lair

"Hey, Michael," Ostin said. He was in his underwear, looking at me from out our door. "You awake?"

"I am now," I said, taking a second to remember where I was.

"I thought you had left me. We just got a call from Gervaso. We've got forty minutes to eat and go."

"I'll be right there."

Ostin nodded and disappeared back into our room.

I kissed Taylor on the forehead. "It's time to wake up."

"Do we have to?"

"This time we do."

She groaned, then slowly pushed herself up. I sat up, stood, and then helped her up.

"What time is it?" Taylor asked.

"I don't know. Ostin says we've got forty minutes. Or we did a couple of minutes ago."

"Okay." She leaned in and we kissed; then she stepped back. She looked like she might fall over. "I'll see you in a little bit."

She walked to her room and knocked on the door. McKenna opened it. "Good morning," she said. "I was about to come looking for you." She waved to me. "Hi, Michael."

"Morning."

I turned and pushed open my door and went inside to shower.

Almost a half hour later Taylor and I walked into the dining room. Gervaso was sitting at a table near the door with Jack, Abi, and Cassy. He waved us over.

"Hey, Tay," Jack said. "Mike."

"Hey," Taylor said.

Cassy was smiling at me. "Good morning, Michael. Do you go by Michael or Mike?"

"Michael. I'm only Mike to Jack."

"My man," Jack said, sounding like Denzel Washington. "I got privileges."

"Michael it is," Cassy said. "I think it's cuter, anyway." She laughed sweetly.

Taylor shot me a look.

"I'd like to talk with you sometime. I have a lot of questions," Cassy said.

"I'm sure there'll be a lot of time to talk on the flight," I said.

"Almost nine hours," Gervaso said.

Jack groaned. "It's really that far?"

"I'm afraid so."

"Well, we'll definitely have time to talk," I said.

"Speaking of time," Gervaso said, "we need to leave in eight minutes, so eat fast."

"Sorry," Taylor said, glancing at Cassy. "We slept in. Together."

Cassy bit her lower lip but said nothing. The tension between them was palpable.

"We'll just grab a sweet roll or something," I said, trying to lighten the mood.

"There will be food on the plane too," Gervaso said.

"Great," I said. "Has Ostin come up yet?"

"He's back in the corner with McKenna," Jack said, pointing.

"Thanks. Come on, Taylor."

We walked over and grabbed plates.

"Didn't I tell you she liked you?" Taylor said.

"She's just being friendly," I said.

"Very." She turned and walked away.

I grabbed a cherry Danish, a hard-boiled egg, some toast, and a glass of orange juice, and carried it over to where Taylor had gone, next to Ostin and McKenna. Taylor looked embarrassed.

"Ostin said he found you guys sleeping in the hall," McKenna said.

"It was quieter than sleeping next to Ostin," I replied.

"I talk in my sleep?" Ostin said.

"No, you snore. Like a chain saw."

He turned to McKenna. "I don't snore."

"Uh, yeah, you do," I said.

"Why are you making these cruel accusations?"

"Because I had to sleep in the hall," I said. "And I got run over by some Chinese dude in a psychedelic green jacket. You definitely snore. If you don't believe me, we can prove it scientifically."

"How would you do that?"

"Easy. We could record you."

"What, with a phone recorder?"

"No, I was thinking more of a Richter scale."

McKenna and Taylor both laughed.

"It's okay," McKenna said. "Real men snore."

Ostin smiled. Then he said to me, "Hey, you should try your Danish baked with butter. The way your mother used to make them."

"I would if I had an oven."

McKenna's eyebrows rose. "Excuse me, but what am I?"

"Sorry, but I don't usually think of you as an oven."

"Give it to me."

I put a pat of butter on top of my pastry and then pushed the plate to McKenna. She put her hand on it. Within seconds the butter was bubbling and the Danish was slightly toasted. She stopped and pushed the plate back to me. "There you go. Be careful, it's hot."

"Thank you."

I had only taken a few bites of my Danish when Jack walked up to our table. "Gervaso says it's time to head down."

I downed my orange juice in one gulp, then grabbed a napkin and my sweet roll, and we all walked out to the elevator. Taylor and I stopped on our floor and grabbed our bags, then went down to the lobby. Ian and Gervaso were standing near the hotel's front doors.

"That's everyone but Welch," Gervaso said.

"He's waiting for us outside," Ian said. "He's reading a newspaper."

"All right, let's go."

After we were in our vans, Welch casually put down his newspaper and walked over to our vehicle and got in. I didn't think that he was being overly cautious. If I had Hatch and his whole army after me, I'd be careful too.

The drive from the hotel to the airport took about a half hour. We set what little luggage we had near the back of the plane, then boarded.

Scott closed the cockpit door, and within fifteen minutes we were in the air. I think that's the best part of a private jet. There's not a lot of sitting around. And you don't have to bring your seat up for takeoff.

Once the plane had settled on a cruising altitude, Gervaso stood up in the aisle at the front of the plane. He steadied himself by holding on to the seats on each side.

"Listen up, all. The flight to Sydney is almost nine hours, so you've got some time to relax. You all look pretty tired, so I suggest that you rest now and we'll talk a few hours before we land. There are some important things we need to go over."

"Sounds good to me," Taylor said softly. "At least the resting part."

We reclined our seats, and she laid her head against me to sleep. We were headed to the monster's lair.

40

Black Mambas, Hatch, and Other Deadly Things

We ended up taking the long way to Sydney, Australia. Usually pilots look for the shortest route between two dots, but in this case that would have basically taken us through a hurricane.

An hour into the flight our pilots informed us that there was a category-five tropical cyclone (which Ostin explained meant there were winds of above one hundred thirty miles per hour) in the area of the Marshall Islands, which were about a thousand miles from Tuvalu and close enough to Sydney that all air traffic had been delayed or rerouted.

We ended up flying from Taipei to Dili, the capital of Timor-Leste—a country I'd never even heard of. Ostin, of course, had not only heard of the country but knew more about it than any normal non-Timorese wanted to know.

He informed us that Timor had been a Portuguese colony since 1520 except when, during World War II, the nation was invaded and conquered by the Japanese, but Timor was returned to Portugal after the war. Thirty years later it declared its independence from Portugal. Nine days after that it was attacked and conquered by Indonesia, which made it part of their country. Kind of like Tuvalu, which was open to attack from the Elgen after they declared their independence from England. Maybe sometimes it's better to just live with the devil you know.

We didn't do anything in Dili. We didn't even get off the plane. It was raining hard, and we waited on the runway while the ground crews refueled our jet, and then we took off again.

From Dili we flew south over Darwin, Australia, then overland to the Australian east coast and Sydney. Once we were over Australia, Ostin began vomiting facts about the country.

"Did you know that Australia was England's penal colony? It's basically where they dumped all the people they didn't want. That's why modern Australians call people from England 'POME.'"

"What's a 'POME'?" Jack asked.

"It's something that rhymes," Tessa said.

"Not 'po-*em*,'" Ostin said. "*POME*. It stands for 'Prisoner of Mother England.'" Ostin continued without taking a breath. "There are more than one million wild camels in the Australian outback. And even Saudi Arabia imports camels from Australia."

"That's not true," Tanner said.

"Completely true," Ostin replied. "Before humans arrived, there were nine-foot-tall kangaroos."

"Now he's just making things up," Tessa said.

"Australians have three times more sheep than people. And wombat poop is the shape of a cube."

"What's a wombat?" Abigail asked.

"Something that poops cubes," Jack said.

"A wombat is a plant-eating marsupial that looks like a badger with shorter legs."

"Is it dangerous?" Tessa asked.

"Does it sound dangerous?" Zeus said.

"No."

Ostin nodded. "They have been known to charge humans and bowl them over."

"Oh, that sounds scary," Tessa said, rolling her eyes. "Getting run over by a short-legged, cube-pooping badger."

"Yeah? Well, there are plenty of things in Australia to be really scared of," Ostin said defensively. "Australia is famous for having a lot of things that can kill you. It has more species of venomous snakes than any other country, including one of the most venomous of all land snakes, the inland taipan. One bite has enough venom to kill a hundred people."

"How do they know it can kill one hundred people?" Tessa asked.

Tanner joined in. "Is that, like, exactly one hundred? Because maybe it's really like ninety-seven people. Or what if it's a hundred huge people versus one hundred little people? The whole 'exactly one hundred people' thing sounds suspicious."

"Didn't we already have a snake conversation in Peru?" Taylor asked me.

"Yes," I said. "But this is a new country."

"Is the taipan as dangerous as the black mamba?" Nichelle asked.

"Yes."

"But it's not as cool."

Ostin's brow furrowed. "Why do you say that?"

"Who doesn't like to say 'black . . . mammmmmbaaaa'?"

Everyone laughed except for Ostin, who was trying to analyze her point. He eventually gave up and continued. "Just so you know, the black mamba isn't necessarily black. The inside of its mouth is."

"Good, that way I'll know it's dangerous after it bites me," Tanner said.

"What is the most poisonous snake in the world?" Tessa asked.

"Snakes aren't poisonous; they're venomous. Poison is something you eat."

"I wouldn't eat it," Tessa said.

"If you eat poison, you die," Jack said.

"I know," Ostin said.

Jack pressed his point. "But you just said poison is something you eat."

"It is."

"But no one *would* eat it," Tessa said. "That's the point."

"Poison is something you eat," Ostin said. "Venom is something you inject."

"Again," Tessa said. "I wouldn't inject it."

"You're talking in circles," Zeus said.

"What is the most *venomous* snake in the world?" Jack asked.

"The Belcher's sea snake is number one. But it's not the most dangerous snake in the world."

"What does that mean?"

"Only about twenty-five percent of Belchers carry venom, and those that do don't really like to bite. But if it does, and it's venomous, you're toast. One bite can kill a thousand people."

"That doesn't make it more dangerous," Zeus said. "What does it matter if it can kill a thousand people or one? Either way you're dead."

"He's got a point," Nichelle said.

"I never said it was more dangerous. You asked which snake was most venomous."

"He's got a point too," Nichelle said.

"The *point* is," Zeus continued, "it doesn't matter if the entire universe implodes on itself or you swallow a grenade, either way you're dead."

"Who would swallow a grenade?" Tessa asked.

"A grenade would never fit down your throat," Nichelle said.

Tessa nodded. "It wouldn't even fit into your mouth."

"That's not the point," Zeus said.

"You just said it was your point," Nichelle said.

Zeus groaned. "I'm leaving this conversation."

"It might fit into Ostin's mouth," Tessa said. "It's pretty big."

"Thank you," Ostin said, though I'm not sure why. "Back to the snakes."

"Oh, thank you," Taylor said. "I was afraid you'd forgotten."

"There's the brown snake, which is known for its bad temper and aggressive nature, which makes it very dangerous. The mulga snake, which puts out ten times the amount of venom in one bite as the tiger snake, the red-bellied black snake . . ."

"Which isn't really black, only its toes are," Tanner mocked.

"Snakes don't have toes," Ostin said. "That would make it a lizard."

"He's so literal," Tessa said.

"It's one of his more endearing qualities," McKenna said.

". . . There's the southern death adder, which is dangerous because it likes to camouflage itself, so it gets stepped on a lot and the venom acts so fast that half the victims die before they can get antivenin. . . ."

"And it has 'death' in its name, which makes it super-scary," Tessa added.

"And then there are spiders."

"Of course there are," Taylor said.

"Can we please stop now?" Abigail said. "I have arachnophobia. I'm not kidding."

"I love that word," Ostin said, ignoring Abigail's request. "My favorite is the Sydney funnel-web spider, which is one of the world's most dangerous spiders. Humans are especially susceptible to its venom."

Tanner asked Taylor, "Why would anyone have a favorite spider?"

"I'll just stick to the ocean," Tessa said.

"You're not safe in the ocean," Ostin said. "Especially not in *this* ocean. It's filled with all kinds of killers."

"Like the great white shark," Jack said.

"Yes, but there's worse," Ostin said. "Much worse."

"What's worse than a great white?"

"There's the blue-ringed octopus, with one of the most toxic venoms on the planet. If it bites you, it causes paralysis within minutes, stopping your heart and lungs."

"I can do that in seconds," Cassy said.

"You bite people and cause paralysis?" Zeus asked.

Cassy laughed. "Sometimes."

Ostin continued. "There's the cone snail. One sting can kill fifteen healthy adults within hours."

"But one sting doesn't kill fifteen anything, because one sting is for one person and you only die once," Zeus protested.

"Don't start that again," Taylor said. "It's a slippery slope."

"There's a fish called the stonefish. Its sting is so excruciating that people die just from the pain. When it comes to killers, most people think of the great white shark as the deadliest creature of the sea, but the box jellyfish has killed more people than all sharks, stonefish, and crocodiles combined. And it's almost invisible."

"That is so comforting," Taylor said. "The invisible killer."

"Like carbon monoxide," Jack said.

Ostin continued. "Even the gentle male platypus has enough venom to kill a dog."

Taylor groaned. "That does it. I'm not getting off the plane."

"Is there anything venomous in Tuvalu?"

Three of us said at the exact same time, "Hatch."

A few minutes later Tessa said, "I know something about Australia. The name 'Kylie' came from the name of an aboriginal hunting stick similar to the boomerang."

"So Kylie just keeps coming back," Zeus said.

"All I know about Australia," McKenna said, "is that they have koala bears, a whole lot of kangaroos, and that famous place where they hold concerts."

"That would be the Sydney Opera House," Ostin said. "Did you know that if all the sails of the Sydney Opera House roof were combined, they would create a perfect sphere?"

"A spear?" Jack said.

"A *sphere*. You know, a ball. The architect was peeling an orange when he came up with the idea."

"A ball or an orange?" Jack asked.

"They're both spheres," Ostin said.

"Then why didn't you just say an orange to begin with?"

"Yeah," Zeus said. "You can't peel a ball."

"I peeled a golf ball once," Tanner said. "It had like a million elastics inside. It moved like it was alive."

"This is making me hungry for oranges," Tessa said.

"We should eat more *bananas*," Taylor said. "I've been slacking off."

"No one ever designed anything to look like a banana," Jack said.

Tessa shook her head. "Can you blame them?"

Ostin sighed. "Also, some shopping malls play classical music in their parking lots at night to scare off teenagers."

"That would scare me," Nichelle said. "More than a wombat."

"Much more than a wombat," Tessa agreed.

In spite of everyone pretty much dissing Ostin (who now looked as if he might lose his mind), I was glad for the conversation. Somehow it made me feel hopeful. I suppose in times of danger it is helpful to cling to mundane things. Like holding on to a life raft in rapids.

While everyone was talking, I looked over at Welch. He was sitting alone, quietly watching us. He had a grim look on his face. I wondered what was going on in his mind. The reality of him being with us was a strange one for all of us, but it had to be especially strange for him. It was hard to believe that this was the same man who had hunted us in our childhood. He didn't look so frightening now. In fact, other than his size, he looked just like any other man you might walk by and not notice.

I remember hearing something from the Bible that said, "Is this the man that made the earth to tremble, that did shake kingdoms?" This was the man who made *us* tremble, who was calling the shots against us in Peru and Taiwan. Now he was sitting with all of us, quietly listening.

I wondered what that felt like, to be cast out from your tribe and to seek refuge among your former enemies. Among the Elgen, Welch was a traitor. I suppose the real question is, you can take the man out of the evil, but can you take the evil out of the man?

Still, the fact that he was going with us to Tuvalu spoke volumes about him. I wasn't sure what Hatch would do with us, but it was a guaranteed death sentence for Welch. Back in Dili, Jack had asked me if I thought we could trust him.

"What are the odds of Hatch forgiving him?" I asked.

"Zero," Jack replied. "Less than zero. Negative zero."

"That's why we can trust him."

"I'm going to talk to Zeus," I said. Taylor scooted back so I could get around her, and I walked down the aisle. Tessa was asleep next to him, listening to music with earbuds. "Hey, can I ask you something?"

"Yeah, bro."

"You don't need to answer if you don't want."

"Ask away."

"What is it between you and Welch? It feels like there's bad blood."

Zeus's eyes narrowed as he glanced toward Welch. "Yeah, there's bad blood. A freaking river of it."

"What happened?"

"You mean other than he was the one who kidnapped me and killed my family?"

"No, that's enough reason to hold a grudge."

"There's more. We were on the outs long before you showed up. Remember when the Elgen found us in the safe house in Idaho, before we went to Peru? There was that one guard who hated me because I shocked him in the shower and he hurt his back?"

That time seemed like a lifetime ago. "Yeah. The one who was torturing you."

"That's the dude. He was Welch's college buddy. Ever since he hurt his back, Welch treated me like trash. Most of the time he called me 'stinky' or 'the pungent one' in front of the other Glows. If it wasn't for Hatch, I'm sure he would have done worse."

"I can see why you hate him," I said softly. "Anyone would. But right now, we can't afford any division between us. Can you forgive him?"

"No."

"Can you work with him?"

He nodded. "Yeah. I can put it aside. For now."

"Then do that. There will be time after to put things right."

"What if there's not?"

I looked at him for a moment, then said, "Then it won't matter, will it?"

He thought about that, then grinned. "You're right."

We bumped fists, and I went back to my seat.

Taylor waited until I had settled in before asking, "How'd it go?"

"Not good," I said. "But we'll survive."

A few minutes later our pilot, Scott, came out of the cockpit. He crouched down next to Gervaso.

"So if he's out here, who's flying the plane?" Nichelle asked.

"His copilot's still in front," Zeus said.

"It doesn't matter," Ostin said. "The plane can fly itself. It's called autopilot. It's like autocorrect."

"I hope it's not like autocorrect," Jack said. "I sent a text to a girl that said I wanted to kiss her. Her father ended up on my doorstep with the police. The autocorrect had changed my text to I wanted to kill her."

Tanner laughed. "That's epic, dude."

"Her dad didn't think so."

"Excuse me," Gervaso said, standing up near the front. "May I have your attention?"

We all stopped talking and looked at him.

"We are currently a little more than two hours from Sydney. After we land, we'll be going to a hotel where we can rest and wait out this storm before we fly to Fiji. Are there any questions?"

"How long will we be in Sydney?" McKenna asked.

"The short answer is, we don't know. The storm has interrupted our timeline. Probably at least a few days. If the boats aren't sailing, it's better we wait in Australia. Fiji's a small country with many Elgen informants.

"The longer answer is, we've got eight days until the Elgen kill the first of their youths. So weather or not, we're going."

McKenna raised her hand. "Once we get to Sydney, can we go out, or do we have to wait in the hotel?"

"You should be okay to go out. Just be smart about it and don't go out alone. Buddy system." He looked around. "Any other questions?"

Ostin asked, "Why didn't we fly directly to Auckland, New Zealand? It's a fifty percent shorter flight to Fiji."

"I'll answer that," Scott said. "Besides the weather, three months ago, the Elgen started running a direct charter from Tuvalu to Auckland, which means there are now full-time Elgen guards and employees at the Auckland Airport. Even though it is New Zealand's largest airport, it's still a single runway, which means—"

Ostin interrupted, probably trying to save face after being publicly schooled. ". . . The odds of encountering Elgen is highly probable and therefore unacceptable. Smart move."

"I'm glad you agree," Scott said, smiling slightly. He gave us a short wave. "I'll see you on the ground."

A moment later Cassy squatted down in the aisle next to Taylor and me. "Hi, Michael. Taylor."

"Hey," I said.

Taylor just kind of nodded.

Cassy asked, "Is now a good time to talk?"

"Sure," I said.

"You can take my seat," Taylor said, abruptly standing.

"You don't need to leave," Cassy said.

"No," Taylor said. "I do. I need to stretch my legs."

I watched her as she walked toward the back of the plane.

Cassy sat down next to me. "I'm sorry, is there a problem?"

"No. She's just a little . . ."

When I didn't finish, Cassy said, "Jealous?"

I nodded. "Yeah. A little."

"I'm sorry."

"It's okay. We've just had a rough go of it lately." I reclined my seat back a few inches. "So what did you want to talk about?"

"I've been waiting to meet you for so long that I feel like I should get to know you better."

"You've been waiting to meet me?"

"For a long time. I've known about you for more than five years. We knew you were out there somewhere before you were found by the Elgen. We were looking for you too. Unfortunately, the Elgen found you first."

"That was unfortunate," I said.

"I'm sorry. We did our best. I've heard about Cell 25."

I hurried to change the subject. "So what did you want to ask me?"

"All right," she said, settling into the seat. "First question. You were the last to find out that there were other electrics. What was it like to grow up thinking there was no one else in the world like you?"

I pondered her question. "Mostly it was lonely. Partially because my mother and I were always hiding and moving. And partially because I always felt like I was different from everyone else and I was afraid of what they would think if they knew the truth. It wasn't until just recently that I learned that almost everyone feels that way. You don't have to be an electric mutant to feel like you're different."

"Or have Tourette's," she said.

"Or have Tourette's," I repeated.

"I was told that you keep getting more electric. Is that true?"

I put my hands out in front of me with the fingers about three inches apart. Electricity began arcing between my hands. "I'm not even pulsing. A few weeks ago, I couldn't do that."

"I've also heard that you can absorb other powers."

"Not always," I said. "It's happened, though."

"Can you absorb mine?"

"I don't know."

"Will you try?"

I thought about it. "No. I can't control it. I'm not sure what will happen with it."

"It's okay," she said. "I really want to see if you can."

When I didn't say anything, she said, "Please."

I breathed out slowly. "All right. I'll try. No guarantees it will work." I put my hand on her arm. "Let's see."

I could feel her, as if she was dissolving into me. Then suddenly she froze. Completely. Her eyes didn't blink or move, she wasn't breathing. "Cassy?"

She couldn't speak.

"Cassy!" I took my hand off, and she fell sideways, completely still. She looked dead.

"Gervaso!" I shouted.

Gervaso jumped up. "What's wrong?"

"Cassy passed out or something."

He grabbed Cassy by the shoulders and lifted her. "Recline her seat all the way."

I pressed her seat button, and he laid her back.

"She's not breathing," Gervaso said. "What happened?"

"She wanted to see if I could freeze her."

"Her heart stopped!" Ian shouted from the front.

Gervaso began giving her CPR.

"It's not working," Ian said. "Her blood's not flowing to her brain."

Gervaso pushed harder.

"Still nothing," Ian said. "We're losing her."

"Let me shock her," I said.

"Hurry," Gervaso said, leaning back. I put my hands on Cassy's chest and pulsed. Her whole body jumped. Then she began trembling and gasping for air.

"She's back," Ian said.

I breathed out in relief. "I'm so sorry."

"It was an accident," Gervaso said. "Abi, come help us."

"Here," Abigail said.

She put her hand on Cassy's head, and Cassy's body immediately began to relax. After a few seconds Cassy opened her eyes and groaned. Everyone was quiet. She looked up at Abi and me.

"Are you okay?" I asked.

"What happened?"

"I froze you. I'm so sorry. I didn't mean to hurt you."

Abigail rubbed Cassy's shoulder. "Are you okay?"

"Yes. Thank you. You have a beautiful gift."

"Thank you."

"How does she look, Ian?" Gervaso asked.

"Heart, lungs, and blood flow look normal."

Gervaso still looked concerned. "How do you feel?"

"I think I'm okay. Just a headache."

He felt her forehead, then said, "All right. Just rest. We'll see how you are after we land." He got up and went back to his seat.

"I really am sorry," I said. "I wasn't trying to kill you. I shouldn't have done that."

It took a moment for her to answer. "It's not your fault. I made you do it."

"That's the problem with taking someone's power. They've been using their powers most of their lives. For me it's like riding a bike for the first time."

A little while later Taylor came up the aisle and knelt down next to Cassy. She put her hand on her arm. "Are you okay?"

"I think so. I'm sorry I've taken your seat. I don't think I can walk just yet."

"No hurry," Taylor said softly. "I just wanted to make sure you were okay."

"Thank you."

Taylor glanced at me, then went to the back of the plane. After a moment Cassy said, "That was nice of her."

"She's a good person," I said.

"I know." She closed her eyes again. "I've wondered what it felt like to be on the other side of my power. It's not so great."

"You do a better job of not hurting people," I said.

"I'll have to remember to go easy."

"I think you just went through more than most."

She said softly, "I know. I think I died."

"What?"

"My heart stopped, right?"

I looked at her quizzically. "Yes, but you were unconscious. How did you know that?"

"My body was unconscious, but I wasn't."

"What do you mean?"

"I left my body. I was, like, floating above my body and I could see what everyone was doing. You reclined my seat and Gervaso gave me

CPR. Ian shouted from the front that my heart was stopped and that blood wasn't getting to my brain. Then you shocked me."

I looked at her in amazement. "That's exactly what happened."

"I could see everything. Ostin was working on a crossword puzzle. He was writing *P-R-O-B-O-S*-something."

I looked back over my seat. "Ostin."

"Yeah?"

"Are you doing a crossword puzzle?"

"I was. Why?"

"Did you write . . ." I looked at Cassy. "What was that?"

"Probos . . . ," she said, struggling with the word.

"'Proboscis,'" Ostin said. "Eleven across, a nine-letter word for a mammal's long nose or snout. That's when I stopped to see how you were. How did you know that?"

"Lucky guess," she said, leaving Ostin baffled. She looked back at me. "The really weird thing, I was able to go outside the plane and travel as fast as it was. Even faster. I went to the front of the plane and watched the pilots. The younger one is asleep. The other was eating a Hershey's chocolate bar." Her brow fell. "Do you think I was dead?"

"I've heard that when you die, you're supposed to see a light."

"I didn't see it," she said. "But maybe it's because I wasn't supposed to die."

"Maybe," I said. "I'm glad it wasn't your time."

"That's a good omen, right? About our mission?"

I thought about it. "Yeah, I think so."

Cassy took in a deep breath. "I still don't feel very good. I think I'll rest a little." She lay back and closed her eyes. Within a few minutes she was asleep. I picked up a *Popular Science* magazine and read.

About a half hour later she woke, rubbing her eyes with her hand.

"How are you feeling?" I asked, setting down my magazine.

"Better."

"I wanted to ask you something," I said.

"Go ahead."

"What's it like, living with the voice?"

"I've been treated really well. I guess I've always considered myself lucky."

"In what way?"

"You know, the Elgen could have found me first. I might have been fighting against you right now instead of with you."

"What do you do with the voice?"

"I'm mostly his bodyguard. This mission is one of the few times I've left him."

"He made you come?"

"No. I volunteered."

"Really? You volunteered for this? Didn't you know how dangerous it was?"

She nodded. "I knew."

"Then why would you volunteer?"

"Why did you?"

I shrugged. "Someone had to do it."

"Exactly." A moment later she added, "And maybe I was bored."

"If you were bored, you could have found something safer to do than attacking the Elgen. Like skydiving without a parachute."

She laughed. "I think there was also some guilt involved."

"Who made you feel guilty?"

"You. Not that I'm blaming you. It's just, you and your friends have been out here fighting this whole time while I'm living safe and in luxury. When I was little, the voice read a quote to me. It was something like, 'You should be ashamed to die without winning some victory for humanity.'"

I looked at her with surprise. "I know that quote. I think it was important to my father."

She slightly nodded. "Then you understand why I needed to prove myself."

"Proving yourself could cost you your life. Is it worth it?"

She smiled a half smile. "Ask me that *after* I die."

I grinned.

"I think the real question is, is an unproven life worth living?"

As I thought about the question, she touched my arm. "I think I should give Taylor her seat back." She started to stand up.

"Cassy. Thank you."

"For what?"

"For being courageous."

She smiled. "I had good examples." She walked slowly back to her seat, stopping to thank Taylor on the way.

Taylor came back over and sat by me. "She's really nice. I feel like such a jerk."

"I'm the one who almost killed her."

We landed in Sydney late in the afternoon, though the rain was torrential and the skies were so overcast that it almost looked like night. The storm was still raging a few hundred miles northeast of us, so there wasn't much we could do but wait it out and hope the storm died before the Glows did.

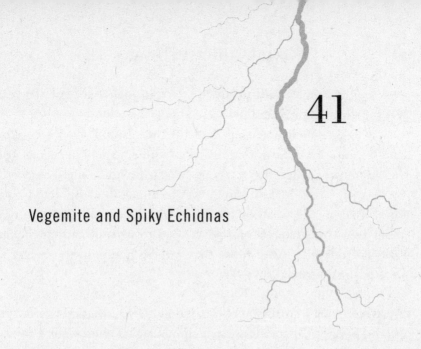

41

Vegemite and Spiky Echidnas

Sydney, Australia

I should have felt safer in Australia than Taiwan. Much safer. As far as we knew, the Elgen had no presence in the country, and, except for the accent, we pretty much looked and sounded like everyone else.

But I didn't feel safer. Maybe it had nothing to do with Australia. Maybe it was just because the clock was ticking down on our mission and we were closer to Tuvalu than we'd ever been.

Still, I'd noticed that in spite of the stress, I wasn't ticking as much as usual. Instead of blinking or gulping, I was sparking more. I wondered if it was just because I was becoming more electric or if my Tourette's was taking a different form.

The weather might have had something to do with my anxiety as well. I think I might have a bit of SAD—seasonal affective disorder— which is just an Ostin way of saying I get blue when the skies aren't blue. And the skies were definitely not blue. I don't think that I'd

ever seen it rain so hard in my life. Not in Idaho, at least. The rain
was practically horizontal.

It was a challenge getting Zeus off the plane. First, we couldn't
land because the runways were backed up because of lightning striking the tarmac. Then there was no hangar for the plane—so even if
we had wanted to make a run for the terminal, Zeus still had to wait
for a break in the weather, which, unfortunately, didn't come until
about two hours later. Even then he had to wear a rain poncho and
carry an umbrella. After more than twelve hours on the plane, we
were past exhausted.

We stayed at a four-star hotel on the Sydney Cove across from the
famous Sydney Opera House, which made McKenna really happy. It
was one of her goals to see the opera house, and now she could see it
from her hotel room.

I didn't care much about the scenery. I just couldn't wait to lie
down in a real bed. After we got into our room, Ostin said, "So,
Michael, going through this storm got me thinking."

"Thinking or talking?"

He ignored my question. "I've been thinking about what would
happen to you if you were struck by lightning."

If someone else had said that, I would have thought they were
crazy, but it was Ostin and that's just the way his mind worked. He'd
think about the strangest scenarios and try to figure them out, which
is why he came in handy in weird places like Elgen Starxource plants
and Peruvian prison cells.

"Probably the same thing that would happen to anyone else," I said.

"I'm not so sure about that," he said. "Did you know that less than
ten percent of ordinary people struck by lightning die? But you're
not ordinary. You might be able to survive a direct strike."

"I'd rather not find out," I said, closing my eyes and hoping he'd
do the same with his mouth.

"I'm not saying you should walk out into a storm with a lightning rod or anything, but it would be interesting to find out. Of
course there's the heat problem. Did you know that the air around

a lightning strike is superheated to more than thirty-three thousand degrees Celsius? That's more than four times hotter than the surface of the sun. That makes McKenna seem like a heating pad. I mean, not literally, but at least her power." He sat down on the near side of his bed. "Just imagine if you were able to absorb that much electricity like you did in the rat bowl. You would be a god."

"I'm not a god."

"With that much electricity people would think you were. People have always associated lightning with gods. That's why the most powerful Greek god was Zeus, the god of lightning. And there was Thor in Norse mythology, Ukko in Finland, Tlaloc the Aztec god, and Indra the Hindu god, all gods of lightning. I could go on."

"Please don't."

"I'm just saying, with that much electricity, you could conquer the world."

"For now I'd be happy to conquer this pillow."

Ostin lay back. "It would be cool. Michael the god."

It's the last thing I heard before falling asleep.

I woke to thunder the next morning. *More rain*, I thought. I walked to the window and opened the blinds. In spite of the thunder, the weather had improved some. There were dark clouds, but it was only lightly sprinkling. Twelve stories below I could see the wet street and harbor buzzing with traffic.

Ostin was still asleep, so I quietly took a shower and got dressed. As I was putting on my shoes, our room phone rang. It was Taylor.

"What are you guys doing today?" she asked.

"We haven't made any plans yet. Ostin's still asleep."

"Is that him snoring?"

"Yes."

"Wow. You weren't kidding. I thought that was thunder."

"Tell me about it."

"So, the concierge told us about a really cool wildlife refuge not too far from here. They have koalas and kangaroos."

"I'm in. Did you ask Gervaso if we could go?"

"He said that the pilots are still waiting on the weather, so we can do whatever we want."

"Where are you now?"

"We're just about to get breakfast. We're in the dining room in the lobby. Want to join us?"

"Yeah. I'll wake Ostin. See you in a minute."

I woke Ostin and told him that I'd meet him in the first-floor restaurant.

"Wait," he said. "I'll come with you." He pulled on his clothes from the day before, then, without even looking in the mirror, walked out with me.

As we walked to the elevator, I said, "Dude, your hair looks like a tsunami."

"What does that mean?"

"It means you should have looked in the mirror before we left."

We found the girls sitting at a table near the back of the restaurant. I was happy to see Cassy sitting next to Taylor. On the other side of McKenna was Tessa. They were already eating.

"Good morning," Taylor said.

"Good morning." I kissed Taylor, then sat down next to her. "They already brought your food out?"

"It's a buffet," she said. "You get it yourself."

"Love the concept," Ostin said, already on his way to the food.

I followed him over to the buffet. The food looked great. Best of all, they had Belgian waffles. When we got back to the table, Ostin began spreading a dark brown paste on his waffle.

"What's that gross-looking stuff you're putting on your waffle?" Tessa asked.

"Vegemite."

"That tells me nothing," she said.

"It's similar to the British Marmite."

"Again, nothing."

Ostin took a bite of the waffle, then said, with his mouth full, "It's a food paste made from leftover brewer's yeast extract."

"I think I just threw up in my mouth," McKenna said.

"I'd rather eat my shoe," Tessa said.

"It looks like something from the bottom of your shoe," Cassy said.

"I'll try some," I said, feeling brave. I put just a little on my English muffin, but I still almost gagged. "Why would you eat that?"

Ostin shrugged. "I don't know. Why do people eat oysters?"

"A dare?"

I noticed Welch sitting on the other side of the restaurant eating alone. After a few minutes I got up and walked over to him. He looked up as I approached.

"Hi," I said.

He looked up, then motioned to the chair across from him. "Have a seat. Coffee?"

"No, thanks," I said, sitting.

He took a sip. "How are you feeling about things?"

"I have to admit, it's weird having you here."

"I was thinking the same thing. What Hatch would give to be in my shoes right now."

"If Hatch were here, I'd electrocute him."

"So would I. That is, if I could." He took a bite of a croissant and chased it with more coffee. He looked at me, then said, "I'm worried for you."

"I'm worried for all of us," I said.

"Yes, appropriately. But I'm especially worried for you. In Hatch's mind you have become his prime nemesis. He believes that you're the final obstacle between him and his plans. He doesn't just want you dead; he wants you to pay for the humiliation you've caused him and the Elgen."

"I'll keep that in mind," I said.

"I wouldn't, if I were you. It might slow you down. The only way you'll ever be safe is to kill him. Keep *that* in mind."

He went back to his meal as if I wasn't there.

Nice chat, I thought. I got up and rejoined the others.

* * *

After everyone was done eating (except Ostin, who was technically never done eating at an all-you-can-eat buffet), we walked out to the front of the hotel to get taxis to the wildlife refuge. There were nine of us, as Abigail, Ian, and Nichelle had joined us, so we took two cars.

"What's the place called?" Ostin asked.

"Featherdale," McKenna said. "It sounds cool." She grabbed his arm. "I get to see a koala!"

Ostin was smiling, not because of the koala but because McKenna was holding his arm.

"Where's Zeus?" I asked Tessa.

Tessa pointed to the sky. "He's staying in. He and Jack are playing video games."

"And Tanner?"

She shrugged. "Who knows?"

Featherdale Wildlife Park was forty minutes from the hotel and was worth the ride. The park was cool and the crowds were light, probably because of the rain. Australia not only has the most dangerous animals; it has some of the strangest ones. I mean, a platypus? It's like a failed cloning experiment.

At McKenna's insistence, our first stop was the koala sanctuary, where Taylor and McKenna got to hold a koala. Then we went to the crocodile feeding, followed by a visit to the kangaroos, wallabies, potoroos, and pademelons. I had never heard of the last two animals, but they were also marsupials and basically looked like rabbit- or hamster-size kangaroos.

There was also an animal called a quokka, which looked like a rat but walked like a kangaroo. The animal came from the island of Rottnest near Perth, which was so named because a Dutch explorer thought the animals were rats and called the island Rattennest— Dutch for "Rat's Nest"—which was later changed to Rottnest.

Next we went to the echidnas exhibit. I had never heard of them either, but they were pretty awesome. They looked like tiny anteaters with big snouts and spiky quills. They walked funny, sticking their legs straight out like alligators.

"Echidnas and platypuses are the only surviving mammals that still lay eggs," Ostin said. "Echidna babies are called puggles."

"I thought a puggle was a mix between a pug and a beagle," Taylor said.

"That's just a designer dog thing," Ostin said. "Echidna puggles came first."

Peculiarly, even though there were at least fifty people at the echidnas exhibit, the animals pretty much ignored everyone but us. At one time I had six of the animals trying to crawl on me.

"Look," Taylor said. "They like us."

"That makes sense," Ostin said. "Echidnas are monotremes, the only land mammals that have evolved electroreception. Platypuses and echidnas can see electric signals. You're drawing them like a moth to light."

Ostin was most excited about the feeding of the Tasmanian devils. The only thing I knew about the Tasmanian devil was what I saw on the cartoons when I was little, but they truly are vicious little creatures. They not only have the strongest bite for their size of any living mammal, but they can take down animals four times their size. And they eat wombats, cube poop and all.

"I keep seeing this word 'marsupial,'" Tessa said. "What does it mean?"

"It means they come from Mars," Ostin said.

Tessa's eyes widened. "Really?"

"No. There is no life on Mars."

Taylor and I looked at each other in surprise. "I think Ostin just told a joke," she said.

The park was a nice reprieve from the dread I had been carrying around. The only time I felt jolted back to reality was while we were eating lunch at the café and McKenna said, "I want to take a koala home."

"We're not going home," Tessa said.

Everyone went quiet. After a moment Taylor said, "I am."

* * *

Before going back to the hotel, we took the taxis a little farther to see the Blue Mountains—so called because of a peculiar blue haze in the air around them. Ostin told us that the mountains are covered by eucalyptus forests and the eucalyptus oil in the air causes the bluish-gray hue.

We got back to our hotel around seven. We ate dinner at a nearby Chinese restaurant called Fortune Village, then headed back to the hotel.

"We girls are going window-shopping," Taylor said.

"Do you want us to go with you?" I asked.

"Only if you really want to shop."

I thought about it, then said, "I'd rather cut that little thing under my tongue with rusty scissors."

"Me too," Ostin said.

"Me three," Ian said.

Taylor smiled. "I figured. See you back at the hotel."

As Ian, Ostin, and I walked back to our rooms, Gervaso stopped us in the hallway.

"How was your day?" he asked. His voice and expression were somber. Something was clearly on his mind.

"It was good," I said. "We went to the wildlife refuge."

He slightly nodded. "I just talked to the pilots. The storm in the South Pacific has been downgraded again. We leave for Fiji tomorrow."

"What time?" Ostin asked.

"Noon. Spread the word." He turned and walked off.

"Noon it is," I said.

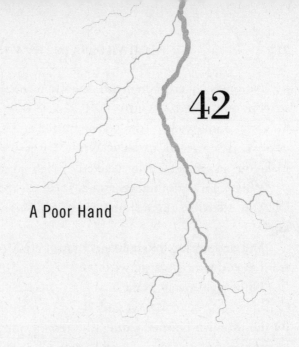

42

A Poor Hand

The next morning, Ostin and I went down to breakfast together. Tanner, Jack, Zeus, Tessa, and Abigail were already there. Everyone looked tired.

"Good morning," I said.

"Is it?" Tanner replied.

I ignored him.

"How was the park?" Zeus asked.

"Kangaroos and koalas," I said. "What's not to like?"

"Did you know kangaroos can box?" Jack said. "I'd like to try boxing one. I hear they're pretty good."

"It's cruel," Abigail said.

"Boxing *is* cruel," Jack replied. "That's the point."

"I didn't know it had one," Abigail said.

"Sounds like everyone's having grouchy flakes for breakfast," Ostin said.

"No one's cheerful on death row," Tanner said.

"I'm out of here," I said.

Ostin and I walked over to the buffet tables. I got a stack of pancakes and some link sausage. While I was waiting for the chef to make me an omelet, Taylor walked up behind me.

"What's up with the cheer squad?" she asked.

"You talked to them, huh? They could use a cheerleader. Know any?"

"Not anymore. McKenna and I saved a table over there. Far away from the table of gloom."

"I'll be right over," I said.

By the time we finished eating, the rest of our group was in the restaurant, including Gervaso and Welch, who sat alone in a corner and spent more time talking than eating. I couldn't hear them, but their facial expressions seemed especially tense. When Gervaso stood, we all got up to leave.

Hardly anyone spoke as we took our bags out to the shuttles and drove to the airport. The weather had cleared up, with just a few scattered clouds, not that you could tell. We had brought our own storm cloud. Only McKenna seemed cheerful. I don't think she had rose-colored glasses; she just preferred being happy. I was grateful for that.

We boarded the plane at a quarter of twelve. Even Scott and Boyd, the pilots, seemed more sullen than usual, taking our luggage from us without the usual greetings. After we were airborne, Gervaso stood up at the front of the plane.

"Let me have your attention. We've had a few days of reprieve and anonymity. Those days are gone. From here on out we are on the battleground. My contact in Fiji informs me that the islands are crawling with Elgen, many of whom are not in uniform.

"Fiji is Tuvalu's front porch, so the Elgen are making a point of knowing who is playing in their yard. They will want to know who you are and what you are doing there. So take no chances and stay invisible. That means no wandering off. No being alone. Talk to no one. Under no circumstances are you to speak, type, or write the word 'Elgen.' If someone asks you why you are there, you must assume they are informants.

"Our flight is four and a half hours. Tonight at dinner we will be meeting with my friend who will be sailing us into Tuvalu. He's taking a great risk in transporting us, both to his job *and* his life. I do not want him endangered any more than he has to be. His name is J.D. and, as I said back at the ranch, he took a bullet for me. I'd do the same for him. Don't make me." He looked around the cabin. "All right, then. Captain Welch has asked to say a few words."

Welch stood. "It's no surprise to any of you that I consider this a highly risky mission. I did not say *suicide* mission, but I do not suspect that we will all return. This is our Normandy beach. The Elgen do not expect us to make such a bold move. If they did, I would call it off immediately. I agree with Gervaso that it is our best chance to deal the Elgen a fatal blow.

"But make no mistake, this is like walking into a rattlesnake den with a machete. No matter how many snakes you kill, someone is still going to get bit.

"So you know, I will not be captured. For me—perhaps for all of us—being captured is the same as death, only one that Hatch can prolong and enjoy. So the only option for me is to fight to the death. I suggest you come to a similar conclusion. I hope it doesn't come to that." With that, he sat down, leaving us all in a state of despair.

"If that was our pregame inspirational speech," Jack said, "I can wait for halftime."

The clouds inside the plane were thicker than those outside it. Then, in the midst of it all, Ostin turned encyclopedia on us again.

"Hey, it's time for facts about Fiji. Did you know"—I don't know why he asked that, as we never did—"Fiji has a population of almost a million people and is made up of 332 islands? About one-third of them are inhabited.

"The international date line runs through the Fiji island of Taveuni, so you can be in two days at the same time. Also, there's a red-and-white flower in Taveuni that blooms nowhere else in the world."

"If I see it, I'll pick it and you can wear it in your hair," I said to Taylor.

"It's probably protected," Taylor said.

"Fijians used to be cannibals," Ostin said. "People used to call the place the Cannibal Isles. The last guy they ate was a missionary named Thomas Baker. Natives said he was doing okay until he touched the chief on his head. That's a big 'don't do' in Fiji. So they ate him."

"The lesson I'm taking from this is don't touch anyone on the head," Taylor said.

"So you can eat people, but you can't touch them on the head?" Jack said. "That's messed up."

"*Crazy* messed up," Tessa said. "So, Michael, they won't arrest you if you pick that flower; they'll eat you."

"They don't eat people today," Ostin said. "That was a long time ago. But they still sell cannibal forks."

"What's a cannibal fork?"

"I think that's pretty self-evident," Tanner said. "It's a fork for eating people."

"Can we not talk about eating people?" Abigail said. "It sounds like something Hatch would do."

"Don't give him ideas," Nichelle said.

"Hatch doesn't need help coming up with evil ideas," Tanner said. "He's a freaking evil idea factory."

Ostin continued. "The cannibal fork, or as it's called in Fijian, the *ai cula ni bokola*, was used during ritual feasts by those considered by the tribe too holy to touch food, such as their chiefs and priests.

"One of the Fijian tribal chief's most important ceremonies was the eating of their tribe's enemy. Since the chief couldn't use their hands for this important ritual, they came up with a special fork. Forks became a way to show the chief's power. The fancier the fork, the more important the owner."

"That's some freaky kind of status symbol," Tessa said.

"I'd like to see them try to eat me," Zeus said. "I'd light them up like a Christmas tree."

"They wouldn't eat you," I said. "They'd worship you. You'd be the Fijian god of lightning."

"Were the people of Tuvalu cannibals?"

Tanner said, "We should ask Welch."

"I know things about Tuvalu," Ostin said.

"Of course you do," Tanner said. "We should ask Welch."

Ostin ignored the slight and continued. "Did you know that Robert Louis Stevenson visited Niutao? That's the island we're going to. The one Hatch named Hades."

"Who's Robert Lewison?" Tessa asked.

Ostin raised one eyebrow. "Oh, please. Really? What did they teach you at the academy?"

"How to take over the world. Mostly."

"I'm down with that," Jack said.

". . . Stevenson is only one of the greatest writers of all times. Ever heard of *Treasure Island*? Or Dr. Jekyll and Mr. Hyde? *Treasure Island* alone has more than seventy-five movies, television shows, and stage productions."

"So what was he doing in Tuvalu?"

"He was visiting Australia when he decided to book a trading steamer called the *Janet Nicoll*. They anchored off Niutao for a while to take on copra."

"Who's Copra?" Zeus asked.

"I know this one," Tessa said. "He's that movie director. He did that one Christmas movie where that guy rips off a bank, then meets an angel—"

"It's called *It's a Wonderful Life*," Taylor said. "And he didn't rip off the bank. The stupid old guy lost the money, and it was stolen by the evil old dude in the wheelchair."

"Potter," McKenna said.

"Yeah, that one," Tessa said. "Except he wasn't a potter; he was a banker."

"His name was Potter," McKenna said.

"Oh, yeah."

Ostin just looked at them like they'd lost their minds. "*Copra* is dried coconut meat. It's where they get coconut oil."

"Like any normal human should know that," Taylor said.

"I'm sticking with the movie director," Tessa said.

For a moment Ostin was speechless. "Anyway, while they were picking up copra, Stevenson's wife, Fanny, wrote about it. She published her story under the title *The Cruise of the Janet Nichol*."

"I like that," Taylor said. "The *Janet Nichol*. Why do they name ships after women?"

I shrugged. "I don't know. Why do they name hurricanes after women?"

"I know," Ostin said. "It's because . . ."

McKenna and Taylor both looked at him.

"Uh . . . because they're powerful."

I grinned at him. "Good save, man. Good save."

"He's getting good at this," Taylor said.

"Stevenson said something I think is relevant to our situation," Ostin said. "'Life is not a matter of holding good cards, but of playing a poor hand well.'"

"We've got the poor hand part right," Tanner said.

Ostin looked at him with an uncharacteristic dark glare. "He also said, 'The world has no room for cowards.'"

Tanner said nothing.

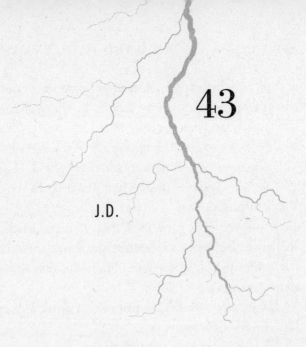

43

J.D.

Our plane landed on the Fiji island of Viti Levu, the largest island in the Republic of Fiji and the location of the nation's capital city of Suva.

As we got off the plane, the air was hot and especially humid, even more than in Taiwan, which I suspected had something to do with the recent storms. I wasn't sure that we were through with them. Even though the sky above us was blue, I noticed a mass of accumulating dark clouds in the east.

There were more non-Fijians around us than I expected, with a lot of tourists from Australia and New Zealand. After Gervaso's talk, I found myself suspicious of everyone. Anyone could be an Elgen.

We split up into three groups and took taxis from the airport to a hotel near the center of the island. Gervaso told us that the hotel had not been checked out for security, so at his friend's suggestion, we met up in a small café called the Bad Dog. It was a simple burger and pizza joint with a lot of wood paneling and vines growing across the ceiling. Gervaso spoke briefly to the woman at the counter, and she led us to a back room.

"We're safe here," Gervaso said. "We can talk."

"When are we going to meet your friend?" I asked.

"Soon," Gervaso said. Then his expression changed. "Actually, that's him right now."

I followed his gaze to a man coming in through the door. He looked to be about Gervaso's age, short with dark brown skin contrasted by piercing blue eyes. He had a shaven head, and a large scar ran across his throat and jaw.

He limped toward us, leaning on an ebony cane inlaid with red, blue, and yellow gems.

"J.D.," Gervaso said, standing.

The man smiled. "Gervaso, my friend."

The two men embraced.

"I did not think I would see you in my part of the world."

"Appropriately, fate is not through with us," Gervaso said. He turned toward us. "Everyone, this is my friend Captain J.D." He looked back. "J.D., these are my friends."

J.D. nodded. "Your friends, my cargo." As his gaze panned over us, he stopped on Taylor. "And beautiful cargo."

Taylor blushed a little. The captain stepped forward, offering his hand. "Lovely lady, what is your name?"

"Taylor," she said, extending her hand uneasily.

He raised her hand to his lips and kissed it. "I might just have to keep this one for myself."

Taylor looked uncomfortable with his comment. Blinking, I stood up and put out my hand so he would release Taylor's. "I'm Michael."

He took my hand but suddenly jerked back. "You shocked me."

Gervaso frowned at me even though I honestly hadn't intended to shock him.

"Must be static in the air," I said.

J.D. grinned. "Indeed. You must be Michael Vey. Am I to understand that this ruby belongs to you?"

"She's my girlfriend," I said. "Not a rock."

He raised his hands. "Forgive me. I meant no offense, brother. You are a lucky man."

"Thank you," Taylor said softly.

He looked at all of the girls. "So many beauties." Then he turned to Gervaso. "There is one extra with you."

Welch stood. "I'm John," he said. "John Watts. I was a last-minute addition to the party."

J.D. looked at him with a peculiar gaze, then said, "Mr. Watts, welcome to our adventure." He looked back at us. "Have you ordered any food yet?"

"No," Gervaso said. "We were waiting for you."

"Please, allow me." He turned and raised his hand to signal a server standing outside the door. "You all like pizza, yes?"

"Yes," Ostin said.

"Here, they have cannibal pizza."

"I just threw up," Taylor said.

"Do not worry your pretty face," J.D. said. "It is not man flesh. It is lamb meat."

"Not much better," Taylor said.

"Speaking of man flesh," Jack said. "I hear that you took a bullet for Gervaso."

J.D. cocked his head. "Oh? Where did you hear that?"

"Gervaso," Jack said.

J.D. lifted a fork and rammed it into his leg so it stuck.

McKenna screamed, and J.D. smiled. "Yes, I took a bullet. But I got this leg as a souvenir."

"Always dramatic," Gervaso said. "You always were."

A waitress walked into our room, and J.D. ordered eight pizzas and five garlic breads, plus bottles of water and grape juice. Surprisingly, the cannibal pizza was actually my favorite.

By the time we finished our meal, it was dark outside and the restaurant was mostly empty. Gervaso walked over and looked out the door, then shut it. "Ian, keep an eye out," he said.

"Yes, sir."

"I'd like you all to hear from Captain J.D.," Gervaso said. "He will go over our plan."

"Thank you, my friend," J.D. said. He looked us over. "You missed a very big storm. There was a lot of flooding. It's just today that the city is back to normal.

"As you know, this adventure we are on is very risky. The plan was to leave tomorrow. That is, if we are crazy enough to stick to that plan."

"What do you mean?" Gervaso asked.

"When you got off the airplane, did you see the clouds in the east? There is another big storm coming. It is scheduled to hit the islands about three days from now."

Gervaso's face turned pale. "The same time we arrive in Tuvalu."

"That means we can't sail back," Zeus said.

"We can in the *Joule*," I said.

Gervaso breathed out heavily. "How long will the storm last?"

"The weather service says three days."

"We'd never survive three days in Tuvalu. So what are our choices?"

"We stay in Fiji another week."

"And abandon Tara and Torstyn," Welch said. "They'll be fed to the rats by then."

"Better them than us," Zeus said.

"There's another choice," I said. "We leave as expected and steal the *Joule*. Wasn't that the plan all along?"

"But this way there's no backup plan," Tessa said.

"I know." I breathed out heavily. "I think we all know that there never was a failure or retreat option. What were we going to do if we failed—try to sail back? There's no way that we could go undetected. The Elgen have planes, missiles, and speedboats. They'd just sink us at sea." I shook my head. "There's no turning back. There never was."

"Burn the boats," Ostin said.

"What?" Tessa asked. "Burn what boats?"

Ostin breathed out. "Cortés sunk his ships so that his men would have to conquer or die." He looked around at all of us with a serious expression. "It's happened throughout history. The Chinese warlord Xiang Yu at the battle of Julu ordered their ships to be burned so there could be no retreat. So did the Burmese King Bayinnaung when facing a superior army. They both went on to win their battles." He looked at me. "There is no other option. We burn the boats."

I think that might have been Ostin's most courageous moment.

Gervaso looked around the room, then turned to J.D. "Will you sail?"

He thought for a moment, then nodded. "If you will go, I will sail."

Gervaso took another deep breath. "If anyone wants out, now is the time. Just raise your hand."

I looked around the room. I kind of expected Tanner to raise his hand, but he didn't. No one did. After a minute Gervaso said, "Okay. We leave first thing in the morning. May God sail with us."

As the rest of us were leaving, Ostin walked up to J.D.

"I'm Ostin. I don't mean to bother you, but I was wondering how you reached a contractual relationship with the Elgen. Did they come to you, or did you go to them?"

J.D. looked at him with an annoyed expression, then turned away without answering.

"It was a valid question," Ostin said softly.

That night most of us gathered in Jack's room to play cards. In the middle of our second game, Ostin said, "I've got a bad feeling about this J.D. guy."

"Why?" Zeus said. "Because he stuck a fork into his leg?"

"Prosthetic," Ostin corrected. "He's rude. And I don't like the way he looks at me. He's got the look of a cat outside a birdcage."

"Maybe he just hates teenagers," Zeus said.

"He doesn't hate Taylor."

"Don't go there," Taylor said.

"Maybe he just hates you," Zeus said.

"That's understandable," Tessa said.

Ostin looked at her. "What do you mean by that?"

I changed the subject. "No, Ostin's right. I can't explain it, but he seems a little . . . off."

"Hey, the dude saved Gervaso's life in Iraq," Jack said. "He took a bullet for him. What more endorsement do you want?"

After a moment I said, "You're right. It's probably just nerves. How far are we from Tuvalu, anyway?"

"Gervaso said it's a three-day trip from Fiji," Ian said. "If we leave around noon tomorrow, we'll arrive Saturday night. There's nothing to do, so you might want to get some magazines. Lots of magazines. And seasickness pills."

Taylor nodded. "Lots and lots of seasickness pills."

44

Leaving Fiji

Wednesday morning I woke to the crack of thunder. I sat bolt upright in bed. I showered, which seemed a little redundant since the entire outside world was already water and I'd no doubt be sick of it by the end of the day. At least this water was hot.

We met up for breakfast at the café across from the hotel. I had a loaf of native sweet bread and some Fiji gram tea.

Tessa looked out at the weather. "I thought it wasn't supposed to rain for another three days."

"That's when the tropical storm hits," Ostin said. "This is nothing. It's just inclement weather."

"Inclement," Tanner said. "Why can't you just say *bad* weather like a normal person?"

"Because intelligent people use the most exact word to precisely communicate their intentions. I don't suspect you'd know anything about that."

Tanner was speechless.

"Touché," Tessa said.

Taylor glanced over at me. "Never seen that before."

"He's figuring it out," I said.

After breakfast we all followed Gervaso down to the harbor. As we walked down the dock, our boat bobbed up and down in a turbulent sea, pounding against the rubber-tire bumpers on the dock.

"Are we really going to sail in this?" Taylor asked.

"J.D. says it's no problem." I looked into her eyes. "At least we won't sink."

"Just throw up a few hundred times," Taylor said. "I should have gotten some of those seasickness patches."

"I can help," Abigail said. "Seasickness is a specialty of mine."

"Maybe the bad weather will help conceal us," I said. I turned toward Zeus. He already looked green. "How are you doing?"

"This isn't going to be good," he said.

I shook my head. "No, it's not. You sure you want to do this?"

"I'm sure I *don't* want to."

"I hear you, Zeus. I hear you."

45

Nike Landing Team

In spite of the weather, the first day sailing was boring and uneventful, which, all things considered, was a good thing.

It rained most of the day, so we were stuck together below deck. Nobody had much to say. Maybe the boredom wasn't such a bad thing. At least it made us hungrier for action.

Jack had brought his playing cards, and we played like a hundred games of Texas Hold'em. We even let Ian play, which is kind of ridiculous, since he could see through the cards and always knew what everyone else was holding.

The second day was a little better. The weather calmed some, and although the skies were still gray, the rain only fell intermittently throughout the day. Zeus even came up on deck for a while.

We tried fishing. Jack borrowed poles from one of the deckhands, and Ian was especially useful. He'd tell us where the fish were or if one was about to bite. I hadn't ever thought of all the things Ian's power could be valuable for, but he'd be especially great at oceanography, as he could see reefs and all sorts of marine life.

He also saw a sunken galleon. We were going too fast to be sure, but he thought it had chests filled with gold doubloons. Jack got the GPS coordinates from the boat's first officer so we could go back someday and check it out.

Taylor caught a halibut. Ostin caught a twelve-foot hammer-head shark, though I'm not sure that "caught" was the right word. "Annoyed" is probably better. The monster fish yanked the pole out of Ostin's hands, and everyone laughed about that except the guy from the crew who actually owned the pole. He was pretty mad. He called Ostin an *oolu-cow*. None of us knew what it meant, except maybe Ostin, who turned bright red. The crew member told Ostin that he'd have to buy him a new fishing pole.

It was nice to be above deck and be able to take our minds off things for a while, especially Zeus, who was pretty much confined below deck the whole time. It wasn't just the rain or the threat of hitting water. Just seeing it made him crazy anxious. I could under-stand. It's how I would feel if we were sailing on an ocean of sulfuric acid. I couldn't help but feel he was suffering more than the rest of us. But there was no way around it. In the end, there would be plenty of suffering to go around.

We didn't see a whole lot of J.D., as he spent his time up in the boat's control deck. Gervaso spent a lot of time with him. At night Gervaso would tell us what they had talked about: the old days, old friends, changes in the military, and what J.D. knew about the Elgen.

I didn't see much of Welch either, as he kept mostly to himself. That second day Taylor woke me in the middle of the night.

"Michael."

It took me a moment to remember where I was. "Taylor?"

She was kneeling on the floor near my bed. Even in the darkness I could see that she had been crying. "I had a dream."

I took her hand as I sat up. "Tell me about it."

"We were on an island. It was small, like fifty feet. And we were with some other people. I don't know who they were; they looked like island people. And suddenly we were surrounded by crocodiles. Thousands of them. They were coming from every side. We kept fighting them back, but they just kept coming. And then there were too many of them and they started eating our people.

"They were just about to eat us when lightning hit and killed all the crocodiles and everything turned to glass. . . ."

Her words trailed off into silence. For a moment neither of us spoke. Then I said, "That's good, then. Right? The crocodiles were killed."

Taylor looked into my eyes. "No, it's not good. The lightning hit you. And I couldn't find you." Her eyes welled up.

"Come here," I said. She climbed up onto my berth with me and I held her. "It's just a dream," I said, forcing the words. "It doesn't mean anything. It's just a dream."

I barely slept the rest of the night.

Late afternoon of the third day the storm returned in force. At times the waves were big enough to make me wonder if the ship was going to tip over. We were all seasick.

The sky was dark long before nightfall, and as we neared Tuvalu, the rains were torrential. We knew we were close as we huddled beneath the deck, trying to get a little sleep before our first test. A little after ten at night Gervaso came and found me.

"Michael, it's time we brought everyone together. We're an hour from docking on Nike."

"Any sign of trouble?"

"No. The Elgen are expecting us." He corrected himself. "Hopefully not us, the boat. We'll meet in the mess in ten minutes. I'll get Welch."

I got Taylor, and then we gathered everyone to the dining room. Gervaso and Welch were already there, bent over a map. They had taped the corners of the map to the main table and were drawing on it in pencil. They stopped when we arrived.

"Hurry in," Gervaso said. "Gather around the table. We haven't much time."

We surrounded the table.

"The original Nike landing team consisted of Michael, Taylor, Ian, Zeus, Tessa, McKenna, and Jack, with Michael leading. But with this weather we'll have to take Zeus out of the mix."

Zeus looked too sick to care.

"I think we should bring Nichelle to take out the cameras," I said, glancing at her. "She'll also be valuable in case Quentin decides not to cooperate."

"Good call," Gervaso said, looking at Nichelle. "You good with that?"

"I'm good," she said. "May I drop Quentin once, just for old times' sake?"

I looked at her. "No."

She grinned. "Never hurts to ask."

"I'm coming too," Welch said. "Quentin should see that I'm with you. He's going to be disoriented enough."

"Like you being with us won't be disorienting," Jack said.

"Just us rescuing him is going to be disorienting," I said. "But I agree that Welch should come. In case things go wrong, he knows the Elgen procedures."

Gervaso said, "That leaves me, Zeus, Cassy, Ostin, Abi, and Tanner to hold the boat."

"We can do it," Zeus said.

"If our cover is blown and they attack the boat, our goal is to get onshore. We'll have better odds fighting on land. Michael, if that happens, we'll radio you, and your team can flank them from the rear."

"We can do that."

Gervaso leaned back over the map, touching it with a pencil. "This is where we'll be docking. The landing team will be wearing rain ponchos and getting off the boat with the rest of the loading crew, then they'll gather here behind the warehouse.

"The central square is less than a quarter mile from the dock. You'll use this trail right here. It's an old goat path the natives use.

It's not lighted. You can take it all the way to here, the outer wall of the square." He touched the end of the pencil to a point near the center of the map. "From here you'll take out the lights and cameras, then advance to here. Taylor will reboot the guards, and Michael and Jack will take them out."

"With pleasure," Jack said.

"I can help," Welch said.

"Good," Gervaso said. "Nichelle, we're going to use the weather to our benefit. Don't take out the lights and camera until there's a lightning strike. Then, with Tessa's help, blow them. With luck the Elgen will assume it's the weather.

"At that precise moment, Taylor will reboot the guards, and Michael, Jack, and David will take them out: Jack and David at the prime minister's cage to the west, Michael at Quentin's cage to the east.

"Once they're down, McKenna, Tessa, and Nichelle will come around to the back of the cage. The cage has a built-in door lock and also a chain with a padlock. McKenna will melt through the bars and chain to get Quentin out. He's not going to be in very good shape, so you'll probably need to help him walk. You might even have to carry him.

"As soon as you have him, get back to the boat as soon as possible." He looked around the table. "All clear?"

"Crystal," I said.

"Good." He leaned back. "You know, this weather is a blessing. Chances of running into anyone out there are much less likely."

"Where do we get our ponchos?" I asked.

"Come with me. You'll suit up with the boat's crew. The rest of you, eat a banana or something."

PART EIGHT

46

A Bonus

Captain J.D. had planned to reach Niulakita, the first of the Tuvalu islands, around seven p.m., but the weather had set the boat back nearly four hours. When the island was within sight, J.D. radioed in. "Come in, Nike port. This is *Risky Business*, do you copy?"

"*Risky Business*, this is Elgen base Nike port. We copy you. Provide passcode."

"Yes, Elgen base. *I-L-K-M-E.*"

"Passcode clear. What do you have to report?"

"Cargo is secure and complete. I am prepared to deliver."

"We are pleased to hear that, *Risky Business.*"

". . . And tell the general that I brought him a bonus."

"You can tell him yourself, *Risky Business.*"

There was a brief pause. Then a new voice came over the headset. "This is Admiral Hatch."

Captain J.D. was a bit ruffled to have Hatch actually speak to him. "Admiral. This is an honor."

"What is this bonus you spoke of?"

"The man you've been looking for. The one they call Welch. I understand there is a million-dollar bounty on his head."

Hatch couldn't believe his good fortune. "Please repeat, Captain."

"I have the fugitive EGG Welch. He is with the children."

A dark smile crossed Hatch's face. "And to think I said there is no God. Everything changes today." He turned back to the microphone. "You just earned a million dollars, Captain. What is their plan?"

"They first plan to sail to Nike to rescue the Glow Quentin. Then they sail to Hades to rescue the other two Glows."

"Torstyn and Tara," the radioman said.

"We could sink the boat before it reaches us," the Zone Captain behind Hatch said.

"Admiral, please don't sink my boat," J.D. said.

"We won't sink your boat," Hatch said, even though he was considering it. After a moment he said, "No, let them follow through with their plan. Alert no one. I don't want them to know we are aware of them."

"We attack them in Nike?" the Zone Captain asked.

"No, too much possible collateral damage. We'll let them rescue Quentin and sail to Hades. We will bring them all together and destroy them once and for all. Radio me after you leave Nike."

"Yes, sir. Over."

Hatch took off his headset and stood back from the microphone. "Today I will feast on my enemy."

PART NINE

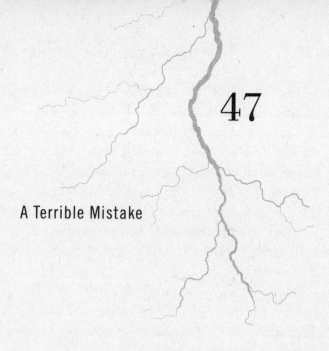

47

A Terrible Mistake

It was a little past three in the morning when we reached Nike. The rain fell in great sheets illuminated by the shore's electric lighting. From where I was watching, the island looked deserted. As Gervaso said, it wasn't the kind of night someone was going to be out on a midnight stroll.

Our team had put on our rain gear and had blended in with the rest of the loading crew who were preparing the crane to lift the crates from below deck. They were carrying canned goods from New Zealand: concentrated milk, butter, cheese, and frozen beef.

As our boat edged up to the main loading dock in front of a landing with warehouses and parked forklifts, there was a bright flash of lightning, followed just two seconds later by a clap of thunder.

"That was close," Jack said.

"Let's hope the lightning keeps up," Taylor said.

I looked up at the angry sky. "I don't think we'll have to worry about that."

There were three lights on the dock as well as lights inside the warehouse offices, but I couldn't see any movement, at least not the human kind. The wind was strong and anything not bolted down was flapping or swinging. The waves had also kicked up, and J.D. revved the engine in reverse to keep us from slamming into the dock.

Then two Elgen wearing rain gear emerged from the warehouse. Both carried flashlights, and one of them made hand signals to the control deck.

Three of our crew members came out holding lines and threw them to the men, who grabbed them and wrapped the ropes around the dock's heavy cleats and secured them. Another man walked out in rain gear carrying a radio.

Our crew members lowered a plank onto the dock, and one of our crew walked down to the man holding the radio. The two of them walked back to the warehouse.

"That's your cue," Gervaso said. "Go."

The eight of us climbed down a ladder near the front of the boat. Then, one by one, we sprinted across the deck into the shadows behind the warehouse, then into the forest.

We met up in a grove of breadfruit trees about fifty yards from the dock. In our outfits I couldn't tell who was who.

"Who's here?" I asked.

"Everyone's here," Ian said.

"You lead us," I said.

We followed Ian along a narrow grass path through the dense forest. The sound of the rain covered our footsteps, and it only took ten minutes to reach the center square.

The center was dark. There were only a few lights in the square, and raindrops fiercely pelted the tops of the two monkey cages, pouring down the sides of the cages in a steady waterfall. The cages were dark inside, and I couldn't see any humans, but Ian could.

"Quentin's in the corner of the east cage," he said. "In the back."

"How does he look?"

He turned to me. "Like a man in a monkey cage."

There were two guards, one for each cage, standing at attention with rifles. They were dressed alike, wearing hats, black knee-length jackets, thick-soled shin-high boots, and pants with a purple stripe down the side. They stood perfectly still as the water bounced off the crowns of their hats and ran down the brims and their shoulders. They seemed to be in an almost trancelike state.

"There's a sign that says 'King of the Monkeys,'" Ian said, shaking his head.

"Should I reboot them now?" Taylor asked.

"Cameras first," I said. I could see at least six cameras, revealed by the red diode on top of them. Four of them slowly panned the square. I turned to Ian. "I count six. What have you got?"

"There's fourteen," he said.

"It's good to be you," I said. "Are there any other guards nearby?"

"Just the two."

"Let's keep it that way. Are you ready, Nichelle? Tessa?"

"I'm ready," Tessa said. "You?" she asked Nichelle.

"Just waiting for lightning."

We didn't have to wait long. In less than two minutes there was a double strike of lightning to the east of us. Nichelle's hand was already extended. The lights went out.

"Did we get all the cameras?" I asked Ian.

"No. There's one camera next to the building that's live. But I don't think it's panning."

"Will they see us?"

Ian looked at it, then said, "No. Not if we stay close to the cages."

"Then let's do this. Everyone back off a little." I turned to Taylor and nodded.

Taylor looked toward the guards, holding her hand up to her forehead. Suddenly the guards froze. One of them dropped his rifle.

"Now," I said. I reached out and pulsed. A massive wave blurred the air, sizzling with the rain it devoured. Both of the guards were knocked off their feet. A few of the monkeys fell off branches as well, screeching loudly.

"That's always cool to watch," Jack said. "Let's go."

We ran toward the cage.

Jack and Welch grabbed the guards and dragged them over to the back of the east cage, then handcuffed them with their own cuffs.

That's when I saw Quentin. He was dirty and huddled in the corner of the cage. He had partially covered himself with some of the dead palm leaves, but he was still shivering in the cold. He looked pathetic, and in spite of our history, I felt pity. Even the smell of the cage, somewhat dampened by the fresh rain air, was torture.

"Quentin," I said.

He looked up at me, and his eyes showed his disbelief. "Vey?"

"It's me."

"Kill me. Please."

"I'm not going to kill you."

Welch walked up behind me. "Quentin, it's me. We're getting you out."

Quentin rubbed the water that was running down his face. "Why are you with Vey? I'm already losing my mind."

"No," Welch said. "We're working together. Now move away from the back of the cage. Hurry."

As soon as he did, there was a brilliant orange-blue light behind him, followed by the sound of water hissing and monkeys screeching as they fled to the far, opposite corner of the cage. Even fifteen feet away I could feel the air warm up around me.

McKenna stood on the platform behind the cage with Tessa supporting her, McKenna holding the metal chain in her hand, which was too bright to look at.

In less than a minute the chain slid from around the cage's bars like a metallic snake, then fell to the ground.

"That's one," Ian said. "Now the door lock."

McKenna examined the lock assembly, not quite sure where to touch. She put her hand on the bolt and heated up. The entire unit turned orange-red but didn't collapse. The heat was intense enough that we were all sweating, but still the lock held.

McKenna's power was different from Bryan's, as Bryan could

force heat in a direct, concentrated path, while McKenna created more heat but in a broader circumference.

After a minute I said, "This is taking too long."

"I can't do it," McKenna said.

"Ian, what's wrong?" I asked.

He looked at the door for a moment, then said, "McKenna, ignore the lock. The weakest part is the hinges. Other side."

McKenna and Tessa moved on the platform. McKenna could get her fingers around the hinges, which meant she could better control the heat between them.

I looked around the square, then at Jack. "Anything?"

"Nothing," he said. "We're alone."

Luck seemed to be on our side, which was something I wasn't accustomed to. It was also something I didn't trust.

The top hinge broke through in less than a minute. "Got it," McKenna said. She grabbed the bottom hinge and heated up.

Just a half minute in, the second hinge creaked as it twisted and then broke through and the heavy metal door fell back toward the exhausted girls. Welch must have guessed what was going to happen, because he had run up behind them and grabbed the heavy door as it fell, pushing it to the side. The door landed with a sharp crash on the wet cobblestone below.

"That could have cut off my leg," McKenna said.

"It didn't," Welch said. "Now get back."

Tessa helped McKenna down to the base of the steps, where Nichelle handed her two open bottles of water.

"Q," Welch said. "Let's get out of here."

Quentin forced himself to his feet. He was basically naked, wearing just a loincloth. Welch took his hand and helped him to the cage entrance.

"Can you walk?"

"Yes," he said, though he seemed unstable on his feet.

"He doesn't have shoes," I said.

"He does now," Nichelle said. She had already removed one of the guard's boots. "His feet looked about your size."

Quentin stared at her. "Nichelle?"

"You never know who you're going to run into at the zoo," she said.

Welch put the shoes on Quentin's feet and laced them up. I gave him my poncho to wear. "Hurry," I said. "We've got to get out of here."

Quentin looked over at the other cage. "We need to rescue the prime minister."

I glanced at the cage, then at Jack, who was shaking his head.

"Not now," I said. "We're out of time."

Jack and Welch both took one of Quentin's arms, and we ran directly into the shadow of the forest, retracing our route along the goat path. We were slightly slower with Quentin, but we still made good time.

We stopped at the side of the warehouse. For some reason, the dock lights had been turned off and our boat was a dark silhouette against the turbulent sea.

"How does it look?" I asked Ian.

"Peaceful."

"Why are the lights out?"

"Maybe the storm took out the generator."

"It's a Starxource plant." I took out my radio. "Gervaso. Are we clear?"

There was a burst of static, then Gervaso's voice. "We're clear."

"Why are the lights out?"

"I don't know. They just turned them off. Do you have him?"

"Yes."

"We'll meet you at the aft ladder."

We moved in the dark to the back of the boat, then crossed the dock in small groups, first Tessa, Nichelle, and McKenna, followed by Jack, Welch, and Quentin.

Taylor, Ian, and I waited until last to make sure no one had followed us, or to reboot any warehouse crew that might take interest in us. No one did. I'm sure it was the hour, but it still worried me that the security was so lax. It seemed suspicious.

I was the last one on board, and Gervaso helped pull me up on deck.

"I sent everyone below," Gervaso said. "Come with me." We climbed to the boat's upper deck.

"How did everything go?" he asked.

"We had a little trouble opening the cage, but otherwise everything went as planned. It was easy."

Gervaso's brow fell. "Easy?"

"I know. When has anything with the Elgen been easy? It could be a trap."

"Maybe. Or maybe they're just overconfident. Like they were in Peru." Gervaso breathed out. "For now we keep to the plan until we know otherwise. Come with me. I need to report to J.D."

I followed Gervaso into the control room.

The captain spun around as we entered the control deck. "You made it, my friends," he said, sounding relieved. "Did all go well?"

"As planned," I said.

"Very good. And everyone is on board?"

"Yes."

"Even Mr. Welch?"

I thought it odd that he had singled him out. "Yes."

Gervaso looked at J.D. with a peculiar expression, then said, "We're all here. We need to go." He turned to me. "Let's go back down, Michael."

Gervaso and I walked back out of the control deck into the rain. When we were on the main deck, Gervaso said, "I've made a terrible mistake. I think we're in trouble."

My chest froze. "Why?"

"We never told J.D. what Welch's real name was."

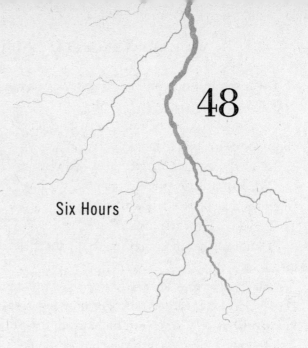

48

Six Hours

The boat was untied, and we pushed away from the dock into the turbulent channel. From Nike we would sail north. Hades was the Elgen's prison island and the second-northernmost island of the Tuvalu archipelago.

Just as the weather service had predicted, the storm was getting worse and the waves were now white-capped. The boat slammed angrily against the dark waters. At twenty-five knots it would take us about seven hours to reach our destination. That would make our arrival time around noon, but considering the weather, we'd probably arrive much later. And now we realized that there was a good chance we were sailing into a trap.

"What do we do?" I asked Gervaso.

"If he's collaborating with the enemy, we can't let on that we know. Not yet. We're surrounded by the Elgen's most fortified bases. If the Elgen attacked now, we wouldn't last five minutes."

"We could go back to Nike and attack their headquarters. If we could capture Hatch . . ."

"We don't know that Hatch is even there. And if we make J.D. turn around, the Elgen will know something's wrong. They'll be waiting for us." He looked at me. "We need to talk to Welch. Get Jack, too."

I went down to the eating quarters, where Welch, Jack, Zeus, and Nichelle were sitting around Quentin at the main table. There was bread, crackers, cheese, and sliced meats, and Quentin, who was now wrapped in a dry blanket, was eating ravenously. He stopped eating when he saw me.

In the light I was stunned by how different he looked. Broken. Humble. He was anything but the cocky rich kid I'd met in Peru. I guess living in a monkey cage will do that. So will Cell 25.

"Michael," he said, starting to stand.

I raised my hand to stop him. "Just sit."

"Thank you," he said, slightly collapsing. "My quads are pretty cramped. Welch just told me that we're going to rescue Torstyn and Tara."

"We're going to try."

"Let me know how I can help. I'm the reason they're there."

"No," Welch said. "I am."

"Hatch is," I said. "And we'll definitely need your help." I turned to Welch. "Gervaso needs to see you. You too, Jack. He's on deck."

"All right," Welch said.

They both stood, and I led them up top to Gervaso, who was standing in the dark midship beneath a canopy.

"Yes, sir," Welch said.

"Have you talked to the captain alone?" Gervaso asked.

"Captain J.D.? No. Why?"

"He knows who you are."

Welch's face tensed. "Is he Elgen?"

"I don't know."

"What's the plan?" Jack asked.

"That's why I wanted to see you. If this is a trap, we'll need a solid base to fight from. Or should we go straight to the *Joule*?"

"Not at this hour," Welch said. "No one, not even an EGG, would visit the *Joule* in the middle of the night. There's too great a chance they'll submerge."

"Why is that?" I asked.

"*Joule* protocol is that a false submersion will go unpunished. A non-submersion, even in practice, when one is required, results in automatic death to the captain. The odds are that they'll submerge and stay down for days. Maybe weeks."

"We can't take that chance," I said.

"What island do we go to?" Gervaso asked.

"We have three options," Welch said. "Hades, Hephaestus, and Demeter. Hades is the prison island, Hephaestus is the Elgen manufacturing, and Demeter is agriculture."

"Which one would you choose?"

"Hades will have more stationed guards, but there will also be weapons and fortifications to dig in. We could also release the GPs and native prisoners to fight with us. Hephaestus is just factories, no food or weapons. They could quarantine the island and starve us out. Demeter has food, but it's just fields and jungle. Little weaponry. All we'll have to fight with is what we have on us. I'd go with Hades."

"Me too," I said.

"Hades it is," Gervaso said. "There's still hope that we're wrong about J.D."

"How are we going to know for sure?"

"Taylor," Gervaso said. He looked around. "Jack?"

"Yes, sir."

"Tell everyone they have six hours to rest and they're going to need it. They need to be ready for battle."

"Yes, sir."

"At ten I'll need you, Michael, Welch, Zeus, Ian, and Taylor to come with me to the control deck."

"Yes, sir," Jack said again.

I went below deck to check on Taylor but found her, Nichelle, and McKenna sleeping. I lay down next to Taylor, my heart pounding wildly. Not surprisingly, I couldn't sleep, and an hour later I got up and went back up top. In spite of the weather, Welch was sitting on a bench smoking.

I sat down next to him. For a while neither of us spoke. Visible to the east of us was a long strip of land.

"What island is that?" I asked.

"Hatch calls it Plutus. It was Nukufetau. It's where he's building the bullion depository, his own private Fort Knox."

Even though our visibility was limited by darkness, rain, and fog, I could see that there were cranes and massive construction going on.

"Look," Welch said softly, pointing to a shadow in the water. "There she is."

What I saw looked like a large, rectangular buoy.

"What is it?"

"The *Joule*."

I had seen the *Joule* only once before, in Lima, just before we sank the *Ampere*, only this time it was mostly submerged, exposing only the conning tower. Again it was docked close to shore.

Welch took a long drag from his cigarette and stared out in silence.

"I thought Elgen guards didn't smoke," I said.

"They don't." He offered me the cigarette. "Want one?"

"I'm fifteen," I said.

"Not tonight you're not."

"I'll pass," I said.

After a few minutes he said, "I hope I get to die slowly of cancer."

After a half hour I went back down to our quarters. Ostin was asleep and snoring loudly, which this time made me happy. It was familiar and peaceful in its own way.

I worried about him. Quentin felt remorseful that he'd dragged Torstyn and Tara to their deaths, but, in my own way, I was just as guilty. Ostin wouldn't have been here if it wasn't for me. He'd probably be graduating from Harvard at seventeen and getting a job with the highest bidder, Elgen Inc. That's what I was thinking about when I fell asleep.

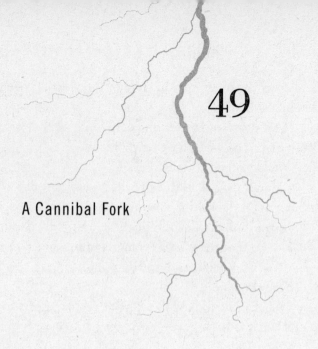

49

A Cannibal Fork

"Michael, wake up." I looked up to see Gervaso standing above me. "It's time."

It took a moment for recognition to sink in. I was hoping the night before had just been a nightmare. It was, just not the sleeping kind.

It was ten o'clock in the morning, not early, but I'd still only gotten a few hours of sleep. And it didn't look like morning. There was no sign of the sun.

After I got up, Gervaso and I went around waking everyone and telling them to eat and prepare to dock. Then Welch, Jack, Taylor, Ian, Zeus, and I followed Gervaso up to the control deck. Ostin came as well, even though he hadn't been invited.

Outside the door to the control deck Gervaso said to Taylor, "I need you to stand next to J.D. I need you to read his mind."

We still hadn't told everyone else about our concern, so Taylor looked surprised. "Why?"

"We have reason to believe that he's working with the Elgen."

Taylor blanched. "I'll stay close."

We walked into the control deck single file. There were three crew members along with Captain J.D., who was in his chair. The men were speaking in Fijian but stopped as we entered.

"Good morning, friends," J.D. said. "You see our destination ahead, just as planned."

Ahead of us in the far distance was a sliver of land. It looked bleak, like a South Pacific version of Alcatraz. It had a five-hundred-meter-tall radio tower held up by guy wires stretching hundreds of yards in each direction. A series of red lights flashed near the top of the tower. A light plume of steam rose above the island, mixing in with the dark, low-lying clouds. The Elgen had burned almost every tree on the island, leaving it black and desolate.

"There's your Hades," J.D. said.

"Yeah, it looks like hell," Jack replied.

"Why is there steam coming off the island?" Taylor asked.

"It must have a small Starxource plant," Ostin said.

We were all quiet. There was a dark foreboding, made more so by the lightning and weather.

"Did you see that?" Taylor asked. "Lightning just struck the tower."

"It's the tallest thing around for a thousand miles," Ostin said. "It probably gets struck hundreds of times a year. And technically, it's a mast, not a tower."

"What's the difference?" I asked.

"Towers stand on their own. Masts have wires that hold them up."

"It's a tower," Jack said.

As we neared the island, we passed several Elgen shuttles. One of them looked like some kind of a prison barge with barred windows.

"Where's the prison?" I asked. I'd seen a map of the island, but it was different seeing the land in real life.

"It's on the other side of the island," J.D. said. "There are two docks, an old one and the new dock for the prison. We will dock on this side. Otherwise we will be seen by the prison guards."

I turned to Ian. "Can you see anything?"

"There's activity at the far dock. It must be a changing of shifts. There's a boatload of guards leaving."

"Maybe that's a good thing," I said. "The new guards will just be settling in."

"I don't see new guards," he said.

"They wouldn't come and go at the same time," Ostin said. "The old guards won't leave until the others have taken their place."

"That's what I mean," he said. "I don't see any guards at all. I see a lot of prisoners in their cells, but no guards."

"That sounds like an evacuation, not a shift change," Gervaso said.

"Why would they all be leaving?" I asked.

J.D. glanced at me. "You never know, Mr. Vey. The Elgen are always changing their ways."

"We've got trouble," Ian said. "There are two very large boats coming our way. I've never seen them before."

Welch's brow furrowed. "What do they look like?"

"One of them looks like a destroyer. The other one has a huge deck with helicopters on it."

Welch's brow furrowed still deeper. "It's the *Edison* and the *Franklin*, Hatch's new attack boats."

"It's no problem," J.D. said. "They're just on patrol."

"Are you sure?" Taylor asked, walking up close to the captain.

J.D. put his hand on Taylor's shoulder. "Don't worry, honey. Everything will be just fine."

Taylor's face turned ashen, and then she shoved the captain away from her. J.D. laughed and turned to me. "You have a feisty girl there, Mike."

"You were right," Taylor said to us. "He's betrayed us. He sold us out to Hatch."

Jack and Welch pulled out guns. One of the crew members reached for a gun, and Zeus blasted him against the wall.

"What is this about?" J.D. said, trying to act innocent.

"You tell us," Gervaso said. "Tell us why you betrayed us."

"Why would I do that? You are my friends."

He even sounded like a liar.

"He's not a friend," Taylor said. "He's a traitor. He sold us all out for money. He wants the million-dollar bounty for Welch, and he asked Hatch if he could own me. As his pet."

"I'm going to electrocute him," I said.

Before I could shock him, Gervaso knocked him out of his seat with a punch. Then Gervaso jumped on him and continued to beat on him until his face was bloody. "Tell us what you did."

J.D. cried out, "Okay, okay. I will tell you."

Gervaso leaned back, his fists red and covered with blood. "Are the Elgen waiting for us?"

J.D. looked up at us from his back, terrified. "Yes."

"We're dead," Jack said, taking over the boat's steering.

"Not before he dies," Zeus said. "I'm going to fry him slowly."

"No," Gervaso said. "Not yet. We need to know what he's arranged. Taylor, come touch this scumbag. I need to be sure he's telling the truth."

"I'd rather touch vomit."

"He is vomit," Jack said.

Gervaso turned back to J.D. "If you lie once, Zeus will burn off your feet. Do you understand?"

"Just give me the word," Zeus said, grabbing the man's ankle.

His voice quivered. "I understand."

"What arrangement did you make with the Elgen?"

"I told Hatch that I would bring all of you to him."

Jack groaned out.

"Why didn't the Elgen attack us at Nike?" I asked.

"Hatch wanted you to get to Hades. Then he was going to send his forces to surround the island."

"To capture us?"

J.D. didn't answer.

Gervaso repeated more forcefully. "To capture us?"

"No. He intends to kill everyone in battle." He glanced at Taylor. "Except this girl. And Vey. He has ordered Vey to be taken alive. He has special plans for Vey."

"What kind of plans?" I asked.

"An ancient Fiji tradition. He said to prepare the *ai cula ni bokola*."

Ostin looked at me with horror. "It's what I was telling you about. It's the cannibal fork they used to eat people."

For a moment I was speechless. "Hatch is planning to eat me?"

Taylor covered her mouth as if she were going to throw up.

"The general plans to serve you for the feast to celebrate the end of the resistance."

I looked at J.D. "You knew this, and you were still going to deliver me to him?"

"What he does with you is not my business."

"How much did they pay you for us?" Jack shouted. "Thirty pieces of silver?"

"How could you do this?" Gervaso said. "I trusted you."

"I needed money," he said.

"For what?"

". . . For drugs."

Gervaso's fist balled up. "You pathetic piece of crap. When did you become a junkie?"

"It's your fault," J.D. said. "After I got shot saving you, they put me on painkillers. I got addicted. When the painkillers stopped working, I needed something stronger. If it hadn't been for you, I wouldn't be a junkie. You share the blame."

Gervaso spit on him. "You had a choice. Everyone has a choice. You took the cowardly way.

"And if you couldn't handle it, you should have put a gun to your head instead of ours."

J.D. was quiet for a moment, then said, "You're right. I should have. But I didn't."

"No, you didn't. But before we're through, you're going to wish you had."

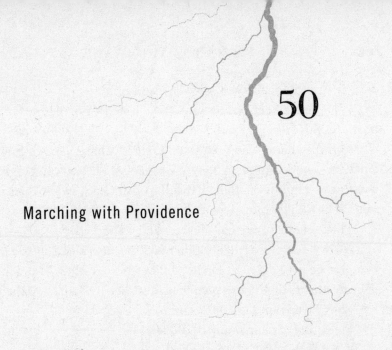

50

Marching with Providence

Gervaso took control of the boat while Jack, Zeus, Ian, Taylor, Welch, and I rounded up the rest of the *Risky Business* crew and brought them down to one of the berths. We tied them up, leaving them in a row on their stomachs. Everyone except for J.D., who we kept tied up on the control deck.

"If the boat sinks," Jack said to the crew, "you drown. Choke on that karma."

We returned to the control deck and told them what had happened. It was like reading the jury's verdict of death. Everyone was quiet. Only Tanner seemed undisturbed, which was disturbing in its own way. I couldn't get Hatch's plan for me out of my mind.

"Maybe J.D.'s lying," Tessa said. "Maybe he just made the whole thing up."

"That would be like confessing to a murder you didn't commit," Jack said.

"He's not lying," Taylor said. "He sold us."

"We've got to get out of here," Welch said. "We've got to turn the boat around."

"And go where?" Gervaso said. "We don't have enough fuel to get anywhere, we're not fast enough to escape their boats, and even if we could, the cannon on their battleship can shoot more than twenty miles. They'll just blow us out of the water."

"Then where do we go?" Tessa asked. "The *Joule*?"

"No, we don't have that option now," Gervaso said. "It's too far. Our best chance is to dig in at Hades and defend ourselves. Hatch built an inescapable prison to keep people in. Let's see if it can keep them out."

"They'll surround us," Jack said.

"We're already surrounded," Welch said.

"What if they decide to just starve us out?" Tessa asked.

"The prison's got to have food and supplies," Welch said.

"No," Quentin said. "Hatch isn't that patient. He'll fight."

"We've got to reach the island and break into prison before they reach us," Gervaso said. "Jack, get us there."

"Yes, sir." Jack pushed the boat's throttle all the way, and the front of the boat lifted with our speed.

"What do you see, Ian?" Gervaso asked.

"The *Faraday* is being loaded with soldiers. It looks like they're bringing their whole army."

"Fifteen of us versus ten thousand of them," Welch said.

"Seventeen of us," Quentin said. "We've got Tara and Torstyn."

"And the prisoners and GPs," Welch said. "They'll fight. There are at least two hundred being held captive. They'll fight for their lives."

Gervaso turned to Welch. "Is there anything we should know about how the Elgen will fight?"

"Hatch likes spectacle. There's no other reason why he didn't just sink our ship. He did the same thing to me. If he weren't a slave to his ego, he would have just executed me on the spot. Instead, he wanted to make a show of me being fed to the rats. I think this is what he's doing now. The final battle of Elgen versus Electroclan. He wants a spectacle, something for the history books."

"The bigger army doesn't always win," Ostin said. "Like George Washington crossing the Delaware to attack Trenton. He was outnumbered, with two thousand hungry, sick, poorly equipped soldiers when they attacked the superior, well-armed, rested mercenary Hessians—the most feared, well-trained soldiers in the world. Washington not only won, but he didn't have a single soldier killed or wounded. Providence marched with them that day." As if to punctuate the point, lightning lit the sky around us, followed by a loud thunderclap.

Welch looked up at the sky, then said, "Let's hope providence is with us, too."

51

The Island of Hades

We put a long chain, with a padlock, around J.D.'s neck, partially to secure him and partially so Taylor wouldn't have to touch him to read his thoughts.

As we neared the island, Gervaso said to J.D., "You need to help us dock. Remember, if the boat sinks, you're going down with it."

"The island is surrounded by reef," he said. "You have to dock the boat at the dock."

"He's telling the truth," Taylor said.

Welch, Gervaso, Jack, and I looked over a map of Hades. "That reef will be an advantage," Welch said. "It means they can't run their boats in all at once. After we disembark, we'll blow the dock. They'll have to swim in to get us. It's not easy to win a war waist-deep in water."

"That will slow them down," Gervaso said. "But not much."

"Maybe long enough for us to thin them out," Welch said.

* * *

The island of Hades was about a mile in circumference, flat and oddly shaped, like an amoeba. The water surrounding it was light and shallow, with a wide, coral reef visible from where we were, a hundred yards out. Surrounding the island was fine white sand, dark beneath the clouds. Under different circumstances it might have been a nice place to vacation.

There was an old town on the west side of the island. At one time there had been a post office, a community center, and a church. Now it was deserted except for a few apartments kept for the guards. At one time the island had been lush, completely covered with various palms, mostly coconut and breadfruit trees, but that was before the Elgen had burned the land, clearing it for the prison. The prison sat on roughly thirty acres on the west side of the island and was surrounded with two twenty-two-foot-tall chain-link fences topped with four feet of razor wire.

About fifty yards out from the prison fence the Elgen's GPs and slave labor, taken mostly from the Tuvaluan natives, had been forced to build an outer wall made of concrete. It was shorter than the other fence but still daunting—ten feet high with razor wire. The wall had been built for prisoners, but it had also been built as a protection from the sea and was added after a cyclone had hit the island, damaging the original construction. Its construction reminded me of what we saw in Taiwan's Starxource plant. "Creepycrete," Taylor called it, drab, formless construction based on the lowest denominator of function.

The entry to the prison was on the north side of the island, where the main dock was built. The Elgen guards had filled the last of the shuttles and were about to push off. To avoid them we sailed west, circling the island clockwise. As we came around the island, Jack slowed the boat down slightly. "I'll wait until you give me the go-ahead," he said to Ian.

"Are you sure it's not a trap?" I asked. "Why didn't they blow the dock?"

"Why are they leaving at all?" Zeus asked.

"Maybe the dock's booby-trapped."

"That would be the smart thing to do," Ostin said.

"I don't see anything, but I'll keep looking," Ian said.

Gervaso looked over the island with binoculars. "No, they're giving us the prison. Apparently Hatch wants a fight."

A few minutes later Ian said, "We're clear. The last of them just circled the bend."

"Got it." Jack hit the throttle, and we sped east along the north bank of the island toward the prison.

By the time we reached the dock, there was no one in sight. The dock led to a landing, with a road leading to a break in the concrete wall. There were towers on every corner of the wall, but they appeared to be deserted as well.

"Why would they just desert it?" Tessa asked.

Ian surveyed the site once more, then said, "It's still clear."

"We're going to have to blow the dock," Gervaso said.

"Then I'll move the boat after we dock," Welch said. "Just in case we need it."

Welch took over the boat's controls and brought us up to the dock. With the size of the waves rocking our boat, we hit the side pretty hard, throwing us all to the port side of the boat.

"Nice landing," Tanner said.

"Like to see you do better," Tessa said.

"C'mon," I said.

Jack and I jumped out onto the dock, and Ian and Tessa threw us the ropes so we could tie the boat onto the cleats. One by one everyone except Welch got off.

Zeus and Gervaso, using towels from the bathroom, blindfolded J.D. and his crew. Then Jack, Zeus, and I took them off the boat.

After everyone was off, Ian and I untied the ropes, and then Welch started to pull away from the dock. Suddenly one of the crew members pulled off his blindfold, then jumped in front of the boat into the sea, which was stupid on many levels. I couldn't figure out what the guy's plan was. Was he trying to get cut up in the boat's propeller? Or was he planning to swim twenty miles to another island during a raging storm?

Zeus, covered in a formfitting rain suit and two ponchos, reacted quickly and shocked the dude just as he hit the ocean. The sound of electricity striking the water was like dropping ice into a pan of sizzling bacon. The man went under for nearly a minute, then popped back up. "I give up!" he shouted. "Don't shock me. I give up."

"Swim to shore," Zeus said. "Next time I won't let you surrender."

As we walked off the dock onto the island, I felt a dark, eerie feeling of desolation. A line from the Bible came to me: *Though I walk through the valley of the shadow of death, I will fear no evil* . . .

Except I definitely feared. I was terrified of the evil to come.

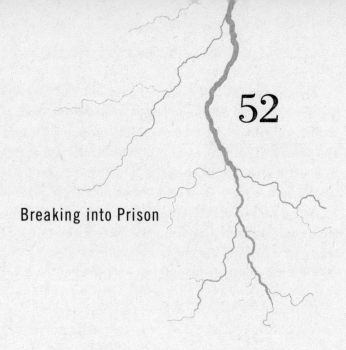

52

Breaking into Prison

Welch anchored the boat about a hundred feet east of the dock and about sixty feet from shore, just outside the reef. He had to swim in to shore, and he was soaked and dripping when he caught up to us. Actually, with the exception of Zeus, with the amount of rain falling we were all soaked by the time we reached the prison's main entrance.

Unfortunately, the guards had locked up after themselves. Ian examined the kind of lock used, then turned to McKenna. "It's mechanical. The best thing would be for you to melt the bolt."

"I can do that," McKenna said. She walked up to the door, pushing her slim fingers as far as she could between the crack. Her hand immediately went bright white. It took less than a minute for the metal to turn to molten steel and collapse.

"Anything waiting for us behind the door?" Gervaso asked.

Ian shook his head. "Just prisoners."

"Let me go first," I said. "Just in case." I put an electric field around me and pushed the door open and walked through.

As Ian had said, there was no one in sight. I turned back toward the others. "Come on."

Gervaso was the first through the doorway, followed by the rest. The next door wasn't locked, but the power had been shut off inside the building. The room smelled musty like mold and was lit only by our glows, especially mine, which was now as bright as a sixty-watt bulb.

"I can help," McKenna said. She lit up, brightly illuminating the room.

"How do we turn the power back on?" Gervaso asked Welch.

"The place is powered by a mini Starxource plant," Welch said. "Whenever there's a plant, there's a central power office. It should be near the entrance." He turned to Ian. "Just look for a room with thousands of wires moving into it. All roads lead to Rome, you know? Just find a wire and follow it."

Ian began panning across the room, then stopped. "It's over there. It looks like a bowl of copper spaghetti."

"That's the place. I can turn it back on. I'll need some light."

"I'll go with you," McKenna said.

"Me too," Ostin said.

They walked off down the hall, and a few minutes later the lights came on. When they returned, Welch was carrying a roll of paper in his hands. "I found this."

Gervaso stepped forward. "What have you got?"

"It's the building schematics. The Elgen usually keep a set in the main control room. We can use it to plan our defense."

"What are we going to do with these clowns?" Jack asked, nodding toward J.D. and his crew.

"There's plenty of cells to lock them in," Welch said. "That hall to the right leads to the interim cell. It's the closest to the command center."

"How do I open the cell doors?" Jack asked.

"Everything can be controlled from the central control panel," Welch said.

"I can do it," Ostin said. "The controls will probably be similar to the academy's."

"Just hurry," Gervaso said. "We haven't much time."

Jack and Zeus hurried off down one hall with J.D. and his crew, while Ostin and McKenna returned to the hallway they had just come from.

Welch took the plans over to a desk and laid them out. The paper had a complete diagram of the prison complex, including the apartments outside the main walls. The prison was shaped like a U, with the open end facing west. The north corridor was where the guards quartered, and there were administrative offices and a small arms closet. At the end of the corridor was the mini Starxource plant.

The eastern corridor was for the laboratory and experiments, and for the scientists' convenience, the southern corridor was lined on both sides with cells for GPs. Cell 25 was located at the opening of the south corridor. The control room was located on the west side of the east corridor. Above it was the main tower, which had glass on all sides like an airplane tower. Next to it, in a separate building, was the radio tower and building.

"I need a pen," Welch said.

"Here's a pencil," Taylor said.

Gervaso, Welch, Ian, and I crouched over the map.

"First we need to blow that dock," Gervaso said, looking up at Welch. "That's the priority. Do they have explosives? Dynamite? C4?"

"They wouldn't need them here. I'm sure they have grenades and some RPGs, something to sink a boat."

"Where would they be?"

Welch tapped his pen on the map. "The small arms armory is right here, but the heavy weapons cache should be here, in the center of the guard complex."

"That's outside the prison," I said. "Why would they do that?"

"In case there's a revolt, the prisoners can't get to the big guns."

Ostin and McKenna ran back into the room. "What's next?" Ostin asked.

"We need to free Tara and Torstyn," Quentin said. "They can help us. Especially Torstyn."

"Nichelle, Taylor, and I will go with Quentin to free Tara and Torstyn," I said.

"What about me?" Ian asked.

"We need you up in that tower," Gervaso said. "With Tanner." He turned to Welch. "We'll need radios."

"Radios should be in the prison armory with the weapons," Welch said.

"Jack can free and arm the rest of the prisoners," I said. "Just like he did at the academy. Zeus and Tessa can go with him."

"What if they have electric collars?" Ostin asked.

"We'll have to shut them off. That's work for you."

"Just like the academy," Ostin said.

"After I find the explosives, I'll blow the dock," Gervaso said. "As soon as I return, we seal off the place. Jack will take his prisoners to guard the walls. Ian is stationed here in the main tower so he can keep everyone apprised."

"What if they start shelling us first?" Ian asked.

"Are there bunkers?" I asked. "Anything underground?"

"Most Elgen facilities have secret passageways that aren't on the plans," Welch said.

"Like the Weekend Express at the Peru Starxource plant," Ostin said.

Welch looked at him. "Exactly."

Ian panned the ground. "There's a tunnel near the entry that runs underground. It's deep enough to provide shelter."

Gervaso looked at Ian. "Where does it go?"

"It leads outside the fence to the guard complex."

Ostin said, "The Elgen don't know that we know about it, so they'll probably try to enter in through it and ambush us."

"Which means we can ambush them while they're trying to ambush us," Gervaso said. "I'll go out the tunnel to blow the dock, then set up a nest at the inner end of the tunnel. How do I get to the tunnel?"

Ostin looked at the map and said, "North corridor. There's a utility closet next to the arms closet. There's a trapdoor in the floor."

Just then Jack and Zeus returned. Gervaso said, "Come over. We don't have much time." He looked at Ian. "We're vastly outnumbered, so communication is crucial. We'll move to wherever the Elgen are so we're always matching them.

"We'll break up into four groups. Michael, after you and Taylor help free the prisoners, you, Ian, Tanner, Nichelle, and Taylor take the main tower. You're squad A, our eyes and ears. Tanner, you do what you do. Just one aircraft could take us out."

Tanner looked at us dully, but said nothing.

Gervaso looked at him. "You good?"

"I'm good," he replied.

Then Gervaso turned to Jack. "You, Zeus, Tessa, Cassy, and Abi are squad B. You take the prisoners, arm them, and set up defenses on the ground inside the outer wall. Jack, you're the general. I want you and the others commanding from up in the towers. I don't want any of you in the line of fire. Just keep the Elgen outside the concrete wall. If they break through, push them back. That's where the real battle is. If we can keep them from breaching the wall, we can win this."

"What about us?" Ostin asked.

"You and McKenna take the command center. You'll have access to all the cameras, communication, sirens, hydraulics, door locks, and electrical power. You can cut power where needed and use the cameras to help communicate to us what's going on."

"Welch and Quentin will take Tara and Torstyn and guard the north gate. After I blow the dock, most of the attacks will probably come from the east. If that changes, Ian will know long before they reach us, and Jack will send his forces to back you up."

Welch said, "If Hatch hasn't executed them yet, there's at least twelve former Elgen guards in the cells. I can take them as well. They're well trained and they know how the Elgen fight."

"Perfect. Just keep those gates closed."

"There's a problem," Quentin said. "I put some of those prisoners in here. They're going to want to kill me, not fight with me."

"Times have changed. They can fight with you or die at the hands of the Elgen."

"Guys, we're missing the point," Ostin said.

We all looked at him. Jack crossed his arms at his chest. "What point?"

Ostin adjusted his glasses. "We came to steal the *Joule* and end the Elgen. What better chance will we get than right now, when the entire Elgen guard has us surrounded? There won't be anyone left to guard the *Joule*. It's ripe for the picking."

"Yes, except they have us *surrounded*," Jack said. "So how are we supposed to get away from the island?"

"Easy," Ostin said. "We can assume that Hatch is expecting J.D. to drop us off and head back to Nike in the *Risky Business*. Therefore, Welch, Quentin, Tara, and Taylor can take J.D. and sail right through the blockade. They'll steal the *Joule* and come back for us."

Jack shook his head. "We're hopelessly outnumbered, and you want to send away some of our best fighters?"

"Well, that's the point, isn't it?" Ostin said. "We're hopelessly outnumbered. We're probably going to lose the battle, but this way we can still win the war."

We were all quiet for a moment. Then I said, "He's right." I looked at Welch. "What do you think?"

"It might work."

"Gervaso?"

He frowned. "Ostin's right. It's our best chance to capture the boat. And we've got a better chance of escaping than fighting."

"No offense," Jack said, looking away from Welch. "But if the former Elgen steal the boat, what guarantee do we have that they'll come back for us?"

Gervaso looked at Quentin. "We don't."

"So do we send one of our team with them?"

"We're all the same team," Welch said. "We can't afford to weaken our forces any more than we already have."

"That sounds suspicious," Jack said. "I need a guarantee."

I thought a moment, then said, "There aren't any guarantees anymore. We just have to trust them."

"We'll come back," Quentin said. "If they don't kill or capture us, we'll return for you."

"If they capture us, they'll kill us," Welch said. "But you have my word. If we make it, we'll come back."

"The word of an Elgen," Zeus said.

"Former Elgen," Welch replied. "Like you."

Before it could escalate into anything else, I turned to Jack. "So then you'll have to take the prisoners and cover the north gate as well."

Jack still looked uncomfortable. "Michael, I'm not good with this."

"I could go with them," Cassy said. "Keep them honest."

"We need her here," Zeus said.

"If our best shot is the *Joule*, she should be there," I said. "She could help them. She might be able to stop them from submerging."

Welch looked at her. "That's fine. She's powerful. And Michael's right, she could help us take the boat."

"It's your call," Gervaso said.

"The *Joule* is most important," I said, looking at Cassy. "Are you okay with that?"

"I'm okay with whatever you need."

No one else spoke up, so I said, "Then it's settled. Welch and Quentin will free Tara, Torstyn, and the guards. Jack will take charge of the prisoners while Welch and company take J.D. back to the *Risky Business* and sail for the *Joule*."

"I should help them release Torstyn and Tara," Nichelle said. "We don't know what Hatch has done to them. Just in case . . ."

"That's a good idea," Welch said.

"We'll go out the tunnel," Gervaso said to Welch. "I'll blow the dock while you return to the *Risky Business*. Then I'll secure the tunnel. If it's a small enough space, one machine gun could hold it—if we can find a machine gun."

"There should be one in the armory," Welch said.

"There is," Ian said. "I can see two of them."

"All right," Gervaso said. "We have a plan and not much time. Let's go. Weapon up first."

We hurried to the armory. The door had a combination lock like a bank vault. Ian turned the dial just four times, then turned the handle and it clicked, releasing the door.

"I've always loved that power of yours," Quentin said.

"Me too," Ian said.

Gervaso pushed opened the door and stepped inside. The supply room was about the size of our apartment back home in Idaho. One wall had three rows of rifles, forty or fifty in all, Russian-made AK-47s. Beneath them were stacked boxes of ammo. Against the far wall were two RPG launchers, a dozen submachine guns—Israeli UZIs—and about fifty handguns.

"Look at this," Gervaso said, crouching down next to the largest of the guns. "They've got some M2s—fifty-caliber Browning machine guns. That will stop anything in that tunnel."

"I've found something better," I said. "A flamethrower."

"That's exactly what I need for the tunnel," Gervaso said.

The opposite wall was a candy shop of destruction—everything a soldier of fortune could dream of. Inside the various cubbies were land mines and rocket-propelled grenades, tear gas, concussion grenades, and smoke bombs.

"This is good," Gervaso said. "There's enough here to blow the dock. Ostin and McKenna, grab some radios, then head back to the control room. You're going to have to start opening the cell doors so we can release the prisoners."

"After we help suit up," Ostin said.

"I'll help you set up the tunnel," Jack said to Gervaso.

Taylor and I helped Gervaso, Jack, Tessa, and Welch get weapons. All Zeus took was a grenade and a bulletproof vest. Jack took an UZI, two handguns, a grenade belt with six grenades, and an ammo pouch. He grabbed two strings of machine gun ammo and draped them crisscrossing over his chest. He also threw the flamethrower over his back. He looked commando.

Gervaso took the machine gun and as much ammo as he could carry.

Ostin calibrated all the radios, six of them, one for each group, and handed them out. "Testing, testing."

"They're working," I said.

"Remember, we're on channel seventeen, as in seventeen electrics."

Gervaso clipped a radio to his belt. "All right. Let's get going. Michael, you guys get up there. They might be getting close." He turned to Ian. "Remember, you're our eyes. Just let us know what's going on. The more information we have, the better."

"I'll do my best."

Gervaso started walking toward the tunnel, then abruptly stopped and turned back. "One more thing. If something happens to me, Michael's in charge."

No one said anything, but Taylor gave me a sympathetic glance. Gervaso took a deep breath, then said, "All right. Good luck, everybody. Semper Fi. We'll see you when this is over."

I looked at Gervaso, then suddenly stepped forward and hugged him. "Be safe, man."

"You too. Keep them all safe."

After he was out of sight, Taylor turned to me. "You don't think you're going to see him again."

"Of course I will."

She knew I was lying even without touching me.

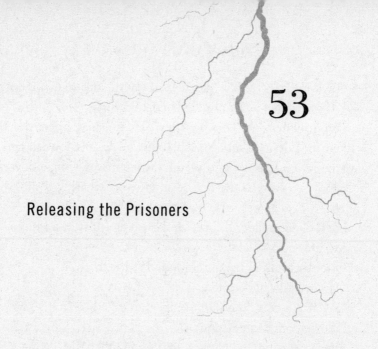

53

Releasing the Prisoners

"**W**e need to help them release prisoners. Then we'll join you up top," I said to Ian and Tanner.

"No worries, man," Ian said.

They left for the tower while Taylor, Cassy, and I joined up with Welch, Quentin, and Nichelle near the end of the southern corridor. They were just about to enter one of the cells. "Who's in there?" I asked.

"Torstyn," Welch said. He lifted his radio. "Command center, you there?"

"Roger," Ostin said.

"Open cell door 003."

There was a slight pause, followed by, "Opening cell door 003 and turning off RESAT."

There was a sudden squeal of air followed by the click of a lock.

"Taylor, Cassy, and I had better stay in the hall for now," I said. "We don't want to completely freak him out."

Quentin nodded. "No worries." He pushed open the door and walked in. Nichelle and Welch followed him. I looked through the glass panel on the door to watch. Torstyn was lying sideways on his bed, looking away from the door. He was wearing a pink jumpsuit. He rolled over to see who had come for him.

He looked ragged, thinner and weaker. Most of all he looked confused. "Quentin? Welch?"

Quentin walked up to the bed. "It's me, man."

"And me," Welch added.

"What are you doing here?" Torstyn asked. "What's going on?"

"We've come to rescue you."

His expression changed when he saw Nichelle. "What's she doing here?"

"Calm down, microwave," Nichelle said. "We're on the same side. Who do you think freed your bro here?"

"She's telling the truth," Quentin said. "Michael Vey and the Electroclan freed us. But we're going to have to fight our way out of here."

"Vey?"

Taylor, Cassy, and I stepped into the room. "Yeah, us."

Torstyn just stared at us for a moment. "Tara?"

"No. I'm Taylor."

"We're on the same side now?"

"We're all against Hatch," I said. "That puts us on the same side."

"I know you're pretty weak," Welch said. "But we don't have a lot of time. Hatch and the guards are on their way. We have a boat. We're going to sneak out the back."

"All of us?"

"No," I said. "Just you guys. We're going to try to hold this prison."

Quentin helped Torstyn up.

"You freed Tara?" Torstyn asked.

"That's where we're going next," Welch said.

We walked out of the cell. Taylor looked inside the slit of the door two cells down. "There's my sister."

I lifted my radio. There was ambient noise and talking from Jack and Zeus, who were gathering up the GPs.

"Ostin, this is Michael. Do you read me?"

"Copy, Michael."

"Open cell 005. And turn off the RESAT."

"On it."

The door clicked. Quentin pushed the door open, and he, Torstyn, and Nichelle stepped inside. I stood with Welch and Taylor in the doorway.

Tara was also dressed in a pink jumpsuit. She looked like she had aged ten years. "Q?"

"I'm so sorry," Quentin said. He walked over and hugged her. "I never should have dragged you into this."

Tara looked afraid and confused. "Where's Hatch? Is he dead?"

"No. The Elgen are on their way. We're going to fight them."

"Us?" She lay back down. "We can't beat them. No one can stop Hatch."

"We can," I said, stepping forward. "I've beaten him. I'll do it again."

"Vey?"

"And I'm here," Taylor said.

Tara stared at her twin. "What are you doing here?"

"I came to save you."

"But . . . I'm your enemy."

"You're my sister. Let me help you." Tara looked at her twin in disbelief, then fell into Taylor's arms and wept.

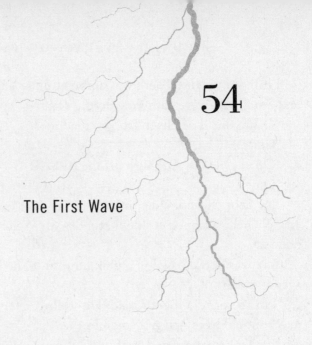

54

The First Wave

"You guys need to get out of here fast," I said.

"Do you have any food?" Tara asked.

"Yeah, we're starving," Torstyn said.

"I'll take them to get something to eat," Cassy said.

"I'll go with you," Nichelle said.

"Michael," Welch said. "Come with me to free the guards. They should see me first."

We passed a room where Abigail was alone arranging tables in long rows.

"What's she doing?" Quentin asked.

"Turning it into a hospital," I said.

Welch, Quentin, and I freed up nine Elgen guards who had run afoul of Hatch. Welch thought there were more. There were, but they had already been executed. Not surprisingly, the remaining guards wanted revenge on Hatch.

"Listen up," Welch said. "Hatch and your former brotherhood are descending on this island. They will not be taking prisoners. Neither will we. Fight as if your life depended upon it, because it does."

We led the men down to the supply closet and armed them. The guards found Elgen uniforms and put them on, though Welch handed out a roll of security tape for them to wrap around their arms to keep from getting accidentally shot by the other prisoners.

As we were finishing up, Jack, Tessa, and Zeus returned.

"The tunnel is armed," Jack said. "Gervaso has gone out to blow the dock."

"Alone?"

"He said we couldn't wait any longer." Jack looked at the guards. "Who are they?"

"These are all the former Elgen guards," Welch said. "Three of them were ZCs. They are leaders. They're now your soldiers. They're under your command."

Jack looked them over. "Fall in, soldiers."

The men lined up against the wall.

Jack looked natural commanding. "Men, we're under attack. We've got to arm and manage two hundred prisoners. Each of you will take a squad of twenty prisoners. It is your responsibility to get them armed and guard the section I give you. Understand?"

The men shouted, "Yes, sir!"

"I told you they were well trained," Welch said. "Now we've got to go. Let's get the boat captain." He looked at Torstyn and Tara, who were still wearing their pink outfits. Their hands were filled with food. "Change your clothes; then eat," he said. "We're going to get the captain. We're leaving the second I return."

"Taylor and I will go and start freeing prisoners," I said to Jack. "We'll send them back to you." I lifted my radio. "Ostin, we're going to start letting the prisoners out. Get ready."

"Roger."

Taylor and I ran down to the south cells. The door was locked. "Ostin, open the main door to the south cells."

"Roger that."

"Who's Roger?" Taylor asked.

"It's just a radio thing," I said. I pushed open the door and walked into a dim, long, narrow hallway. There were about twenty doors on each side, each filled with GPs in various states of mental trauma. I walked up to the first door and looked in through its acrylic slot window. I counted five Tuvaluan men, all with electric collars and dressed in orange jumpsuits. They must have heard us coming, as they were huddled at the back of the room. "Open S-001."

"Opening S-001." The door unlocked. "Collars off."

I opened the door. The GPs didn't move.

"Déjà vu," I said. "Just like the academy." I looked at the men. "You can speak."

No one did.

"Maybe they don't speak English," Taylor said.

"I speak English," one of them said with a British accent.

"Good. We are here to free you. But we have to fight against the Elgen. Will you help?"

"Yes."

"What's your name?"

"I am Enele Saluni, grandson of the prime minister."

"After we overthrow the Elgen, your grandfather will be free to rule again," I said. "But right now the Elgen are coming and we need your men to fight."

"The Elgen are coming here?"

"All of them. To destroy the prison."

"Do we have weapons?"

"For everyone," I said.

Enele turned and spoke in Tuvaluan, and the men immediately stood at attention.

"We will help," Enele said.

"We've got to let everyone out," I said. "We'll need everyone."

We walked out, then opened the first four doors on the south side of the hall, releasing twenty prisoners. I led them back to Jack, leaving Taylor with the radio and Enele. When I returned to the armory, Welch was standing there with J.D., another crew member, Quentin, Tara, Torstyn, and Cassy.

"Everyone ready?" I asked.

"Where are we going?" J.D. asked defiantly. He must have figured out that he had nothing to lose, as he'd already lost his previous humility.

"There's been a change of plans," Welch said. "You're going to sail back to Nike just as you told Hatch you would."

J.D. scowled. "And if I refuse?"

Welch's eyes narrowed. "Imagine what it would feel like to have your hand in a microwave oven for sixty seconds. Torstyn can show you how that feels. And then he will melt your eyes, your tongue, then your brain, in that order. Do you understand?"

J.D. swallowed. "Yes."

"Yes, what?"

"Yes, sir."

"Torstyn, these are Hatch's friends and collaborators. If they make one wrong move, melt them. Slowly."

"Just give the word," Torstyn said, staring hatefully at J.D.

"Let's go." Welch lifted his radio. "Come in, Gervaso."

"Gervaso, copy."

"This is Welch. We're headed down the tunnel. Just didn't want you to shoot us."

"I'm headed out now for the dock. Good luck."

"Roger," Welch said into his radio. Then he turned to his group and said, "Let's go."

I looked at Cassy. "Good luck."

"I'll make sure they come back, if I have to drive the boat myself," she said.

As we were parting, our radios squelched. "This is Ian. We've got small rafts landing on the west side of the island. Three of them. Here they come."

"Looks like some of our guests arrived early," Welch said. "Let's get this party started." As the others began climbing down the ladder to the tunnel, Welch turned to me. "If we don't come back, it's because we failed or are dead. You can trust us."

"I do," I said. "Good luck."

"Just hold out." He turned and followed the rest of his group down the tunnel. Jack and his soldiers were standing quietly, sizing up the GPs.

"That's all there is?" one of the guards asked.

"It's just the first group," I said. "We think there's about two hundred. Not all of them speak English. Not all of them are fit to fight."

Jack turned to the GPs and asked, "Who speaks English?"

Three of the men raised their hands.

"Get up here," he said to the biggest. "You're second-in-command of the squad."

There was at least one English speaker for every ten natives, which was all we needed. While Taylor and I were releasing prisoners, Jack had established a chain of command with the guards and gone over the map of the installation, establishing their battle stations. He had also distributed radios to each Squad Captain.

With the guidance of a former Elgen Zone Captain, Jack created a plan to hold the outer wall.

The group of prisoners I had just brought were assigned a leader, and the man created the first squad, arming his men and leading them out to defend the west wall, where the Elgen had started landing.

By the time I returned to the south corridor, Taylor and Enele had released nearly a hundred prisoners.

"We better stop for now," I said to Enele, a little nervous of so many unstable men roaming free. "We'll need a little time to assign them to squads."

"Do not worry," Enele said. "They will follow directions."

I led the men back to the armory, where Jack and the guards divided them up while Taylor and Enele freed the rest. There were more prisoners than we expected, two hundred and thirty-two in all, so Jack created an extra squad, with Enele in charge.

* * *

After all the men had been sent out in squads, Taylor and I climbed the stairs four stories to the central watchtower. As we entered the observation room, we saw Tanner sitting cross-legged on one of the shelves, looking out through binoculars. He was wet, and there was a pool of water beneath him. He had opened a window and rain was blowing in, drenching him.

He's lost it, I thought.

Nichelle was on the west side of the tower, and Ian was on the east side talking into his radio. He didn't need binoculars. It didn't even matter what side he sat on.

He turned toward us. "Guys, this rock is starting to crawl. I'm having trouble keeping track of them all. The first major wave is about to hit the west shore. Did you get my message about the early rafts?"

"Yes, we heard it. Did you warn Gervaso?"

"I don't know if he heard me. He didn't answer."

"If he saw them, he turned his radio off so he wouldn't give himself away."

Tanner spun around on the counter. "Hey, kidlings. There are more binoculars over there on that shelf. These things rock."

"Thanks," Taylor said warily.

We each took a pair. Then I walked over to Nichelle. "How are you?"

"You know, the sea scares me. I didn't want to tell you that on the boat. Thought it might worry you. But I think the devil rides the waves."

I looked out and saw the first flotilla of Elgen boats approaching the island.

"He definitely is today," I said. "How's Tanner?"

She just shook her head.

Just then, over the radio came, "Ian, this is Gervaso. Do you read me?"

PART TEN

55

Blowing the Dock

After Gervaso had established his machine gun nest at the inside neck of the tunnel, he grabbed the backpack he'd filled with explosives and, carrying just a Beretta handgun, crawled out the outer end of the tunnel. Just as he was about to surface, his radio squawked.

"Come in, Gervaso."

"Gervaso, copy."

"This is Welch. We're headed down the tunnel. Just didn't want you to shoot us."

"I'm headed out now for the dock," Gervaso said. "Good luck."

"Roger."

Gervaso turned off his radio and climbed out of the tunnel. The rain was pouring down, and the ocean looked pitted from a million raindrops.

He didn't see anyone, so he crossed the road to a row of charred bushes and began crawling toward the dock. When he got there, he waded into the water beneath the dock, carrying his backpack. To blow the dock he would have to link the explosives together, connecting them close enough to each other so they would trip each other, resulting in complete annihilation.

Because of the turbulence of the sea, the waves kept slamming him into the underside of the dock, and it took Gervaso nearly twenty minutes to set the explosives, ten minutes longer than he had planned. It made him nervous. He suspected that the Elgen would be landing soon—if they hadn't already.

After he finished setting the detonator, he again looked around to make sure he was alone, tossed his backpack into the sea, and then climbed to the top of the dock. He stopped to look out toward the sea. Through the rain and darkness he could see the *Faraday* about eight hundred yards out. That meant serious trouble. The *Faraday* was capable of transporting more than thirty-five hundred soldiers. If they all were allowed to dock, men would pour out faster than they could handle. The prison would be overrun.

He looked around. The *Risky Business* was still where Welch had left it. He wondered where Welch was. He lifted his radio and turned it back on. "Ian, this is Gervaso. Come in."

"This is Ian."

"We've got Elgen to the north in the *Faraday*. They're going to try to dock."

"I can see it. Does the dock still stand?"

"I'm about to blow it. Did Welch get out?"

"They're out of the tunnel. He shouldn't be far from you now."

"Roger. Over."

"Over," Ian said.

Gervaso returned the radio to his belt. He knelt down on the dock and hung over to check his wiring once more, then stood. As he turned to go, he saw the shadows of Welch and his team creeping beneath the cover of the wall.

Finally, he thought. Gervaso raised his hand and shouted in a muted yell, "Good luck."

The shadows stopped. Then a gun opened fire, hitting Gervaso in the chest and knocking him back onto the dock.

Bleeding, Gervaso slowly pulled himself around to see who had fired on him. The men he'd mistaken for Welch's group were Elgen guards. They walked toward him, their guns pointing at him.

"Expecting someone else?" a guard asked.

Gervaso feebly lifted his handgun but was hit two more times from Elgen bullets as the squad stepped up onto the dock. Gervaso gasped for breath as he reached into his pocket and rolled over to his stomach, bracing for the next round.

"Finish him," the captain said to one of his men.

The front guard, barely older than twenty, walked on the blood-soaked dock until he was next to Gervaso. He pointed his gun at the back of Gervaso's head. "Good-bye, man."

Gervaso rolled over to look the young guard in the eyes. In his hand Gervaso held a grenade, its pin already pulled. "Yeah, good-bye."

"Hit the deck!" the guard shouted, but it was too late. The grenade blew, igniting the chain of explosives. The entire dock exploded in a blinding flash. When the smoke cleared, the dock, the Elgen, and Gervaso were gone.

PART ELEVEN

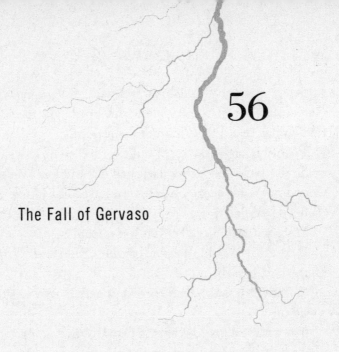

56

The Fall of Gervaso

"Gervaso!" Ian shouted.

I turned around. Ian was paralyzed.

"What happened?"

His voice was strained. "The Elgen got him."

"What do you mean, 'got him'?"

"They . . . got him."

"We've got to rescue him," I said.

Ian just looked at me, his eyes welling up with tears. "He blew the dock. He's gone."

For a moment I couldn't speak. Then I leaned over, resting my hands on my knees. "No!" Tears began to fill my eyes, then fall, spattering on the already wet floor. "No."

"I'm sorry, Michael." Taylor put her hand on my back. After a minute she said, "You're in charge now."

I stood back up. I caught my breath, then lifted the radio. In the strongest voice I could muster I said, "Everyone, this is Michael. Gervaso is gone, but he blew the dock. He gave his life for us. Remember that. Don't let him die in vain."

I could hear Jack scream out over a distant radio. The sound of it made me feel even sicker. Jack had already lost Wade, now Gervaso. Gervaso was his hero. His mentor. A second father. A better father than his real one.

I radioed Jack directly. "I'm sorry, man."

"I knew I shouldn't have left him," he said. "I'm going to take them apart myself."

"I know," I said. "Just keep it together. We've got a long night ahead of us."

The radio snapped. "This is Ostin. We're going to need someone to take the tunnel. Gervaso has the gun nest set up but it's wide open. I'm detecting movement near its mouth."

"I'll take the tunnel," Zeus said.

"Roger that," I said. "Zeus has the tunnel. Don't let anyone in!"

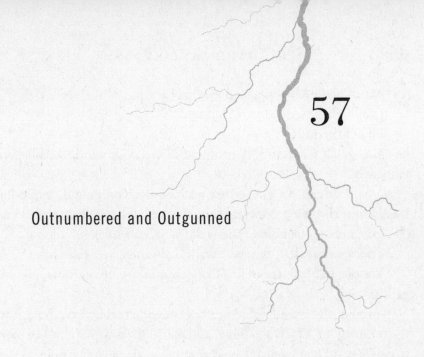

57

Outnumbered and Outgunned

The *Faraday* docked as close as it could get to the island without hitting reef, about two hundred yards out to sea. I wished I had something to blow it up with. The *Tesla*, the Elgen's landing tender, had begun transporting troops to the reef, dropping them in the water, then returning for more.

More guards came from the west, arriving on rafts and smaller boats. Within a half hour there were hundreds of troops surrounding the compound.

"They just keep coming," Taylor said. "Like ants at a picnic."

Suddenly Ian shouted, "We've got two helicopters inbound. They've got missiles."

"Where?" Tanner asked.

"Three o'clock."

Tanner lifted his binoculars. "There they are."

"How far out can you bring them down?" I asked.

"Now," he said. He reached out his hand.

"Lead helicopter is down," Ian said.

"I'll get the next."

"You got it," Ian said. A moment later he shouted, "Missile was launched!"

A fiery streak hit the outer wall of the compound, exploding loudly and throwing concrete and twisting rebar. When the smoke cleared, there was a hole in the wall the size of a truck.

"There's a break in the west wall!" I shouted over the radio.

"We see it!" Jack shouted. "Concentrate fire at the hole. No one gets in."

Through the haze I could see fire spewing through the hole from the mouths of Elgen machine gun barrels, answered by our own troops. Then Elgen guards began running in through the hole.

Dozens fell before Jack's forces, but the Elgen kept pouring into the break. Even though the prisoners had stopped hundreds, they were soon overwhelmed, outnumbered, and outgunned. Jack's men were forced to fall back behind the chain-link fences, which separated them from the guards but not their bullets.

Then the Elgen turned their guns on the towers. They couldn't hit me, as I could repel everything they had, but I was concerned for the others.

"Everyone down!" I shouted. "I don't want to deflect something into you."

The number of Elgen in the yard just continued to grow. Our tower sounded like it was being chipped apart piece by piece, splinters and plaster and dust clouding the air.

I lifted the radio. "Jack, fall back!" I shouted. "Get your men into the buildings. The Elgen have taken the grounds." I looked out over the flow of Elgen guards. "There's nothing we can do to stop them."

"They're going to set explosives on the prison walls," Ian said.

"We're so dead," Tanner said.

"Shut up!" I shouted. "Stop saying that!"

PART TWELVE

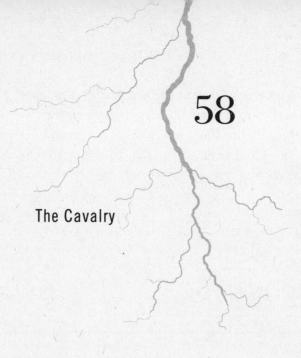

58

The Cavalry

From the center of our fortress, Ostin and McKenna watched the attack unfold around the compound on a panel of screens. If it wasn't for the occasional sound of explosions rattling the room's walls, it would have seemed more like a movie than an actual battle.

"They've breeched the wall," Ostin said calmly. "Everyone's falling back."

McKenna looked at him. "What do we do?"

"In the movies this is when the cavalry rides in."

"It's not the movies. And we don't have a cavalry."

The monitors showed guards flooding into the complex by the tens, then hundreds. The prisoners who hadn't made it behind the chain-link fence were shot down. The grounds were littered with bodies. Jack had already lost a third of his forces.

Ostin looked at the screens for a moment, then over at the central control panel. "Battery power at ninety-seven percent, estimated battery life thirty-six hours. That should be enough." He examined the panel again, then said, "I have an idea." He looked at McKenna. "Maybe there is a cavalry."

PART THIRTEEN

59

Already Lost

The dark grounds below us were chaos. The screaming of fallen prisoners echoed amid the hellish landscape of rain, smoke, and fire. The Elgen forces flowed in like demon shadows, darkening a courtyard lit only by gunfire or grenades. Occasionally, lightning would strike, illuminating the grounds for a second, like a strobe, capturing the dying and killing in frozen, violent stances. That's when we could see just how many there were of them. It seemed like thousands.

"They're setting explosives on the outer fence," Ian said.

"That's the last thing keeping them from the building," I said. "Once they reach the building, it's over."

"We could have used Cassy," Taylor said.

"Jack!" I shouted. "Hit those guys on the south perimeter. They've got explosives."

"Got them."

Taylor said, "Michael, what's going on over there?"

At the end of the north corridor, beneath the flume of the Starxource plant, a door opened, revealing an intense red glow that seemed to be growing brighter. Suddenly a steaming flow burst from the door. It was glowing orangish-red, like a stream of lava spewed from a volcano.

"What the crap is that?" Ian said.

It was something I had seen before.

"It's genius," I said. "Ostin is a freaking genius." Then the sound caught up to us, a loud screech like the painful squeal of a train's brakes. "It's rats. Ostin must have released them from the Starxource plant."

Even in the mini Starxource bowl there were tens of thousands of the hungry, electric animals. The ravenous rats swept across the yard in a powerful, glowing surge, running at the guards, drawn to them by the smell of death and meat.

The Elgen in front were the first to fall, vainly firing their guns into the mass, which was like shooting arrows to stop a river.

The swarm of rats broke against the men like a wave hitting the shore, covering and devouring them, pouring over each other, as the guards were stripped of their flesh.

The guards at the rear ran to escape the onslaught, some successfully, some not.

It took less than three minutes for the guards to evacuate the complex. At least those who could. Those who didn't make it out were devoured.

The river of glowing fur continued out the breaches in the wall, chasing the guards outside. The sounds of screams and machine guns echoed in the distance.

I lifted my radio. "Ostin, you're a freaking genius."

"Roger that," he said. "Tell me something I don't know."

"I can't. There's nothing you don't know."

"Well, we emptied the yard for a moment."

"More than just a moment," I said.

"It's a reprieve," he said. "Not a victory."

"What do you mean?" I noticed that the glow below us had began to dull. I looked through my binoculars. The rats were falling to their sides, steaming and twitching until the entire ground was a gray, writhing carpet of wet, smoldering fur.

"What's going on?" I asked.

"It's the rain," Ostin said. "Water kills them."

I looked around. "Jack, let's get the prisoners back out there and collect the Elgen weapons. Let's get their machine guns on the breaches. They'll be back."

"Sooner than you think," Ian said.

Just then a loud explosion rocked our perch. At first I thought lightning had struck the grounds, because smoke was rising from below us, but when I looked out toward the fence, I saw a large gap wide enough to drive a tank through. Then another blast hit.

"It's mortar fire," Ian said. "They're shelling us."

Another projectile hit the tower to our east and blew it apart, leaving just a few bricks and mangled rebar. Then a second tower was hit.

"We've got to get out of here," Taylor said. "They're aiming for the towers."

"Too late!" Ian shouted. "Incoming!"

A mortar round broke through the glass of our tower. I reached out to deflect it just as it blew. The shrapnel scattered away from me, covering the western wall. The explosion rang in my ears as smoke filled the room.

After a moment Taylor coughed, then said, "You saved us."

I rolled over to my side, trying to catch my breath as the smoke cleared.

"Oh no," Nichelle said. "Tanner?"

I sat up. Through the smoke I could see Tanner lying on top of a desk against the west wall. His arm was dangling over the side, and I could see blood dripping from his fingers.

"Tanner!" I shouted.

All of us ran to his side. He was mostly covered in the chalky plaster of the wall, except where the red of his blood had seeped through and stained his clothes and the dust crimson. There were holes all over his body. Shrapnel. I looked over at Ian, who looked horror-struck. He lowered his head as he shook it.

Somehow Tanner was still conscious.

I touched his shoulder, one of the few places not soaked with blood. "I'm so sorry."

Tanner grimaced in pain, then said softly, "You were right, man . . ." His chin quivered, and a thin stream of blood fell down from the corner of his mouth. "I tried. I just couldn't do it. All those people I killed."

"It wasn't your fault," I said. "It was never your fault. Hatch made you do it."

"Maybe . . . God will see it that way." He looked into my eyes. Then his gaze froze and his hand went limp.

"No," I said. "Tanner, I'm sorry."

Taylor started crying.

"I killed him," I said.

Nichelle put her hand on my arm. "No, you didn't. The Elgen did."

I stood there, the world spinning around me. I had already lost two friends. No matter the outcome, I had already lost. After a minute Ian said, "Come on, Michael. We've got to get out of here."

I just knelt down next to Tanner's body. "I'm so sorry."

Taylor put her arm around me. "Please, Michael. Ian's right. We've got to go or we'll all die."

I looked back up. Ian and Nichelle were looking at me and there was fear on their faces.

"C'mon," Taylor said, gently pulling me. "We've got to go."

I forced myself to my feet. We took the stairs back down into the prison, barring the door behind us. At the end of the hallway we could see a group of GPs crowded inside. The lights inside the building were flickering.

I was having trouble concentrating. "Ian, what's going on?"

"The guards have taken the grounds again. There're more of them. They just keep coming."

Just then Tessa's voice came over the radio. "Michael, they broke through the north gate. We can't hold them. We're falling back inside."

"The second fence is down," Ian said.

"Everyone into the prison," I said.

"It's going to be hand-to-hand combat," Ian said.

I looked at him. "No, it's not. They're going to bury us alive."

Just then the ground beneath us shook.

"It came from over there," Ian said. "It's the tunnel."

"Zeus!" I lifted my radio. "Zeus? Are you there? Zeus, what happened?"

Nothing.

"Zeus!"

There was a burst of static, then, "I'm here. I couldn't hold them anymore so I blew the outer tunnel. I'm coming up."

I breathed out in relief. "Meet us in the east corridor. Ostin, Jack, everyone, meet in the east corridor. Now!" A horrid little voice said to me, *We'll die together in the east corridor.*

60

The Radio Tower

The prison's east corridor was crowded and full of panic. The few GPs who had survived were terrified or unconscious. Most were injured, some dying. Abigail was walking around the cafeteria caring for the wounded, comforting as many as she could. She had run a wire between a dozen injured men and was holding the end of it, taking away their pain. She was trembling and pale.

"Abi!" Taylor shouted. "Come with us!"

Just then there was an explosion and the door at the end of the south corridor blew across the hall. Almost immediately dozens of guards started running in.

"They're inside," Taylor said.

At that moment something inside me cracked, and rage as hot as lightning pulsed through my body. I felt insane. My Tourette's went crazy and I started twitching uncontrollably.

The guards immediately set their guns and began firing at us, at me, the glowing target, but I was so electric that nothing could hit me. Nothing could hit any of us. Then I shouted, "Stop shooting at us!" I reached out at them and pulsed with all my anger.

The shockwave I emitted rattled the walls and broke against them like an explosion, evaporating everything that had stood in the path.

"Michael!" Taylor gasped.

I looked down at my hand. It was flashing between flesh and electricity. At moments I could see through it. I was pure electricity.

"What's happening to you?" Taylor asked.

My body was now glowing brighter than a lightbulb. "I don't know. But don't touch me."

"Michael," Ian said. "They just took the south and north wings. We need to evacuate."

"To where?" Taylor said. "There's no place else to go."

I looked around. There was only one place left, the radio room next to where the radio mast was mounted.

"Outside," I said. "Where's the rest of the clan?" I lifted my radio. "Everyone hurry!"

Just then Ostin and McKenna ran up, followed by Tessa and Zeus, who was covered in dirt. Then Jack came. He was covered with dirt, and his shirt was torn and bloody where a bullet had grazed him.

"Everyone outside," I said. "To the radio building."

Fortunately, the walk to the radio building and tower was covered by a fiberglass canopy, which provided shelter for Zeus.

"What are we going to do out here?" Taylor asked.

"I just need to think," I said. "Away from the chaos."

"We shouldn't be by this mast," Ostin said. "If lightning strikes, it could kill us."

"As opposed to the Elgen?" Jack said.

"Lightning never strikes the same place twice," Taylor said. "I already saw the tower get hit."

"That's a myth," Ostin said. "The Empire State Building was once hit forty-eight times in less than a half hour."

"Michael, what's going on with you?" Jack asked. "You're, like . . . electric."

"I know." I looked up at the tower. "Ostin, are you serious about this tower getting struck by lightning?"

"As a heart attack, man. We need to move."

"I'd rather be electrocuted than shot," Ian said.

"Give me odds," I said. "What are the odds this will be struck again?"

"Too good," Ostin said. "That thing's five hundred meters. We've got to get away from here."

"Give me odds."

"I can't," Ostin said. "There are too many variables."

"For once in your life just guess!"

"Eighty-two point four percent!" he shouted in frustration.

"Good enough," I said. "Zeus!"

"Yes, sir."

"When you blew the tunnel, did you blow the whole thing?"

"No. Just the end so they couldn't get in."

"How many can fit in there?"

He looked at me quizzically. "I don't know. Maybe fifty. Why?"

"That's where you're taking everyone." I opened the west door of the radio building and started walking toward the base of the tower.

"What do you mean?" Jack asked.

"Michael, what are you doing?" Taylor said, coming after me.

I turned and looked at her. I wanted to kiss her, but I knew I couldn't do it without hurting her. I was way too electric. "Just make sure everyone's down in the tunnel by the time I reach the top."

"The top of what?" She looked at the tower, then back at me, panic in her eyes. "The tower?"

"I love you. Remember that. I'll always love you." I turned back and walked toward the center of the tower, where a ladder climbed the latticework to the top.

"You promised you would never leave me!" she shouted after me.

"I know," I said. "If it was my choice, I wouldn't. But it's not anymore."

"Michael, what are you doing?" Ostin said, coming out of the building. "Get away from the tower."

"I know what I need to do. I just need more electricity."

He looked at the sky, then back at me. "Michael, that's a billion volts. It will probably kill you."

"We're already dead, man."

Taylor shouted frantically, "Jack, stop him! Please!"

Jack ran to me. "Michael, don't do this."

"I don't have a choice."

"There's always a choice. I won't let you."

"You don't have a choice either. You can't stop me."

"Yes, I can." He grabbed me by the arm. Just touching me shocked him. His arm shook, but he didn't let go.

I looked at him calmly. "You need to let go, Jack."

"You're not climbing that thing, man. Look how bright you are. You're like a beacon. The Elgen will shoot you off before you reach the top."

"No, they can't touch me. It's our only chance. Now let go."

"I won't do it, buddy. I can't lose you. You're all I have left. You're my friend." His eyes welled up with tears. "You're my best friend."

I looked Jack in the eyes. "You once said you'd take a bullet for me. You need to let me do the same. That's what I'm doing." Limiting myself as much as possible, I pulsed. I was so electric that my mildest was enough to throw Jack back, unconscious. I pointed to Zeus. "I'm counting on you, Zeus. Get everyone you can into the tunnel."

I turned back, grabbed on to the ladder, and began climbing.

PART FOURTEEN

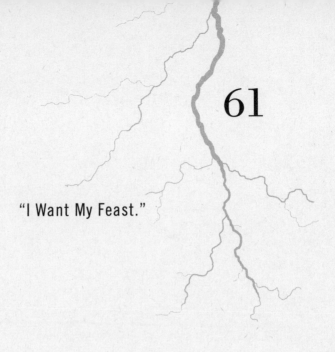

61

"I Want My Feast."

"**W**hat is that?" Hatch shouted, staring through his binoculars from the *Faraday*. "What's that climbing the radio mast? That light?"

One of the officers lifted his own binoculars. "It's not a light. It's a person." He turned to Hatch. "I think it's Vey."

"Why would he climb the tower?"

"He must be trying to escape."

"To what?" Hatch said. "He's either an idiot or a coward. Shoot him down. I want every gun on him. I want the tower brought down if you have to, just bring him down. I want Vey's body. I want my feast. I will have my feast."

PART FIFTEEN

62

Tempting Lightning

I hadn't considered whether or not I had the strength to make the climb, only that I needed to do it. My clothes were drenched and I was winded just a few hundred feet up, maybe just 10 percent of the way to the top. Usually when you climb a ladder, you're on an incline, leaning inward. A vertical climb is much more difficult, as you are moving straight up. It feels as if you're being pulled backward.

Within fifteen minutes my friends, who were still huddled around the base of the tower, looked like miniatures—like the plastic army men I used to play with when I was a child.

As I climbed higher, I could feel the change in the atmosphere. The air seemed more electric—more charged—and my body tingled with the added power. My clothes began to burn.

It wasn't hard to tell when the Elgen army had spotted me. I could see the fire from gun barrels pointed at me, popping like thousands of camera flashes at an NBA play-off. The bullets began whizzing by me like angry wasps. Then bigger things, projectiles, began flying toward me. I didn't mind that they were shooting at me. I hoped they would. It meant they weren't shooting at my friends, and I was so electric that I easily repelled everything the Elgen sent my way. At this point I think I could have repelled an airplane.

My biggest concern was that they might take out the tower. When I was halfway up, one of the shells exploded next to the tower about fifty feet below me, and the entire tower shook. My feet slipped, and for a moment I hung seven hundred feet up by just my hands. Had I not magnetized, I probably would have fallen. I wondered if they would cut the guy wires. I wondered if they would be willing to bring this whole tower down just to get to me. *Of course they would*.

It took me more than a half hour to reach the top of the mast. Twenty feet before the top was a horizontal beam that hung out about thirty feet in each direction.

At the very top of the mast a red light flashed. I put my hand on the plastic shell of the light, pulsed, and blew it out, not that it helped my situation any, as I was now glowing brighter than the light, but the thing annoyed me.

Lightning flashed in a cloud a few miles off, and the accompanying thunder was louder than I had ever heard it before.

I leaned heavily against the tower's rungs, breathless and dripping with sweat and rain. I was mildly afraid of heights—most people are, I guess, but I was really high up and hanging on to thin wet bars by very little. People have BASE jumped from lower heights.

That's when I realized that, in the unlikely event that I somehow survived a lightning strike, I would never be able to hold on to the tower, and I would fall to my death. As I looked up at the churning, groaning sky, I hooked my arm over the highest rung, then undid my belt. Not only did my mother always buy belts bigger than I needed, since I was still growing, but I had lost weight over the last few months, so the extra length of the belt wrapped halfway around my waist. Taylor had once threatened to cut it in half. I had at least ten inches to work with.

I ran my belt over the rung, then buckled it back on so it would hold me, the same way the utility guys fixing power lines did back in Idaho. I noticed things like that. As a child, I was always looking for someone else who might be electric too.

That high up I could see the entire island. I could see all the way to one of the other islands. If I was Ian, I probably could have seen Fiji. There were more Elgen than I imagined. Thousands and thousands. Even as the prison fell, more were coming from boats, more were marching to finish us off. I now understood that we had never really had a chance.

Dozens of Elgen boats surrounded the entire island. I wondered where the *Risky Business* was. I wondered if they'd made it through. I wouldn't put it past Hatch to just kill J.D. and keep the million-dollar bounty he'd put on Welch. Maybe I should have just electrocuted J.D. back on the boat.

I looked straight down below me. My friends were gone. All of them. I felt relieved and sad at the same time. I was truly alone.

It was at that moment that I realized that I would never see any of them again. My eyes welled up, and my tears mingled with the driving rain that stung my face. Peculiar thoughts crossed my mind. Was I enough? Had I been the man I should have been? I wished that I hadn't caused my mother all the pain I did. I hoped she wouldn't miss me too much. I wondered what would happen to her.

Just then a bullet struck an iron rung below me. It rang like a bell, awakening me from my thoughts. I thought it was strange that it didn't concern me. I suppose accepting your death is liberating that way. All I thought was, *That was a good shot, dude. You almost got me.*

I've heard it said that your life flashes before you before you die. I don't know if that's true, I don't know whether this counts or not, but memories suddenly began flooding into my mind.

I remembered my mother and me eating at PizzaMax.

I remembered the first time Taylor invited me over to her house and gave me awful lemonade, and learning, for the first time in my life, that I wasn't really alone.

I remembered standing on Jack's doorstep asking him to drive me to California and the look on his face.

I remembered the party when I knocked Corky over.

I remembered the time at the academy when Zeus had blown a bullet out of the air that Hatch had fired at me. That was still pretty cool.

I remembered Taylor's dream about the crocodiles and lightning and the island of glass. I was sorry that I would never completely understand what it meant.

I remembered hundreds of hours with Ostin, video games and Shark Week, wasted time that now seemed anything but wasted. How grateful I felt to have him in my life. I regretted dragging him into this all, but I was glad that he had become someone powerful and that he had found McKenna's love.

I remembered my mother telling me about my father's death and then standing next to his grave. I wondered if I would see him soon.

So many memories. Most of them recent, it seemed. I suppose I had lived more life in the last year than most people live in eighty. That was good. Because I knew that mine was coming to an end.

Suddenly my body began tingling and I felt a wave of electricity pass through me, lifting the hair on my head. I took a deep breath, then held up my hand with my fist clenched.

"Come on!" I shouted to the clouds. To the gods of lightning. "Come on! Just do it! Strike me!"

63

I'm No God

During accidents and other catastrophic events, time seems to slow down, sometimes even to freeze, like advancing one frame at a time on a DVD player.

When the lightning struck, everything froze. Time froze. I don't know how to explain this, but time became light. Light became time. My skin was impossibly bright. I remember thinking that if I weren't electric, the light would have burned the retinas from my eyes.

Next came the sound, like a hundred thousand freight trains running over me. Only this didn't go over me, it went into me, through me. It became *me*. I was lightning. I was pure energy. Maybe for a fraction of one second I felt what it feels like to be God. But I'm no god.

PART SIXTEEN

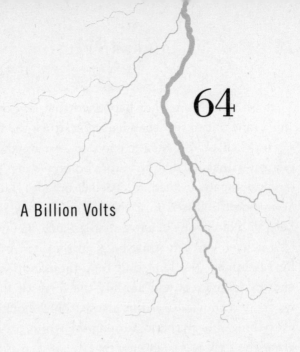

64

A Billion Volts

In 1945, at an army testing site in New Mexico, the first atomic bomb was tested. The explosion was enormous, its energy equivalent to that released by 40 million pounds of dynamite—equal to all the energy produced and consumed in the United States every thirty seconds: That's every car, lamp, diesel, dishwasher, jet airplane, diesel train, factory, everything. However, this bomb's energy was released in a few millionths of a second, and in a volume only a few inches wide.

The resulting explosion was terrible. The hundred-foot steel tower on which the bomb was mounted was completely vaporized. The ball of air formed by the explosion boiled up to a height of thirty-five thousand feet, higher than Mount Everest. For hundreds of yards around the blast site the surface of the desert sand turned to glass.

*   *   *

That isn't far from what happened that day on Hades. Hatch was still a mile out to sea when lightning struck the tower, or, more accurately, Michael Vey. No one had ever seen anything like it. It was like being a witness of that first atom bomb testing. The lightning hit but didn't dissipate. Instead, Michael absorbed it. Like the energy of that atom bomb released in a volume only a few inches wide, Michael held all billion volts in a five-foot-six-inch, 126-pound frame.

Michael Vey did something no one had ever done before. He held lightning. Not long, only for a thousandth of a second, but long enough to redirect and amplify the force of the energy. The pulse he created shot outward in a supersonic shockwave that destroyed everything above ground, turning the white, crystal sand of Hades to glass. The flash was so intense that it was seen as far away as Nike and by pilots in Australia and New Zealand.

The few Elgen guards at sea who survived the blast were blinded by the light, and had Hatch not been wearing his special sunglasses, he would have been also.

All of the Elgen boats engaged in the siege either caught fire or were capsized by the resultant waves.

Hatch, with twelve crew members and his personal guards, escaped in one of the *Faraday*'s life pods, the only one that hadn't been damaged by the heat. Twelve hours later, he reached Nike broken and ranting. He still didn't know that the *Joule* had been stolen.

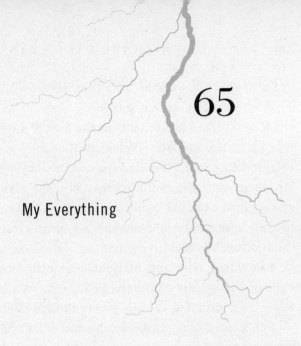

65

My Everything

It was a full hour after the blast that Jack, Ostin, Ian, and five of the natives dug themselves out of the tunnel. They emerged from a small hole, cautiously rising like prairie dogs in a vast wasteland.

Jack was the first to climb out, his hair and clothes dusted white with fine sand. The rain had stopped. The heat of the blast had evaporated or emptied the clouds, and Jack just stood there, dumbstruck, looking around the scorched island in awe. Only Ian, who had watched the transformation from below, wasn't in complete shock. It was as if they had gone into the tunnel, only to have been transported to another planet.

Then the rest of the tunnel's inhabitants, almost fifty in all, began to emerge into the surreal landscape. All were silent, speechless, walking around as if in a daze.

Then the natives began wailing in the Tuvaluan tongue. Many

of them knelt down, touching their foreheads to the earth.

"Unbelievable," Jack said softly.

"It looks like Hiroshima after the bomb," Ostin said.

Jack turned to Ostin. "Was that Michael?"

Ostin just stood there gazing out into the horizon. "It's possible." He turned to look at the tower. Only the clawlike metal supports mounted to concrete pylons remained. All but the bottom five feet of the tower had been incinerated. A lump came to Ostin's throat. "I think it was Michael."

Just then Taylor and McKenna came up out of the tunnel. The sight of the melted world stopped them. "Where's Michael?" Taylor asked. She turned to Ostin. "Where's Michael?"

She looked over to where the tower had been and saw nothing but the ends of scorched and melted beams. "Where's Michael?!" she screamed.

"He's gone," Ostin said. He turned to Taylor. "He's gone."

For a moment she froze. Then she ran to Ostin and shook him. "Don't say it! Don't say it!"

"I'm sorry," he said.

"Don't say it," she said again. She fell to her knees, then to her chest, overcome by the pain of loss. "Don't say he's gone."

Ostin sat down next to her, tears falling down his cheeks. "He was my best friend."

Taylor looked up at him. "He was my everything."

The two of them fell into each other and cried.

"What do we do now?" Tessa said. "We're stuck here."

"What about the *Joule*?" McKenna said.

"I doubt they made it," Zeus said.

Jack shook his head. "If they did, they're probably halfway to Fiji by now."

All was silent again when Ian, who had been quietly looking out into the distance for a while, said, "No, they're not."

Everyone turned. To the north, only about two hundred yards in the distance, the *Joule* was rising up out of the ocean.

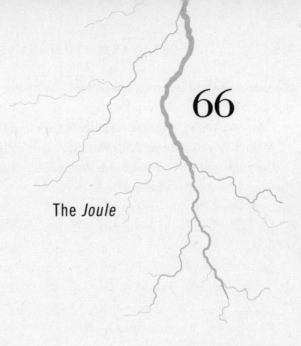

66

The *Joule*

"They did it," Ostin said.

Jack looked at the boat in awe. "And they came back. They actually came back. Michael was right."

A hatch opened on top of the *Joule*, and two figures emerged.

"It's Welch and Quentin," Ian said.

The Electroclan watched as a panel on the *Joule* folded down, with a small boat connected to it. The two figures climbed into the boat, and a mechanical arm lowered them into the sea. There was no sound as the boat headed toward the shore, crossing over the reef, and running up onto the glass beach.

As they stepped out, Welch and Quentin looked around at the devastation. "What happened?" Quentin asked. "It looks like a nuclear blast."

"It wasn't," Ostin said.

Welch looked around for a moment, then at the surviving

members of the Electroclan, and said, "Let's get out of here. Is everyone here?"

"We lost some," McKenna said. "Tanner and Gervaso."

Welch's head dropped. "I'm sorry. Anyone else?"

No one spoke. No one could. Welch looked around for a moment, then said, "Where's Michael?"

Join the Veyniac Nation!

For Michael Vey trivia, sneak peeks, and events in your area,

follow Michael and the rest of the Electroclan at:

MICHAELVEY.COM

Facebook.com/MichaelVeyOfficialFanPage

Twitter.com/MichaelVey

Instagram.com/MichaelVeyOfficial

Look for

MICHAEL VEY

Book 7
Coming in Fall 2017